REVOLUTION ON ST BARBARA

Ernest Masterman, the British Chancellor of the Exchequer, and his wife Sybil come to the small Caribbean island of St Barbara, having experienced revolution elsewhere. The Administrator of the island arranges for them to stay with the island's leading businessman, wily Joseph Mordecai. Mordecai is under financial pressure and conceives the notion of hoodwinking the Chancellor into the belief that St Barbara is on the brink of revolution, which can only be averted by a massive cash grant from the British Government ...

REVOLUTION ON ST BARBARA

Revolution On St Barbara

by
Terence Kelly

Dales Large Print Books
Long Preston, North Yorkshire,
England.

British Library Cataloguing in Publication Data.

Kelly, Terence
    Revolution on St Barbara.

    A catalogue record for this book is
    available from the British Library

    ISBN 1-85389-908-9 pbk

First published in Great Britain by Robert Hale Ltd., 1983

Copyright © 1983 by Terence Kelly

The moral right of the author has been asserted

Published in Large Print 1999 by arrangement with Laurence
Pollinger Ltd.

Dales Large Print is an imprint of
Library Magna Books Ltd.
Printed and bound in Great Britain by
T.J. International Ltd., Cornwall, PL28 8RW.

ONE

Elaine Mordecai came hurrying out on to the terrace. 'P.J's just arriving!' she announced.

Joseph Mordecai lowered the local newspaper unhurriedly. Joseph did nothing hurriedly. An enormous man who had long since abandoned fruitless attempts to keep his body in trim, he had exceptionally bushy eyebrows which he had learnt to use effectively and which now, raised to their fullest extent and combining with a pained look in his eyes, conveyed faint annoyance.

'What on earth does he want?' he demanded.

'How should I know?' said Elaine, starting to tidy up. 'I just happened to see his car turning into the gateway.'

'Leave it alone,' said Joseph, referring to a copy of the *Financial Times* which, held down by a bottle of Dimple Haig, was fluttering busily in the breeze. 'Has he got his flag up, did you notice?'

'Pennant,' said Elaine. 'You make him sound like a taxi-driver. Yes, he has.' She was a small woman, very neat in a pink checked dress which went well with skin a good deal darker than Joseph's. Alert and quick in her movements, with tight black hair and direct no-nonsense eyes, she was one of the few on the Caribbean island of St Barbara who could give Joseph as good as he gave. Ignoring his request, she lifted the bottle of whisky, whisked out the *Financial Times,* folded it once and slipped it under one of the cushions of the swing settee, then continued briskly tidying up. Joseph, meanwhile, regarded her from the comfort of a deep and well cushioned chair of basket weave. Beside him, on a second side-table, was a cut-glass tumbler half filled with his second whisky and soda of the morning and an opened box of Jamaican cigars.

'You don't think,' suggested Elaine, but in a tone which made it quite clear that this was the last thing in the world she expected him to do, 'you should go out and meet him?'

'Must be very important,' Joseph observed, retrieving his newspaper and seemingly becoming absorbed in it, ignoring the light patter of feet on the tiled terrace floor as Carole, his daughter, disgracefully beautiful, all but naked in bikini and hip-length see-through cover-up, came running from the house.

'Daddy!'—her voice was gay and held the

small note of triumph of someone about to deliver a stunning piece of news—'His nibs is here!'

'The Administrator, Carole,' said Elaine. 'And your father already knows—he's just playing his own particular game of bowls.' She addressed herself to Joseph. 'Do we invite him to stay to lunch?'

'No,' said Joseph.

'Do we ask him to come out here?'

'Yes.'

Sydney, dressed in gleaming white shirt, black trousers and black shoes, very crisp with close curly hair and shining eyes, came through from the sitting-room and stood in the wide opening to the generous terrace to announce: 'His Excellency is here, Mistress!'

'Yes, Sydney,' Elaine replied calmly. 'Ask him to join us on the terrace. And Carole, I think you'd better go round the other way and put some clothes on.'

'Stay as you are,' said Joseph.

'Stay as you are,' Elaine corrected herself. 'We are to be caught unawares. The Mordecais relaxing in their garden on a Sunday morning.'

And she put the soda split and a crown cork she had picked up back on the side-table.

'Sir Peter!' Elaine said warmly. 'This *is* a surprise!' And Joseph (timing it to perfection) was laying aside the newspaper and rising to his feet.

'Morning, Elaine,' said Jeffery-Smith, who knew them very well. 'I can't tell you how sorry I am to disturb you on a Sunday morning.' Determined to give no impression of being rushed, he was terribly exposed.

'Not a bit of it, man,' said Joseph agreeably. 'Delighted you should drop in on us.' And, with a faintly reproving glance, 'Carole, dear, I think you ought to go and put more clothes on.'

'No, please,' Jeffery-Smith said hastily. 'Not on my account.'

Carole caught the all but imperceptible nod of her father's head.

'That's all right, Sir Peter,' she said. 'I've had my swim.' And, to underline the point, she shook her head so that her wet hair, long and flowing, as dark as her mother's but less coarse, swung, effectively drawing Sir Peter Jeffery-Smith's attention. Carole had inherited much of Joseph's skill.

'Won't be long,' she said gaily. 'Don't go away before I come back, will you?'

Jeffery-Smith's eyes followed her as would the eyes of any man with blood still flowing in his veins, for Carole was a joy to look at, an exquisite creature with flawless coppery skin who was totally of a piece with the glorious sun-drenched morning

10

and the dancing lights of the inviting pool at the terrace end. Jeffery-Smith had intended to make the request which had brought him across the island to Joseph Mordecai's weekend home courteously but succinctly and, successful or unsuccessful, be gone in a matter of minutes. But he had been out-manoeuvred, knew it—and accepted the situation.

'What,' said Joseph, the instant Jeffery-Smith turned back to him, 'would you like to drink?'

'I'm afraid I don't have time ...'

'Nonsense, man,' interrupted Joseph engagingly. 'After driving all that way!'

'All of eleven miles?'

To a degree the two men understood each other. It was essential they should. Joseph Mordecai was by far the island's richest and most successful businessman. There were few things in which he had no interest and many which he controlled. In most Caribbean islands there are powerful families—Henriques, Matalons, DaCostas, Mussons, Issas—whose names are locally legendary and who exercise an influence over their compatriots which in relative terms is even greater than that of, say, the Mitsubishis of Japan and the Rockefellers of America. In St Barbara there was no such family; there was simply Joseph Mordecai. He owned the telephones,

11

the Ford agency, the cement factory, the largest dry-goods store; most of the worthwhile spirits were in his keeping as was the leading brand of cigarettes. He grew sugar, citrus and bananas and had developed the only shopping centre. With insatiable enthusiasm he was continually branching out into fresh directions; if a new factory began to rise on the outskirts of Dukestown it was as likely as not another Mordecai enterprise. There was only one direction against which he resolutely set his face and that was politics. Joseph Mordecai, the island joked, was neither a member of the P.N.P. or the P.L.P.—he was of the P.I.P.—the Party in Power.

Jeffery-Smith liked the man. 'He can sniff a profit quicker than a mosquito finding blood,' he was inclined to say. 'But he'll never suck you dry—if it's only so that he can come back another day for more!' He also found him a useful ally. The Queen's representative needs his own representative amongst the business community. By definition he is apart; he must find the way to be accepted and respected and these are two very different things which can pull in opposite directions. Also Jeffery-Smith was not St Barbaran; he was English. However accepted, however respected, he could never be seen as anything but

12

transient; the island's inner councils were closed to him.

Joseph, for his part, considered Jeffery-Smith a happy choice. St Barbara, a hiccup of some mountain range, was several hundred miles from any other land and escaped many of the influences which created difficulties elsewhere. Politics, like Carnival soon to be upon them, was more a quinquennial diversion than a serious affliction and the lushly beautiful island surrounded by a sea which teemed with fish was able to support its comparatively modest population with at least life's basic necessities. There was no need for a firm hand upon the reins—a gentle touch now and then was all that was required. Shrewder by far than he tried to make himself out to be, Joseph was quite aware of Jeffery-Smith's limitations and regarded them as advantages. Government House was a focal point which served a useful purpose. To be invited to one of the limited dinner parties where the best food, wines and service on the island could be found, was a goal to which the up-and-coming could strive and until the time came when their names had been added to the list of the select, they could be kept happy by invitations to one or other of the not infrequent drinks parties on the lawns. His own commercial prowess shut the

13

door against many of his would-be rivals personal ambitions and Joseph Mordecai was quietly grateful that social aspirations should at least partially fill the gap.

Joseph was a fixer and everybody knew it. If Jeffery-Smith ran into problems outside his bailiwick, he knew where to turn, and, on the other hand, a nod and a wink from Joseph could be relied upon to secure that invitation dear to some matron's heart.

So the two men, and for that matter their wives, shared an understanding sufficiently close as never to run the risk of becoming over intimate. It might be 'man' and 'Joseph' on the terrace of Spoon Point, Mordecai's weekend home, but it was invariably Sir Joseph and Mordecai in public.

So Jeffery-Smith, although he could ill afford the time, accepting he would never get away from Spoon Point without at least one drink inside him yielded gracefully.

'Thank you, I'd love a gin and tonic.'

'Splendid,' said Joseph, as if he had won an important concession. 'Now sit down please, man, while I fix it.'

Jeffery-Smith sank into a replica of Joseph's chair of which there were half a dozen on the terrace. How civilized this is, he mused, gazing across parkland studded with graceful coconut palms before ending in the thick bush with which the majority of the peninsula on which the house was built was clothed. This was what he saw when he looked ahead but on either hand there were vistas of great beauty. Below and to his left, beyond the pool, shimmering through a belt of casuarina trees, was the sea; to his right the sea again, a vast *sweep* of sea, studded again but this time with islet after islet, scores of them, of every imaginable shape, some hardly larger than mere rocks, others quite substantial, of a hundred acres or more, all tossed as if at random into the sapphire ocean, all girt with the white of surf and the gleaming green of deep clear water over sand. How civilized and peaceful.

'Now, Peter,' Elaine, equally at ease in one of the many chairs, interrupted his reverie helpfully, 'tell us why you've come to see us.'

'Yes,' he answered gratefully. 'Well I've just had the most unexpected news. Ernest Masterman and his wife will be landing at Siparia' (which was the tiny airport serving St Barbara) 'in ...'—he glanced at his watch—'exactly one hour and ten minutes time ...'

'Ernest Masterman! You don't mean ...'

'That's exactly what I mean, Elaine! The Chancellor of the Exchequer!'

'Lawks!' said Joseph cheerfully.

'You may well say lawks.' There was

15

rugged satisfaction in the tone.

'But,' said Elaine 'why here?'

'Being,' said Jeffery-Smith, 'neither politician, travel agent nor doctor, I couldn't say. In fact why anyone with the entire Caribbean at their disposal should choose an island only forty miles long and not ten across and three hundred miles from any land of consequence ...'

He broke off, sensing disloyalty to St Barbara, which he loved.

'Doctor, you said,' mused Joseph thoughtfully.

How the devil does he do it? Jeffery-Smith asked himself. And why does this fellow with his astonishing ability to pick out the cogent points, limit himself to a place like this? Why on earth doesn't he take himself off to Trinidad or Jamaica where there'd be so much more scope? Why not even London or New York?

'Apparently,' he answered, 'the fellow's in a nervous state.'

'Oh?'

'He's flying in from Chile. He's been down in Santiago on this Safeta business ...'

'Safeta?'

If anyone would have known about Safeta, that man was Joseph Mordecai. But Jeffery-Smith was in no mood for delving into the St Barbaran's devious motives.

16

'South American Finance and Economic Treaty Agreement,' he responded briefly. 'He's not too well it seems.'

Joseph chuckled. 'I'm not surprised.'

'No,' said Jeffery-Smith, his sense of humour somewhat under pressure, 'it's not the talks. It's all the frightful trouble they've been having. They ran right into it apparently. Armed mobs in the streets. Tear-gas. Bombing and shooting and Lord knows what ...'

'But,' said Elaine, in her soothing, lilting, West Indian voice, 'what has this to do with us?'

Jeffery-Smith was very fond of Elaine. She was that kind of quiet, unflappable woman on whom you could rely. A Government House party without her to fall back upon was not so different from being an Administrator without an A.D.C. She was attractive, resourceful and imaginative—and she had a sense of humour. To a large degree she made up for the side of Joseph which made him feel uncomfortable. 'Only one damn woman on the island who can manage him,' he was wont to say. 'And that's Elaine. God knows how she does it, but she does!'

'Elaine,' he answered. 'We have less than a hundred policemen on the whole damn island and Carnival starts tomorrow week.

And the man's coming here for a rest. Hah! From Chile of all places! By the time they get going with all that banging and shouting and fireworks and dressing up as American marines, he'll think it's Santiago all over again!'

She shook her head. 'I'm sorry, I'm not with you, man. You've lost me somewhere.'

'We've got the builders in!'

'Oh,' said Elaine.

'How very inconvenient for you,' said Joseph jovially.

Jeffery-Smith groaned inwardly. He's twigged, he told himself—and by God he's going to make me pay for it.

'Inconvenient!' he burst out—and allowed himself the rare luxury of reproaching his masters publicly. 'The damn house has damp everywhere and it's riddled with termites. You know how long I've been trying to persuade them that if they don't do something about it, they won't have a Government House at all! And now, when they finally agree ... half the roof's off, the hall looks like a brickyard ... And some damn, blithering idiot has to divert Masterman and his wife to St Barbara of all places!'

'Divert?' probed Joseph gently.

'He was apparently going to stay in Christiana.'

'You don't mean,' said Elaine with disbelief, 'they take those rumours seriously?'

'It happened in Grenada,' Jeffery-Smith pointed out. 'And damn nearly in Dominica. To say nothing of the Seychelles!'

'Well, yes, but ...' She didn't bother to finish it.

'Someone's obviously got the wind up.'

'The falling domino,' said Joseph, chuckling.

'I agree it's drivel. But you can't tell a signal that! And by the time I got it he was well and truly airborne anyway. Some idiot got the wind up so they shifted the blighter on to us without taking the elementary precaution of checking we could take him. Bloody fools!'

'Em must be pleased,' said Elaine. (Em was Lady Jeffery-Smith.)

'Hah!' Jeffery-Smith sounded as if feeling better. 'She's rushing round like a blue-arsed fly!' Then, hastily, aware this weakened his position: 'Not that there's anything she can do. We can't possibly put him up. This isn't Trinidad. We don't have half a dozen spare suites just sitting around against the possibility that the British Government will be so asinine as to send the Chancellor of the Exchequer off to South America just in time to run into a revolution!'

'And Nethersole's off the island,' Joseph purred.

'So will you put him up?' said Jeffery-Smith rushing to the point.

'Us?' said Joseph, as if such a possibility had never crossed his mind.

'You!' said Jeffery-Smith determinedly. 'I daresay,' he threw in with an offhandedness which didn't deceive Mordecai for an instant, 'I could get you an M.B.E. out of it.'

'Another drink?' suggested Joseph rising heavily.

'What?' Jeffery-Smith glanced at his glass and was amazed to see that he had emptied it. 'No. Thank you, no, but I don't have the time ...'

'Nonsense,' said Joseph taking his glass and crossing to the trolley. 'Gin and tonic, wasn't it?' And, unhurriedly, with much clinking of ice, he began to construct another mix.

'I might even,' said Jeffery-Smith bitterly, as if the words had actually been put into his mouth, 'stretch it to an O.B.E.'

There was no response. Joseph was slicing a lime. Jeffery-Smith looked hopefully at Elaine but her attention was apparently held by the green iridescent flash of a humming-bird marketing an hibiscus bush. Jeffery-Smith was no more deceived than his host had been—loyalty was a first consideration amongst the Mordecais.

Joseph brought the fat glass across, chinking gaily, deliciously cool. 'There,' he said, putting it down beside his guest and very smoothly reaching for his own glass took it to the trolley.

Jeffery-Smith possessed himself with the best patience he could manage. He fancied he could hear his own watch ticking—a time-bomb threatening to destroy the harmony of his final two years of office. Yet nothing would have made him speak ahead of Joseph plumping down cheerfully beside him.

'Cheers!' the latter said at last. 'What a splendid day it is!'

The remark had it come from anyone but Joseph Mordecai would have been fatuous—the only time the weather was discussed by Barbarans was when it was bad.

'Joseph!' Jeffery-Smith pleaded. 'I shall have to gulp this one I'm afraid but ...' And he was driven to break a cardinal rule and look at his watch without reasonable excuse. 'But in fifty minutes I have to be at Siparia meeting Ernest Masterman and his wife without having thought of somewhere to put them up ...'

'Oh I'm sure you'll have no trouble,' said Joseph blithely. 'Must be all sorts of people delighted to put them up.'

'That isn't quite the point is it?'

'Oh?' The massive eyebrows over the rather small eyes were raised expressively.

'There's the little matter of security.'

'Security?'

'And peace and quiet. Why ...' a note almost of triumph warmed the coldness of the Administrator's tone. 'You don't even have a telephone.' And, contradicting himself, he grumbled: 'If you'd had a telephone I wouldn't have had to waste time I can't afford dashing across to see you.'

'Now, man,' joked Joseph reasonably. 'I own the telephones on St Barbara; I don't have to pay for them as well.'

'Look!' said Jeffery-Smith. 'Masterman is bound to be in a jumpy state after Santiago. Or his wife anyway. We've Carnival almost on us and with all the racket they kick up practising ...' He paused, trying to think of some way to put it without demeaning himself to beg and, rather feebly, attempted apeing Mordecai's type of humour: 'The man'll probably think there's a putsch here too!'

'A what!' roared Joseph, delightedly.

'A putsch,' Jeffery-Smith repeated, wishing he didn't have to do so. He had decided to accept defeat and withdraw with such rags of dignity as remained.

'I'm sorry you aren't able to help me

22

out,' he said. 'It was just that I thought with your house so ideally located ...'

'Located?' said Joseph. He sounded interested.

'Well, of course.'

'I don't follow you, man.'

'I should have thought that it was obvious. Being on a peninsula with a neck of ... well it can't be more than a couple of hundred feet at most. And cliffs all round. Must be the easiest house on the whole of St Barbara to provide security and peace and quiet for someone as important as the Chancellor of the Exchequer.'

He turned to look deliberately at the house. Not an over-large house but one of quality. A delightful modern-styled house of cut pink stone with an exciting folded roof. A house set amongst superbly tended grounds, furnished in cheerful, impeccable taste and all its accoutrements—glass, china, cutlery, excellent.

'Joe?' he heard Elaine say.

He stood very still, pretending a continuing interest in bricks and mortar. How much one syllable could convey, he thought.

'No, my love,' he heard Joseph respond.

So that was it—and God knows what the answer was. He turned to take his leave.

'You mentioned,' Joseph lied with outrageous effrontery, 'A C.B.E.'

Jeffery-Smith refused the bait. A C.B.E. was out of the question. An M.B.E., yes. Even, with Joseph the island's leading industrialist, just possibly an O.B.E. But a C.B.E.? Not in a million years. He looked Joseph straight in his small blue eyes in the way which had had many men in Kenya, in the Gold Coast, in St Barbara, shuffling in their shoes. Against Joseph Mordecai it had the effect of a peashooter against a tank.

'I'm sorry.' Joseph was all regret, his face turned somewhat doleful, his rather heavy lips pursed sadly, his mighty shoulders sagged.

'Thank you for the drink,' Jeffery-Smith said with dignity.

'I'd like to help you, man,' Joseph explained as if they had all day to chat and there was no unboarded Chancellor of the Exchequer winging his way across the Caribbean. 'But really I don't think I should.' His fat hands were parted, palms upturned in expressive apology. 'After all it would hardly be fair for me to benefit by such an honour when the one really inconvenienced would be Elaine.'

Good God, thought Jeffery-Smith, the blackguard!

'You'll forgive us, won't you?' Joseph was continuing blandly. 'And give our regards to ...' (and the sudden smile was plain) ' ... Lady Jeffery-Smith.'

'You damn rascal!' cried Jeffery-Smith. Mordecai frowned. 'It isn't possible, you know?' Jeffery-Smith went on and, reversing it: 'You know it isn't possible.' Still there was no reply. 'Very well. A K.B.E. I'll try. Is it a deal?'

'A K?' mused Joseph as at an entirely new idea. 'Well, of course it would help keep the servants ...'

Elaine waited only long enough for the Government House Daimler to move off down the long winding drive towards the gatehouse, pennant fluttering bravely, before turning on Joseph.

'What was all that damn foolishness?' she demanded. 'When you were going to help him out in any case?'

He chuckled and slipped a massive arm around her tiny waist.

'I couldn't,' he replied, 'resist pushing him up from M to K.'

'You,' she remonstrated, 'are nothing but a damn higgler with the morals of a politician and the ethics of the marketplace. Suppose he did get you that damn K? What about me? I'd lose all my friends.'

Joseph chuckled—a belly chuckle, warm, engaging.

'Nonsense,' he said, giving her a squeeze. 'All a K would do would be bring your enemies out into the open.'

'And where's the advantage?'

'Why, my love.' He sounded almost serious. 'You'd have them at your mercy for the first time in your life. You could set them at each other's throats by being nice to one half and inviting the other half to dinner.'

'Huh,' she said, resolved not to be amused. 'All you've done is put the poor fellow through the tortures of the damned to no useful purpose whatsoever. You don't for a moment think you'll get a knighthood, do you? Just for giving him board and lodging?'

'No,' agreed Joseph. But there was something in his tone which puzzled Elaine. 'Not just for that.'

TWO

Henry Cicurel was not the most prepossessing of men. His build was good, if on a small scale, but what happened above his neck rather let it down. He had a very round head and very round eyes and no inspiring features; by no stretch of the imagination could he have been called good-looking.

Henry had come to St Barbara a man searching for a purpose. His father was immensely rich and powerful, owning a chain of stores across the States—a thrusting, decisive entrepreneur with tight lips, strong chin and eyes of glass. In no way had Henry taken after him; in fact Wilbur C. Cicurel had not the least idea who Henry had taken after. It had even occurred to him that perhaps Henry wasn't his son at all but, too immersed in his enterprises the thought having crossed his mind had exited to make room for more important considerations.

Having no other sons, Wilbur C. Cicurel had assumed that Henry would in due course take his place in the establishment and little in life had surprised him more than his son's rebellion. Put simply, Henry wanted to find himself, to be a person in his own right. Having been brought up amongst unlimited wealth, making money meant little to him and Wilbur C. Cicurel, quite baffled (making money meaning everything to him and, so he had assumed, everything to everyone else), had discovered he exercised less power over Henry than over the merest minion in his enterprises. Shrugging shoulders far broader than his son's and telling himself that once the boy learnt what life was all about he would come to heel, Wilbur had dismissed Henry's fatuous plan of travelling through the small islands of the Caribbean until he found one to suit his fancy as romantic idiocy which would die as surely as busy Lizzies in winter-time.

But Wilbur had been wrong. Henry had discovered in the Caribbean something very sympathetic to his nature. To sit in a small boat dangling a line for red snapper under the moonlight was more exciting to him than scouring the sea for marlin in his father's dreadnought; he was more at home amongst West Indians, drinking rum and soda in crude bars made out of upturned car crates, than he had ever been amongst sophisticates in plush establishments off Madison; he preferred being up at dawn to gaze upon a sea stretching to the horizon like grey satin, waiting for the sun to rise and give it colour and turn the dark hills green and deep with shadow, rather than to go to bed at dawn with the stale taste of too much smoke and bourbon in his mouth, and the jangle of too much noise and jabbering in his ears. Above all he liked the people of the smaller islands. He had tried both Trinidad and Jamaica, found much to commend them, yet something lacking. It was only when he began his circuit of Barbados, St Kitts, Grenada, St Lucia, St Vincent and, finally, St Barbara, he had begun really to feel at home. He had chosen the British rather than the American Caribbean for obvious reasons and he had preferred St Barbara out of them all because, being distant from the others and basically untouched by tourism, it had answered his yearning for simplicity. It had been nothing at all to do with Carole Mordecai; he had made his selection before being aware of her existence. He had simply, having decided, walked into Mordecai's Dukestown office and asked Joseph for a job. And Joseph had been delighted to offer one to him: finding men of executive material who could act as links with his overseas contacts who were mostly North American was an ever pressing problem.

Like many young men before him, Henry

Cicurel, bewitched by his first acquaintance with the Caribbean, had decided that here was his Earthly Paradise. It is possible, although not certain (for some men do stay for ever), that he might after a number of years have tired of its limitations, but Carole Mordecai quite destroyed this possibility. He had not merely never seen a girl so beautiful, he had not imagined that a girl so beautiful was anywhere to be seen. She was, in a word, perfection. He adored her. He would happily have thrown his life away for her. He was her slave.

He assumed, as do all men who live in such a manner, that any failures on his part would demote whatever small standing he might have in her eyes. It was beyond his comprehension that business failures were neither here nor there to her. She was uninterested in business. Business was something which went on, something her father did—and, apparently, did far better than anyone else. Things went wrong from time to time—she was perfectly well aware of this—but on the whole things went right. It happened.

So Henry, passing Jeffery-Smith en route, with yet another disaster to report, his heart thumping in his breast at the mere notion of being near his beloved, was more concerned that he should be thought the less of by

Carole than with possible strictures from his employer. But Henry, in thinking this way, was thinking wrongly—that the bicycles had gone to Trinidad was as unimportant to Carole Mordecai as the latest Chinese earthquake.

Elaine, who was rather fond of Henry, saw through the forced eagerness on his round and freckled face and allowed him to open the conversation.

'Say wasn't that P.J?'

'It was,' said Joseph. 'Good morning, Henry.'

'Good morning, Sir. Good morning, Mrs Mordecai. He sure was in a hurry.'

'He had to get back for lunch.'

'Don't be so miserable, Joe,' Elaine interjected. 'The poor man's burning with curiosity.'

'He came,' explained Joseph, 'to offer me an honour in return for putting up the Chancellor of the Exchequer and his wife. He tried an M, and an O, and a C, and we finally ended up with K.'

'Gee!' said Henry, awed.

'No,' observed Joseph, quite unable to resist it, 'that was one letter he didn't mention.'

The joke fell on ground far too disturbed to nurture it.

'But ... but that's a knighthood! Isn't it?'

31

Henry's head jerked round. 'That means you'll be Lady Mordecai!'

'There are,' said Elaine, who had decided the joke was wearing threadbare, 'certain formalities to be gone through first.' She became practical and businesslike. 'I'll leave you to talk whatever it is you've got to talk over.'

And she went into the house.

'Well, now,' said Joseph. 'What have you to tell me?'

Henry was occupying the chair recently vacated by Jeffery-Smith. By sitting on the very edge of it, he conveyed the impression of feeling it would be too great a liberty to make himself at home. And there was something of this in it for it was a rare experience for Henry to be visiting the Mordecais at Spoon Point. But the greater reason was sheer nervousness from the twin influences of the news he had to impart and the imminent possibility that at any instant his Goddess might appear.

'Sir!' said Henry. 'What I've got to tell you ...' But he ran away from it: 'If only you'd get on the telephone! It's difficult to say things on the radio.'

Joseph couldn't see why. What he could see was that Henry was in a very jumpy state; was rather like a runner who'd get across what he had to more effectively if he were allowed to get his breath back first.

'Not a blast!' Joseph said, but very cheerfully. 'For the last time, man, I have no intention of having my weekends ruined by having that damn bell jangling in my ear when I'm just about to drift off to sleep or waking me up when I've just got into it. The advantage of radio communication is firstly that it limits the number of people who can bother you to people who may have something interesting to say and secondly that it's always available when you want to use it yourself and you don't have to stand around waiting for your damn daughter to get off the line.'

'Yes, Sir,' gulped Henry, feeling even more distanced from Carole because her father could refer to her so flippantly. And he got it out:

'All America said No!'

The smile on Joseph's face was wiped away as swiftly as sunlight by cloud.

'Why, man?' And suddenly this was not the Joseph Mordecai of Spoon Point, jovial and rubicund, enjoying his third whisky of the morning. This was the Joseph Mordecai of Commodities & Services Ltd, Dukestown. His eyes were smaller, his lips were tighter, his massive eyebrows closer to each other.

'Seems,' said Henry, 'this time we've lost out to Trinidad.'

'Damn!' said Joseph.

'And that's not all,' Henry went on miserably.

'Not all? What do you mean not all?'

Henry shook a dejected head. 'Adorable are dickering.' His tongue touched his lips uneasily. He scarcely dared to get it out. 'They want,' he said, '30 per cent off our quote.'

'30 per ... ridiculous!'

'What I said to them.'

Henry stood abruptly, and began to pace. 'I tell you, Sir, I'm worried. We lost the jalousies to Barbados and the batteries to Jamaica. Now the bicycles have gone to Trinidad and if we can't take 30 per cent off ...'

'All right! All right!' said Joseph. 'I don't need a catalogue!' He stared at Henry irritably.

'Oh do sit down, man!'

Henry did not sit; but he did stop pacing. He stood marooned, blinking his sad round eyes, his forehead bedewed with sweat, a woebegone figure for all his carefully chosen blue and white cotton shirt and slacks.

'Why,' demanded Joseph, 'did All America say no?'

'They didn't like our price.'

'They expect us to assemble their damn bicycles for nothing?'

Henry did not answer.

34

'Well?'

'They say Trinidad can cut our price to ribbons.'

'Ridiculous!'

'That's what they say.' Of a sudden he was reckless. For months now nothing he'd touched had gone right. Joseph had had an idea; not a new idea for the Caribbean, but a new idea for St Barbara. With little industry of their own, most of the islands had a pool of available and unused labour which could be trained to do simple, repetitive jobs such as assembling bicycles out of components manufactured abroad for sale throughout the area; the operation worked out cheaper than having the entire article made in the U.K. or the States and then shipped out over thousands of miles, often with heavy additions for duties which were waived, or at least ameliorated, if local employment had been given. All that was necessary was to think of suitable items which fitted into this kind of category, seek out the manufacturers of the component parts, fix a deal with them and then throw up simple factories in which the product could be made and stored. And Henry's job had been to fix the contracts. And he was failing. Much more of this and Joseph, he told himself, would abandon the idea. And then where would he be? A washed-up failure!

'What the hell can we do?' he demanded fiercely. 'It's unfair competition.'

'Oh?' said Joseph, scenting something. 'What do you mean by that, man?'

'Trinidad Government's putting up half the money for the factory.'

'The bicycle factory?'

'So Sherwood says.' Sherwood was Henry's contact with All America.

'If,' said Joseph, 'we had to amortize only half the cost of ours ...'

'We could get nearer.'

'You've worked it out?'

'Sure ... I mean, yes, I worked it out. On the 'plane. It's a big part of the oncost ...'

'A very big part.'

Henry sensed a change in Joseph's mood. The irritation had died away; his mind was more engaged in seeking an answer to the problem than lamenting it.

'We had,' Joseph mused, 'exactly the same problem with Barbados, didn't we? They undercut us on that jalousie contract because, like Trinidad, Barbados was helping out with subsidies. Trinidad, Barbados ...'

'And Jamaica! And St Lucia! And if ...'

Henry was in full triumphant cry.

Joseph stopped him, raising a fat, brown hand.

'Please don't shout,' he admonished gently. 'It disturbs the servants and makes them break things.'

He regarded Henry Cicurel in quite another manner, almost paternally. Had Elaine been present she would have warned him to be on his guard.

'You must learn tranquility, man,' he advised. And, looking for inspiration, found it.

'There,' he said. 'Look at that bird.'

'Bird?' echoed Henry, puzzled.

'That one.'

Henry's eyes followed the direction a podgy forefinger indicated.

'That humming-bird?'

'Doctor bird,' Joseph corrected him, viewing the beautiful little creature darting from hibiscus bloom to hibiscus bloom, with satisfaction. 'It gets its name from those two black streamers, you know. They used to remind people of the tail-coats doctors wore in the old days when visiting their patients. It's a *species* of humming-bird, of course. One of the most handsome, don't you think? Now where was I?'

Joseph knew exactly where he was. He was back to working to a plan. Henry was to be lulled into security.

'Ah, yes,' he resumed. 'I was about to say that you would achieve far more by emulating the method of careful selection as practised by that humming-bird in its search for nectar than by pacing up and down my terrace like a man on a tennis court. My great-grandfather came to this island with just a satchel on his back, did you know?'

Henry knew. Everybody on St Barbara knew. It was Joseph Mordecai's pet boast.

'Did he, Sir?' Henry responded dutifully.

'With a satchel on his back,' Joseph repeated comfortably, not in the least taken in. 'In search of business. And once having got here, he didn't rush around like a maniac looking for it.'

'What did he do?'

'Let it come to him.'

'How?'

'By not wasting his time and energy rushing round like ...' He remembered Jeffery-Smith; or rather Jeffery-Smith was very much in the forefront of his mind. 'Like a blue-arsed fly,' he ended. 'And by not beating his head against a wall.' And he went on to explain.

'His philosophy was always to wait for the right set of circumstances to present itself.'

'I can't see,' said Henry, falling headlong into Joseph's trap, 'how *any* set of circumstances is going to present itself in time for us to get that franchise from

38

Trinidad. Or keep the ...'

Again Joseph held up a hand. 'You don't see?'

'No, Sir. I don't.'

Henry shook a head made even rounder by having his hair cut short against St Barbara's heat and because it was better that way for scuba diving.

'No, Sir, I don't.'

'Well, man,' said Joseph genially, 'why don't we explore the situation? Why are we losing all these contracts?'

'All sorts of reasons,' Henry said. 'Most because other islands subsidise their development programmes and this one doesn't.'

'And from where do they get the money to do this?'

'Well ... from their Governments.'

'Who get it from where?'

Henry was baffled. 'Well, taxes. And some get help from the U.K. Or America.'

'Uncle Sam?'

'Yeah. If you like ... Sir.'

'Subsidies from someone else?'

'Right.'

'But St Barbara doesn't?'

'No.'

'Why not?'

Henry shrugged: 'We don't shout loud enough, I guess.'

'What you're saying is that if we shouted

39

louder we might get ... get a grant-in-aid or something?'

'I guess so.'

'And then of course *we'd* be able to subsidise the building of factories for assembling bicycles and batteries and jalousies. And making batik. And things like that?'

'That's right.'

'An interesting thought,' remarked Joseph, as if it was one which hadn't occurred to him before. 'Tell me, Henry, what do you mean by *shout?*'

'I don't know.' Henry shrugged again. 'Make a fuss. Bang the drum. Put the pressure on.'

'And the more pressure, the more grant-in-aid, d'you think?'

Henry laughed—for the first time that morning. But the laugh was bitter.

'It's historical,' he said.

'I must say,' responded Joseph agreeably, 'I do like the neat way you Americans put things. And tell me how much d'you think St Barbara would need to finance the building of all the factories we'd have needed if we hadn't lost any of those franchises?'

'Say ten million bucks,' said Henry largely.

Joseph chuckled. 'Your bucks, man, or ours?'

'Yours.'

'And how much fuss, how much banging of the drum, how much pressure do you think we'd need to get that?'

'To get ten million bucks?' Henry laughed again, harshly this time. 'For St Barbara?! We'd need a revolution!'

'A revolution?'

'Yes, Sir,' said Henry, enjoying himself at last. 'A full-scale revolution!'

Joseph flopped bulkily backwards into the deep comfort of his chair and regarded his young protégé with an expression of admiring delight.

'My dear boy!' he declared. 'What a splendid idea! And what a nose for timing!'

'Eh?' said Henry.

'Why with the Chancellor of the Exchequer coming to stay with us.'

Henry looked blank.

'Will you do something for me?' Joseph said, giving him no time to recover. 'Will you go and ask my wife to come out and join us?'

Henry frowned. He was still trying to puzzle out the penultimate remark.

'Yes, of course, Sir,' he said rather vaguely.

When Elaine came out with Henry, Joseph wasted no time: 'Henry's just had the most marvellous idea,' he said. 'We're going to

41

have a revolution on St Barbara.'

'What!' exploded Henry.

Elaine said nothing. She knew her husband as a man of many parts and this was one she had seen before. Joseph was up to something. The radiance of his smile, the deference to Henry, the headiness of his tone ... this was nothing but an opening gambit. Joseph had a project.

She did not dismiss his affectation as either theatricalism or a wish for cheap laughs at Henry's expense. On the contrary he was in deadly earnest, a man with a plan which he was temporarily covering up with outré humour. She had married a man as cunning as a wagonload of monkeys. She knew instantly that something had been said between him and Henry which had given him an idea which must, in the first instance, be presented under the camouflage of whimsy; that for his plan he would need Henry's help and knew he would never get it if he presented an appeal in a normal straightforward manner.

And it didn't even end there. The name Mordecai was both byword and legend in St Barbara. For generations the family had led in one field or another be it commerce, politics or the law. But Joseph's father by his reckless gambling had brought the house down in ruins and the fragments which remained had been sufficient for only one member to start building it up again. The others, brothers and cousins, had scattered, some to larger islands in the Caribbean, others to America; only Joseph had stayed on. And Joseph Mordecai was a proud man and, acutely aware that if he failed the laughter would have been louder than it would have been with other men, had set about pre-empting that derision by a larger-than-life approach which had become his habit and his stock-in-trade. When you conveyed the impression of not taking something seriously, it did not seem too serious if you did not succeed, while by not appearing to take it over-seriously you undermined the opposition. Elaine knew only too well how difficult a man other St Barbarans found Joseph to better in business. They knew him and yet they didn't know him; they enjoyed his rather zany humour but found it hard to decide where the humour ended and where the cool planning which it camouflaged began. They welcomed him as a character until the moment when his non-conformity across a boardroom table baffled them. They knew perfectly well that behind the bright blue eyes under the best-known pair of eyebrows in St Barbara was a mind which was working overtime, that within the huge, domed, almost hairless head was a brain alert for the slightest opportunity.

They knew these things and yet, in spite of knowing them, found themselves deflected and underwriting the opponent who had set out to have them do just that.

Insofar as it was possible to keep a clear head when dealing with Joseph Mordecai, his business rivals had learnt to work on the principle that the more outlandish his approach, the more likely it was that what was under discussion mattered to him. So now Elaine, who certainly knew him better than any other man or woman on the island, realised that something very remarkable was afoot ... and held her tongue.

Meanwhile Joseph was going on delightedly: 'Isn't it a perfectly splendid idea? And he's going to time it with Masterman being here.'

Henry started on and abandoned a brief defence. 'But, Sir ... you can't really be suggesting ...' How could he go on? This was too absurd; this was idiotic.

Joseph read this as he chose. 'Don't let me steal your thunder, man. It was *your* suggestion.'

'You've never read Plato, Henry, have you?' said Elaine.

'Plato!' Henry was more and more bewildered.

'The Dialogues of Socrates?' Henry shook his head in the slow, blank manner of

44

someone giving up trying to make head or tail of what was going on.

Elaine explained:

'The system is to ask a series of leading questions which inevitably result in a suggestion the questioner wants suggested.' She paused, and ended dryly, looking at Joseph. 'My husband is a great admirer of Plato.'

Just then Carole came out. She had changed into a minute green bikini but around the lower part of it she had tied with a single knot a headscarf of a foulard pattern basically dull pink but threaded with a little green; a sliver of green pant string on one thigh added intriguingly to the effect. Around her neck dangled a necklace of green, pink and amber beads. She stood in the doorway, one knee bent making the scarf split to display a lovely copper upper leg, while one arm, encircled by a pale green bangle, was up behind her head as if putting her hair in place. Elaine wondered how long she had taken working out the pose and colour scheme, ruefully admitting it showed a touch of genius. Henry, she mused, you should take heart—Carole doesn't go to such lengths for everyone.

No such thoughts were occupying Joseph's mind. 'Ah!' he said. 'Carole!'

'You want something, Daddy?'

'No. But Henry does.'

'Eh?' said Henry.

'You were just saying how hot you were, man.' Henry had said no such thing. 'It is hot. And that early-morning flight. And driving here from Siparia ...' He gave Henry no time to spoil his golden opportunity. 'Take him inside, Carole, and show him our selection of bathing-trunks ... Go on, man. We don't have all that time. It's only half an hour to lunch, you know ...'

'So Henry's staying to lunch, is he?' said Elaine with meaning. 'It would of course have been helpful to have known a little earlier.'

'But Henry hadn't made his brilliant suggestion.'

'Brilliant suggestion!' She withered him with her scorn. 'What's all this nonsense, man? I suppose you realise the dreadful state you've got him into? He doesn't know if he's supposed to make sense out of nonsense or humour you as a man who's gone off his head.'

'He's a splendid fellow,' Joseph responded. 'I'm glad I picked him out.'

'You didn't pick him out. He walked into your office and asked you for a job.'

'I didn't have to take him on, you know.'

'Let's not argue about that.' Her voice was brisk. 'What's all this nonsense about a revolution?'

'That, of course, would be nonsense.'

'What are you up to, man?'

Joseph stared at the bush which marked the limit of his generous parkland, bush so thick that one could hardly see a yard into its depths.

'Henry brought bad news,' he said. 'You know that contract for assembling bicycles I was expecting to get with All America? Well, we're not getting the damn thing after all. And we're going to lose that contract for making underwear for Adorable Lingerie unless we can knock 30 per cent off our quote—which is impossible.'

'Well, I'm sorry, of course,' said Elaine, 'but I still don't see what this has got to do with a revolution breaking out on St Barbara.'

'In the last six months,' Joseph said, 'we've lost five contracts to some other damn island. It's very serious, my love.'

'Probably because Henry's not all that experienced. But ...'

'It's not Henry's fault,' Joseph interrupted. 'It's that damn fool Nethersole's.'

'Nethersole's?!'

'Nethersole's. All the other islands get grants-in-aid from one place or another but Nethersole's so damn self-opinionated

47

about St Barbara that all he does is convince London and Ottawa and Washington that it would be taken as an insult for us to be offered one. Then, when we get the chance of quoting for franchises for assembling bicycles, or beds, or whatever, we can't compete because these other islands subsidise the building of the factories while we've got to meet the whole cost out of profit.'

'And it's serious?'

'Damn serious ... Listen, my love.' Joseph was in a rare mood for him at Spoon Point, quietly in earnest.

'We are going to have the Chancellor of the Exchequer staying with us for a few days. P.J's instructions to us will be to ensure that the man, who's probably been shaken by all that's been going on in Santiago while he's been there, has absolute peace and quiet. We're to have no visitors and P.J. will obviously arrange for half a dozen or so policemen to keep intruders out and make sure nothing that's going to upset his own applecart happens to Masterman. We don't have a telephone and we live on a peninsula. Masterman and his wife have never been to St Barbara before. They've been switched from Christiana where there's rumours that idiot Bosworth's about to try and take it over. We know it's nonsense but obviously

Whitehall doesn't or Masterman would still be going there. There's a background of sudden take-overs in the Caribbean. First there was Cuba. Then there was the Anguilla business. Then Grenada got taken over while Gairy's back was turned while he was making a visit to the States. Dominica's been in the news. Same thing. Why not St Barbara? Especially now with Christiana ... And with Nethersole away. History repeating itself ... So! If we could persuade Masterman and his wife there's unrest, trouble brewing, the likelihood of a revolution because the people are fed up with not having jobs, watching all the plums going to more favoured islands ...'

'But they're not.'

'Of course they're not. All they want to do is sit on their arses in the sun, thank God! But Masterman and his wife won't know that. Just imagine you're her. Look at that lot, love!' Joseph spread a massive arm towards the bush. 'Suddenly, quite unexpectedly, you arrive in an island that you mayn't even have *heard* of before. Knowing nothing about it. You're boarded out on a peninsula of several hundred acres the vast majority of which has never been cleared and for all you know could be crawling with revolutionaries. And look at all those islands. Hundreds of them. Ideal places for storing arms in readiness for an assault. I mean, you have to admit, Castro could dump hundreds of men and no one be the wiser until it was too late. Ship 'em over in small fishing-boats or something. Land them at night.'

He could see she was unconvinced, even if, perhaps, a trifle less certain than she had been before.

'Suppose, my love,' he said, 'this was not St Barbara, but Grenada. Suppose it isn't now, but a few years back. Suppose the Chancellor wasn't coming to stay with the Mordecais but with the Degazons. Suppose it isn't Nethersole who's off the island but Gairy. You think if Johnny Degazon suggested to Rosalind what I'm suggesting to you, she wouldn't be saying what you are saying now?'

'But there *was* a revolution on Grenada.'

'Exactly! But you think if Masterman had been staying with the Degazons he'd have seen any of it?'

'He'd have been told ...'

'And believed what he'd been told.'

'So we tell him there's going to be a revolution and he says thank you very much, how much money do we have to give St Barbara to put it down?'

'We don't tell him. We ...' Joseph moved his great hands rather in the manner of a woman winding wool. 'We provide certain ... pointers ...'

50

'Oh, it's ridiculous,' said Elaine. 'I never heard anything so far-fetched in my life. You're just a damn fool, man. A fool puffed up with his own damn cleverness.'

But Joseph would not be swayed.

'If,' he said, 'you grant the possibility, which I think you must, that Masterman and his wife, had they happened to be staying with the Degazons when Maurice Bishop took over in Grenada, would have accepted that a revolution had taken place merely because of enough indications which fitted in with what a handful of people told them, I think you have to admit they can be persuaded we are about to have one here.'

'It's absurd,' said Elaine, rather feebly.

At once, seeing things were going his way, Joseph became less earnest. 'Politics, my love,' he said, 'is the art of the absurd. If you had told any man all the way through from a serf in Russia in the nineteenth century to a twentieth-century Chinese communist with his little red book the things that were going to happen in their countries, they would all have said you were being absurd.' He coined a phrase. 'In politics today's events are yesterday's absurdities.'

Elaine fought a gallant rearguard action. 'You're talking about different situations, Joe. If the Mastermans had gone to stay with the Degazons at the time Grenada had its revolution, the island would have been queuing up with people to tell them what had happened ...'

'*Had* happened!'

'Was happening then.'

'Maybe. But what about what was *going* to happen? Carry the analogy further. Suppose the Mastermans had stayed with the Degazons a month before, a week before, even a day before Bishop took over. D'you think people would have been queuing then?'

It was unanswerable. Elaine had to admit to herself (even if she was not going to admit it to Joseph) that what he said was correct. That theoretically it was possible to create a set of circumstances which could convince even a British Chancellor of the Exchequer that something disastrous was about to occur on St Barbara.

She switched her defence.

'Accepting, which I don't,' she argued, 'that what you say is right, all that would happen would be that Masterman would do something about it.'

'Such as what?'

'Well, man, how do I know? Telephone ... no, he can't. Use your radio then ...'

'The radio's sabotaged.'

'Well ... go and see P.J.'

'How?'

'Borrow a car ... Oh, I suppose that's sabotaged as well. Talk to the police ...'

'That,' said Joseph, 'is a problem.'

'You don't,' said Elaine, 'really mean you're serious?'

'You're persuading me to be.'

'Oh, no!' exclaimed Elaine hotly. 'Don't try putting this on me. Don't insinuate I agreed ... or ... or encouraged ... or ... or ...' She paused for breath. 'And what,' she demanded, 'happens when it all comes out?'

'It won't come out.'

'Why won't it?'

'Because we shall find a way of stopping it coming out.'

'Not *we*. What way will you find of stopping it coming out?'

'That,' admitted Joseph, 'is something I shall have to think about.'

At that moment Henry came out of the house. He looked trim and neat in bathing-trunks with a towel thrown carelessly over one shoulder. Henry looked his best in trunks, being so well made if only on a small scale.

'My dear fellow,' Joseph said jovially, 'how splendid you look.' And to Elaine: 'It's so nice, isn't it, my love, having young people around the house?'

Henry was anxious to get unfinished

53

business cleared up before Carole joined them.

'Sir ...' he began.

'About your revolution?' Joseph interrupted. 'Don't worry. It's on. I've spoken to my wife about it ...'

'Don't tell me she's agreed?!' said Henry, flabbergasted.

'Well,' Joseph temporized, 'let's say that she didn't disagree. And not to disagree is all you can ever expect from a woman, you know, when you put a new idea to her. Women, Henry, are, as you will find, like anacondas: they can swallow the most complicated suggestion in a single gulp but they take a long time over the process of digestion.'

'Cheer up, Henry,' Elaine said grimly. 'I have not agreed.'

'But in the meantime,' Joseph chuckled, 'we may rely on your neutrality?'

'In the meantime,' Elaine said, fuming, 'I shall go and see how lunch is getting on.'

She turned and walked furiously into the house. Henry watched her departure with dismay. This was the woman about whom he cherished dreams, admittedly very faint dreams, of securing for his mother-in-law one day. Now he had turned her against him.

'We've upset her,' he observed gloomily.

But Joseph was all bonhomie and cheerfulness.

'Nonsense, man,' he said. 'Women, as you will find, are all the same. Whenever they are doing badly in an argument, they say something crushing and then go and see how lunch is getting on. The Parthians used to do the same sort of thing with arrows. Where's Carole?'

'Changing into another costume.'

'Costume?' said Joseph. 'Well! I suppose the last one wasn't designed for swimming in. Now sit down, Henry, there are a few details about your revolution I want to discuss with you.'

Henry, with deeply furrowed brow and a worried look in his eyes, stared at his employer, this mountain of a man with his huge domed head and his astonishing eyebrows. He decided on frankness.

'Sir,' he began. 'I don't know quite how to put this ...'

'Then I shouldn't bother to try,' Joseph interrupted genially. 'Do sit down.'

Henry sat.

'Now,' said Joseph. 'You suggested we need a revolution to get money out of the Chancellor of the Exchequer so that we can build our factories. No, please don't interrupt me! But you know, man, it isn't really necessary to go as far as that.' He explained as he had to Elaine,

55

ending: 'So you see all we need to do is to produce sufficient circumstantial evidence for Masterman to jump to his own conclusion there's about to be a lot of trouble in St Barbara and then, when he asks us what we think he ought to do about it, we make our suggestion.'

'Suppose he doesn't ask?' Henry said morosely.

'Oh,' said Joseph largely, 'it isn't very difficult to persuade people to ask you the questions you want them to ask.'

Henry reflected that it was not.

'So,' said Joseph, 'we have to start constructing what is, I believe, known as a scenario. A convincing scenario. Now ...'

He broke off as Carole, dressed in a few squares of green gingham, came through the sitting-room.

'Have you spoken to Carole about your revolution?' he inquired.

'Good God, no! ... I mean ...'

'Splendid,' said Joseph. 'Now leave this to me. Not a word.' He waited until his beautiful daughter was on them.

'Come on, Henry!' she ordered gaily ... And would have passed by without a pause.

'Just a minute, Carole.'

Carole stopped at once. 'Yes, Daddy?' she said, half turning. She really was an exquisite creature. She had inherited her mother's eyes, dark brown almost to black under heavy but carefully drawn eyebrows, her lips were full and eager, her teeth were dazzling, her tawny skin glowed smooth and faultless, her hair, dark, long and flowing caressed her hollowed, moulded back, her limbs were long, fining to tiny wrists and ankles, her high breasts emphasized the firmness of her tight young buttocks. She was all health and youth and vibrant life, yet disciplined and controlled. The man who could break down that control and discipline would, you sensed, know rewards of love vouchsafed to few.

'We've been talking,' lied Joseph shamelessly, 'about Christiana.'

'Oh?'

'Where there's supposed to be a revolution about to break out. Bosworth's rumoured to be about to do a ...' He remembered Jeffery-Smith's word and preferred it. 'To organise a putsch.'

'Yes, Daddy, we've heard all that nonsense,' said Carole a trifle impatiently. She could have conversation with her father any time.

'Yes, but it's interesting,' mused Joseph. 'You think it's nonsense?'

'Everybody knows it is.'

'What would it take to convince you that it wasn't nonsense?'

Carole shrugged her pretty shoulders.

'Well if the Cubans started airlifting soldiers in, I might be convinced,' she said offhandedly.

'They could hardly do that on *our* airstrip,' Joseph pointed out.

'Well, dropped them by parachute or something. Henry, if we're going to have a swim before Mummy ...'

'Just a minute,' said Joseph in a tone which stayed her. 'Any other ideas?'

'Well, I don't know, Daddy.'

'Try, man.'

'Oh, dear.' Carole perched herself on the edge of one of the chairs, as if to indicate she accepted she must satisfy her father before being released but that that release must not be delayed very long.

'I suppose,' she offered, 'that if someone told me the police had gone over ...'

'You think that's important? The police?'

'Well they were the first to go over to Grenada, weren't they?'

'True,' said Joseph thoughtfully. 'What else.'

'Well there'd have to be some shooting and people rushing round with arms, firing their guns, killing each other ...'

'You think that's really necessary? People killing each other? Only one or two were actually killed in Grenada. Would you really want to have someone killed before you could be convinced a revolution had broken out? Or was about to?'

'No, of course I wouldn't, Daddy. But then I don't want to be convinced a revolution has broken out anyway.

'Henry does.'

'Mr Mordecai!' cried Henry, aghast.

'In fact,' said Joseph blandly. 'His idea was that we should have an actual revolution.'

And, having timed it so well, he launched directly into his idea.

It was, again, an exercise in serious intent explained through a gauze of prankishness. Joseph knew exactly what he was doing. He was quite persuaded as to the possibility of his scheme succeeding. But he needed assistance. And here, at hand, was assistance. Carole would need no inducing. To try to winkle money out of the British Government by convincing one of its leading Ministers all hell was about to break loose on St Barbara would be a tremendous lark—right up her street. Her nature was as capricious as his own. But Henry? Oh, another matter altogether. Henry was a serious young man, full of earnest resolve. It was possible that, grudgingly, Henry might agree to play a minor role. But Joseph wanted more than grudging assistance; he wanted full-bloodied, enthusiastic commitment. And, so far as Henry was concerned, Carole was the key. She had bewitched the man. So be it. Thus far Joseph would pimp his daughter.

And so it turned out. Henry was not in a moment changed from a confused and uncomfortable employee into a firebrand revolutionary, but he could not but observe the excitement mounting in Carole, the glee, the growing approval of her father's crackpot project. Indeed he saw more—he saw for the first time how closely father and daughter were identified; there was between them a consentaneity which went beyond mere words—which was blood and humour. The writing on the wall was as bold and clear to Henry as Joseph Mordecai had intended it to be and it said: 'Henry Cicurel! Row in with us or be damned forever pipsqueak!'

So Henry listened with a sense that something quite catastrophic was going to happen, which he was quite powerless to prevent and in which he must, inevitably, be involved.

'That's a very good idea of yours.'
'What, Daddy?'
'A parachute drop.'
For the first time in his life, Henry heard Carole giggle.

'You going to 'phone up Fidel, Daddy?'

'Arms,' said Joseph. 'Supplies.'

Henry swallowed. Somehow he had to get into this conversation.

'You going to drop arms, Sir? Where are you going to get them from?'

'I don't,' said Joseph, 'have to get them. I already have them.' And at Henry's frown, 'Sports and Games, man!'

'Oh,' said Henry, comprehending. 'Sports and Games' was one of Joseph's many enterprises—a shop in Dukestown which supplied everything from duck decoys to marlin lures. There were plenty of shotguns. 'You're going to drop shotguns,' he said, putting thoughts into words rather recklessly.

'Not drop,' said Joseph. 'Sprinkle. And not just shotguns. Revolvers.'

'Revolvers! You've got revolvers?'

'Cases of them. You seem surprised.'

'Well back at home ...'

'You only have to apply for a licence on St Barbara. And someone has to be there to supply.'

And that someone would, of course, be Joseph Mordecai.

'Henry,' said Joseph, becoming very practical. 'As soon as we've had lunch, I want you to drive into Dukestown and collect a good assortment from the shop with plenty of ammunition. And some

61

empty boxes with markings on them showing what they had in them. I'll give you a list.'

'Where do I put them?' asked Henry doing his best to show enthusiasm.

'Where? ... Yes?' mused Joseph.

'I know,' said Carole. 'In the cave!'

'Cave?' echoed a bewildered Henry.

'Where you park your boat,' said Carole somewhat irritably.

There were, at Spoon Point, most things a wealthy man might find useful. There was, for example, an artificial dock with a little jetty in the bay below the house on the eastward side with water deep enough for Joseph's fishing cruiser, *The Happy Day,* and on the peninsula there was a cave which had been improved to provide shelter for it against the risk of hurricanes. Henry, arriving on his boat at St Barbara, had sought permission to moor it there and Joseph had agreed.

'Good idea, Daddy?' Carole queried. 'We could load Henry's boat right up to the gunwales and have old Masterman ...'

But Joseph's head was shaking.

'No?'

'No,' he confirmed. 'Nothing must be traceable directly. But it's a good idea.' He addressed himself to Henry. 'What you must do, Henry, is to run your boat *out* of the cave making sure you leave enough evidence to show a boat has been there recently. I know, run it down to Port Lucea. And when you've done that, run *Happy Day* down there as well to have her bottom scraped or something. All right?'

Henry shrugged helplessly.

'And me?' said Carole eagerly.

'You? You go and have a word with Jorg Jodestal.'

'Who's George Jodestal?' demanded Henry.

'Jorg, not George,' said Carole. 'He's a Norwegian. He does the crop-spraying.'

Henry remembered. He had overnighted at Joseph's banana plantation and the yellow Cessna had come at dawn, its navigation lights like eyes, the spray like a vapour trail. It had been a marvellous thing to watch that aircraft skimming the hill folds. Especially because he held his own pilot's licence, Henry had envied the pilot who was doing something which had struck him as both exciting and fulfilling. Now he was doubtful.

Carole, unaware that any indication of interest she showed in another man made Henry wretched with jealousy (or at least not thinking about it at the time), was eager.

'You want him to come and drop things?'

'Pretend to drop things,' Joseph said.

63

'But why not drop something, Daddy?'

Joseph thought about it.

'Couldn't he drop a parachute and we could smash up one of those boxes you were talking about, Sir? You know, the ones with markings on them?' Henry, determined not to be left out, suggested.

'Brilliant, Henry!' Carole cried. 'We could put it just in front of the bush!'

'I don't have any parachutes,' said Joseph.

'But Jodes ... Jod ...'

'Jodestal.'

'He'll have one most likely.'

'He throws it out of his aeroplane and ...'

'No, Carole,' Henry said, daring to use her name. 'If he's got one and you can get it from him, we could fix it up in a tree. You know, like it's got caught up there. And we smash a box and put that underneath ...'

'And sprinkle a few bullets about the place ...'

'And trample the bush ...'

'We could make a trail towards the cave ...'

'Just a minute! Just a minute!' a delighted Joseph interrupted. 'The first thing is to make sure that Jodestal will help us and afterwards keep it to himself.'

'He'll help. *And* he'll keep it to himself,'

said Carole with such conviction as to lessen Henry's new-found boldness. 'When do you want him?'

'Tonight, if possible,' Joseph said. 'It would be far better to get this thing going ...'

'Before they start getting relaxed and finding their way around the place ...'

'Exactly. Now let me see.' Joseph pulled at his chin with a huge hand soft as if filled with air. 'They'll be arriving between five and six. If we eat at eight, I can have them out for coffee at say nine ... Quarter past. Quarter past nine.' He pondered. 'But will he find the place at night?' Joseph knew nothing of such things; all the flying he had done had been strictly with an airline.

Henry was better versed. Henry had a pilot's licence. Henry could do many things. He could ride, and shoot, and ski on water or on snow. All these and other things had been taught to him by professionals his father had hired at various times. Not only could Henry do these things, he could do them well. Carole had watched him scuba-diving and seen him on one water-ski. She had been impressed. Carole thought far more of Henry than he thought of himself.

'Oh, sure,' Henry said. 'The peninsula sticks out like a finger. He can't miss it. And anyway you could put on the burglar lights ... I mean, there's nothing else. A few lights in Port Lucea. They won't amount to much ...'

'Henry!' cried Carole—wonder of wonders—putting her hand upon his arm to interrupt him. 'Do you know Morse?!'

'Sure, Carole ...'

'Daddy! If Henry had a torch. And he hid himself out there in the bush. On the very edge of it, I mean ...'

And so it went on for quite a little time and, like its predecessor, Carole's third bikini of the morning never did get wet ...

THREE

Life at Spoon Point was almost entirely lived on the terrace, which was delightful by day and magical by night. The lighting was subdued with no glaring bulbs to drench everything in white and attract satellites of insects, and no hard spotlights picking out individual trees and making the surrounding darkness, which was really deep blue, black. There were what were called 'buzz-off' bulbs of an amber hue which, it was said, repelled flying things; there were candles in glass shades and light was allowed to filter from the house itself; even the pool lights, fresh through clear blue water, were only switched on for parties. The principle was that nothing should compete with Nature's light: a million stars so bright as to fill the sky with fire and, in its phases, a moon so brilliant one could actually read big print by it; the faint sheen of the sea with its definite margin against the sky and the haloes around every islet which were the necklaces of surf; the fireflies, flickering like floating sparks, and the brighter luminosity of various kinds of flying beetles, rather greener in colour, bigger and more direct, not intermittent like the fireflies, but winging their way out of coverts at great speed, like meteors.

Tonight, the evening of the Mastermans' arrival, was a dark night, which is to say without a moon, as Carole, loveliness personified in sleeveless dinner-dress, came out ahead to check on the preparations to which Sydney was putting the finishing touches.

She was alive with the excitement of youth which thinks only of the project and ignores its possible consequences; it hardly crossed her mind to calculate the amount of cheek needed for success. In any case her father was a remarkable man who, once he had set his mind to it, could apparently achieve anything. This, of course, is the normal attitude of children towards their fathers but mostly they outgrow it in their teens and often swing violently the other way. Carole had not and, an only child, had deep affection for him.

She was, of course, utterly spoiled and really it was disgraceful one girl should have so much on her side: beauty, wealth, position and a doting father. But such combinations, unfair though they may be, sometimes create young women delightful to have around the place in their ease and assurance and the sparkle their presence

68

can add. Ernest Masterman, certainly, had been quite charmed and even Sybil, his wife, had as her only immediate criticism that a youngster, condemned to live in such a limited society, given the opportunity of sitting at table with such an important Minister of the Crown, should have been giving all her attention instead of so obviously wanting the meal over so as to be off and doing something else.

Sydney had no such reservations. Whilst he had deep affection for and total loyalty towards his Master and Mistress (as without qualification he regarded them), Carole was the light of his life. Being unmarried (seeing no reason for marrying with the Mordecai establishment providing everything a man might reasonably need in life except that particular thing which St Barbarans gave of generously for the sheer fun of its giving and receiving), he felt a proprietary right over Carole verging on relationship, having watched her grow from tiny pickney into the unflawed flower she had to his mind become.

He would, quite literally, have given his life to defend her had that been necessary.

When she came out, he at once abandoned lighting a final table candle against the possibility she might have something more important to command.

'Everything ready, Sydney?' she whispered conspiratorially—for it had been essential to embroil Sydney into the business on the basis that a little game was to be played on the current guests.

'Yes, Miss Carole,' he answered softly.

'Have you lit the mosquito coils?'

'Not yet, Miss Carole.'

'Well I think we'd better. They'll be coming out soon and if she gets bitten it could spoil everything. We can go through the rest while we're doing it. Where are they?'

'On the trolley, Miss Carole.'

Carole went to the trolley, a promising affair stocked with a wide array of brandies, whiskies and liqueurs and several boxes of cigars. In a corner was a small square box of anti-mosquito coils; she took a couple out, carefully because they were brittle things, and handed one to Sydney.

'Mr Masterman's to sit in that chair,' she said, 'and Mrs Masterman in this. So we'd better put one under each. So that they don't see them.'

'Yes, Miss Carole.'

Sydney struck a match to light the coil Carole was holding. To do so he had to stand very near. He was very conscious of her presence, of her perfumed hair, of her very being. He was happy.

'Them slow to light, Miss,' he observed.

'Aren't they? ... Now. The parachute. Did you fix it where Daddy showed you?'

'Yes, Miss Carole. It hanging from the mango tree.'

'And underneath it that box I gave you?'

'Right underneath the tree.'

It had not surprised Sydney excessively when he had accompanied Mr Mordecai, Mr Cicurel and Miss Carole into the edge of the uncleared bush at a time in the afternoon when normally everyone would have been doing anything but clambering around in the heat, that they should have with them such articles as an old parachute and a broken crate. His life was not at all as theirs and it never occurred to him it should be. They did strange things such as skiing on water and flying in aeroplanes and fishing from motor-cruisers. They had their own radio receiving and transmitting sets, they wore strange clothes (like Mr Cicurel that afternoon in a tunic and shorts such as he remembered seeing photographs of British soldiers wearing) and he overheard scraps of conversation about things they apparently found it quite normal to do which mystified him in a vague, detached sort of way. He was neither envious nor critical of their lives—they were simply different from his own.

Equally he had accepted and carried

through to the letter Mr Mordecai's instructions that he was to dress in his chauffeuring clothes and collect from Government House a Mr and Mrs Masterman who were very important guests and to drive them back to Spoon Point, taking a route through Dukestown which would, if possible, avoid any places where there might be Carnival preparations taking place and, so far as he could, avoid conversation with his passengers.

As to how such an unusual thing as a parachute could have been obtained, he gave this no thought at all. Mr Mordecai owned one of the two establishments in Dukestown which could honestly call themselves department stores, to say nothing of various smaller shops of different kinds—if he wanted something for the garden, if Gertrude wanted anything for the kitchen, if Hazel (the general housemaid) wanted anything for the house, Mr Mordecai invariably managed to produce it by the next weekend.

'Did you test the torch before you gave it to Mr Cicurel?' Carole suggested, bending lissomly to put the mosquito coil, propped on its cardboard stand, under Sybil Masterman's chair.

'It shine,' said Sydney proudly, 'like a mongoose eye.' He regarded with pleasure the glowing end of the second mosquito coil and blew on it gently before handing it to Carole. And just then Joseph came out to join them.

Joseph looked expansive—it was the only word. He was dressed in a white tuxedo and black evening trousers and he wore a scarlet cummerbund. He had given much thought to the last and had concluded it was an excellent touch which would support Masterman in a view of him he hoped to inculcate, that he was not merely an eccentric but also something of a fool. That was not the whole of it of course—had it been, Joseph would not have had a scarlet cummerbund in his wardrobe. Truth to tell, Joseph did rather fancy himself as something of a dog in his scarlet cummerbund—but he would never normally have sported it in the presence of a British Chancellor of the Exchequer. But anyway there he stood, massive belly banded in scarlet, the famous eyebrows cocked for action, a vast and genial smile on his vast and genial face, his small eyes bright with anticipation, making his entrance with a baffling:

'How wrong he was!'

'Who?' enquired Carole, not bothering to turn her head away from what she was doing and feeding him good-naturedly.

'Why,' said Joseph, as if surprised he should be asked, 'Robert Louis Stevenson of course. He said that in politics no preparation was necessary.'

Carole laughed—a pleasant sound.

'Well now, Sydney,' Joseph went on, 'when you fetched Mr and Mrs Masterman, did you manage to avoid driving them anywhere where there were Carnival preparations?'

'Until I got to Jemima's Corner, Sir.'

'Oh,' said Joseph, pushing out his lips, the smile fading somewhat. 'And what was there at Jemima's Corner?'

'There was a band, Sir.'

'Oh, dear.' He thought for a moment. 'How was it dressed?'

'Well, Sir,' said Sydney, 'I don't rightly know. I think that maybe they was Assyrians.'

'Assyrians!'

'They had tall hats. Yes, Sir, I think they was Assyrians. We had Assyrians 'bout four years back and I think that is what these were.'

Carole had finished with the mosquito coil and was standing looking from one to other of them.

'Did they see them?' she demanded.

'Oh, yes, Miss Carole, they saw them all right.'

'Didn't they ask you who they were? What they were doing?'

'No, Miss Carole. They never spoke to

74

me at all. Not all the way. Mr Masterman spoke to me when I picked them up, but that was all. Mrs Masterman did not say one word to me at all.'

'Really!'

'Pas devant les domestiques,' Joseph explained, and went on to quote happily: 'Except wind stand as it never stood, it is an ill wind turns none to good.' The geniality was quite restored, the smile back, the tone jovial enough. But there was no mistaking the firmness either. For all the manner in which it might be played, this was a very serious matter. If he pulled it off, Joseph stood to make half a million pounds, maybe; perhaps even more.

'Sydney,' he said, 'timing is going to be very important.'

'Yes, Sir.'

'Mrs Mordecai will tell you when to bring out the coffee.' He glanced at the arrangement of the chairs. 'That one a little further to the right, I think.' Sydney moved it a little. 'Yes,' said Joseph, standing behind it and viewing the distant bush carefully. 'Yes, I think that's perfect.' He waited while Sydney shifted the mosquito coil and then dismissed him: 'All right, Sydney, in you go and make sure Gertrude's got the coffee ready.' Sydney withdrew. 'You're quite sure Jodestal won't let us down?' he went on to Carole.

'Don't worry,' Carole (who found the idea of young men falling down on a promise made to her an almost unimaginable proposition) said reassuringly. 'What time's it now?'

Joseph glanced at a gold wrist-watch on a band of a size commesurate with its owner's massiveness.

'Just gone nine.'

Carole chuckled. 'You've got fifteen minutes filibustering,' she said. 'On your own too.' (Elaine had yet to be persuaded.) 'But I dare say you'll manage.' She kissed him lightly on the cheek. 'You usually do,' she ended. 'Go on. In you go and fetch them.'

But Joseph paused before going into the house and, in fact took a slow and heavy couple of paces across the terrace to peer into the night.

'I wonder,' he mused, 'how Henry is getting on out there.'

There was a small problem to be overcome before Masterman could be lured out—his wife was trying to persuade him to have an early night, an idea towards which, after a long and tiring day, he wasn't ill-disposed. What was worse was that Elaine, who had no idea what had been arranged for his evening's entertainment, and would have liked nothing better than an hour's relaxation without stress before going to bed herself, was on Sybil's side.

'Really, Joseph, if the Minister wants an early night ...' she said rather tartly and not a little surprised at Joseph's 'But you can't possibly go to bed so early, Minister.' —She got no further because Sybil, who always felt that her husband had no need of assistance from anyone except herself, interrupted with a very final: 'My husband is very tired and so am I.' Which should have ended the matter and normally would have.

But she was dealing with Joseph Mordecai.

'My dear Mrs Masterman,' he said most sympathetically, 'that is exactly why you mustn't go straight to bed. You'll sleep so much better when you get relaxed. And there is nothing in the world more relaxing than lingering over a coffee under the St Barbaran stars.'

He spoke with such consideration, so obviously wanting to do all he could to put his unexpected guests at ease that Ernest Masterman was seduced. Moreover he was conscious of a slight sense of guilt by no means new. Sybil was of course a marvel of a woman, unselfish, untiring, the most wonderful support for a man following a political career. Without her help and encouragement he would never have got started; without her unremitting inspiration during the periods when his party had been in opposition or her total belief in his abilities, he would have been a back-bencher all his life at best or (and more probably) chucked the whole thing. He understood: her life was entirely built around his career. She had no other interests. She had set herself a goal—that one day she would be the wife of the Prime Minister and this, not for what she could gain from it, but for him. She was, by nature, a woman who had to follow a cause. In exactly the manner of, say, the spinster in a village who makes herself an indestructible prop to the Rector, she found completeness in her cause, willingly sacrificing energy, time, personal comfort and even the opinion of others.

But she could irritate.

She had, for example, made it painfully obvious (especially to Mrs Mordecai who had clearly only controlled herself with difficulty over dinner), that she had written off this attractive little island and its people as of no account. Sir Peter Jeffery-Smith and his slightly fey but engaging wife, this oddly assorted trio of Joseph Mordecai and his wife and their delicious daughter, this charming house, the superb and unusual dinner, the soft warmth of the night with its lulling sounds and its tempting perfumes ... all this she had dismissed. He must (within the bounds of loyalty of course) do something to redress the balance.

'Well, I must say,' he answered Joseph. 'It *sounds* relaxing.'

'Oh it is. It is,' said Joseph, seizing on this gratefully. 'Such a peaceful island. One knows that nothing, absolutely nothing, is going to happen.'

'Why should anything happen?' demanded Elaine, effectively pointing out two things: firstly that he had overdone it; and, secondly, that Elaine, who over lunch had thrown cold water over the project, had of a sudden realised that what she had assumed she had achieved, she had not achieved at all—that the project was very much alive.

Keeping it from her had been a calculated decision. Joseph was aware that his outrageous plan would not stand up to quiet, considered discussion and too much commonsense from Elaine might have dented even Carole's enthusiasm. So he had played it down, reaping the added bonus that the more naturally Elaine behaved before the Mastermans, the less likely they were to become suspicious.

It had worked like a charm.

Joseph, an excellent judge of character, adept at reading what was passing through the minds of others whilst hiding his own thoughts under a mask of cheerful urbanity, had weighed up his guests.

Sybil Masterman was, he had gleefully realised, precisely the kind of woman Elaine couldn't bear: tight, limited, humourless, single-minded, cold. Already, over dinner, Elaine had been out of character, correct and precise, attentive yet detached. No one could conceive that anything so absurd as what he had put in train could be perpetrated in her house. Sybil Masterman, at least, would consider the things which were to happen absolutely unrelated, more, unrelatable, to the Mordecai establishment. And as for Masterman, Joseph believed he could draw rough parallels with other men he had known whose natural inclinations had been deflected by marriage whilst other qualities, which otherwise might have lurked unknown, had been guided to the surface. Here was a man of considerable self-control, imbued with principles which would never allow him publicly to rebuke his wife, however uncomfortable some of her utterances made him feel. These were the things he must bear in mind.

In the meantime?

In the meantime, yes, he *had* gone rather over the top. Acting larger than life was a useful ploy for camouflaging motives, but what was said must relate to the larger-than-lifeness of himself and not to the thing in hand. He must avoid the kind of self-indulgence which had earned him Elaine's searching look.

'I think,' he suggested to her, 'you should go and see about the coffee, darling, while I take our guests outside.'

And, giving her no time to remonstrate, he at once led Masterman, in dinner jacket, and Sybil, in evening dress, out on to the terrace.

'There,' he declaimed. 'Isn't it a lovely night!' And, as if discovering Carole: 'Oh, there you are, Carole. Isn't it lovely tonight?'

'Yes,' agreed Carole, who simply could not resist it. 'Everything in the garden's lovely.'

'Won't it be a little cold out here?' suggested Sybil, a little suspiciously. And in fact there was quite a breeze, the night breeze from off the hills behind the peninsula.

'Cold?' said Joseph. 'Did you say cold? My dear lady, this is St Barbara—it is never cold in St Barbara.' As usual he sought an ally: 'You don't find it cold, Minister, do you?'

'Not in the least,' said Masterman. 'I only wish I'd taken your advice and not put this damn thing on.' And he fingered the dinner jacket which Sybil,

81

after research into Chile's climate, had decided was all he would need to take with him. 'I've a good mind to borrow that jacket you offered me.'

'Oh, I shouldn't bother,' said Joseph hastily—and at once received support.

'Mr Mordecai is quite right, Ernest. You know how careful one has to be in the tropics.'

'Why don't we all sit down?' said Joseph.

'There are no mosquitos, are there?'

'Mosquitos? In St Barbara? Ha. Ha.'

'Well if you're quite sure ...'

'Oh, yes. Now ...' Joseph manoeuvred himself so as to be correctly positioned. 'Where would you like to sit?' He made as if to pull back a chair. 'Mr Masterman, may I suggest here?'

'Oh, this one will do ...'

'No. No. That palm tree just masks the Southern Cross ...'

'I happen to have seen,' said Masterman with good humour, 'the Southern Cross rather more times than I care to remember.'

'Really,' said Joseph, watching with relief the Chancellor settling into the indicated chair, and, turning his own attention to seating Sybil: 'How did that come about?'

'I was a prisoner of war in Java and the huts were crawling with bugs. So I slept outside.' Masterman chuckled and, as if in remembrance of those days, put a hand up to his thick moustache and pulled a little at the end of it. 'I used to sleep on a concrete step. On an old macintosh. And straight ahead of me was the Southern Cross.'

'Good gracious!' said Joseph. 'How frightful for you. You couldn't have got much sleep.'

'As a matter of fact, I never slept better in my life. Once my hips had got used to it.'

'What were you doing in Java?' Carole, her interest stirred, enquired. A pity he's so old, she was saying to herself. He certainly makes Henry callow.

He smiled at her—and because she was such a pretty girl and the night was so filled with promise, as had been other nights in the tropics he had known in those few, brief, exciting weeks, he forgot for the moment he was sixty. What was her name? he was saying to himself. Julie. That was it. Julie Venema. He had never mentioned her to Sybil. And there was in his wide-set eyes under his strong, if greying, eyebrows much of the wickedness which Julie, half Dutch, half Malaysian, had been unable to resist.

'I was flying Hurricanes,' he answered modestly.

'Oh,' said Joseph. 'You know all about aeroplanes?'

'Yes, quite a lot. Why? Are you interested

83

in aeroplanes, Mr Mordecai?'

'Aeroplanes? Good Heavens, no. Except to fly in of course. Ha. Ha.' Many thoughts were chasing through Joseph's mind. 'So the tropics are hardly new to you, are they, Mr Masterman?'

'New? Hardly!' said Sybil. 'He spent four months in a Javanese jungle while everyone else was spinelessly giving themselves up to the Japanese.'

'I wouldn't say spinelessly,' said Masterman. 'And it wasn't everyone in any case.'

'But you were in the jungle?'

'Yes, Mr Mordecai.'

Dear me, thought Joseph—and decided to change the subject.

'Will you be joining us for coffee, my dear?' he asked of Carole.

'What? Oh.' Carole, who was beginning to find Masterman a fascinating man, pulled herself together. 'Oh, no, Daddy. I think I'll have an early night. What time is it?'

Thank you, thought Joseph, with an excuse to look at his watch. 'It's five past nine.'

And again Carole could not resist it: 'With any luck, I'll have dropped off by quarter past.'

'Off you go then,' said Joseph a little severely, considering his daughter was pushing their luck too far. And he stood, massive, very much the father, watching her make her goodnights.

'I thought,' said Sybil, when she had gone into the house, 'you didn't approve of people going to bed immediately after meals.'

'Well, no, my dear lady,' Joseph responded disarmingly, 'but the young have such good digestions, don't they?' And as Elaine, prompted by Carole's entry, came out: 'Ah, there you are, darling.'

'Carole's gone to bed.'

'She wanted an early night. How's the coffee coming along?'

'You're ready for it?' Her tone was clipped. There were things going on which were being kept from her.

'And waiting,' said Joseph blandly.

'It's as well,' said Elaine, but to herself, 'that the coffee's not out here already. If it were, I'd probably throw it at him.' But she went into the house again to see about it.

'My husband was also in Sumatra,' said Sybil apropos of nothing as Joseph sat in his favourite terrace chair.

'How interesting.'

'He was at Palembang.'

'Oh?' Joseph had never heard of Palembang.

'It's an oil town,' Masterman explained.

85

'Ah.'

'He was there when the paratroops were dropped. All round his airfield.'

'Good Lord,' said Joseph. 'How terrifying.'

'He lead a party of ground staff out ...'

'But I thought ...'

'He was not on readiness that morning.'

'Readiness?'

'My wife,' said Masterman, 'was a WAAF ... Women's Auxiliary Air Force. She knows all the terms. Readiness is the state of being detailed to be ready to fly when required. You take turn and turn about. I happened not to be on readiness at the time the paratroops were dropped.'

'And they were all around you?'

Masterman raised his eyebrows and nodded slightly.

'That's right. It was quite exciting.'

He was trying to make his mind up about his host, suspecting there was rather more to Joseph Mordecai than met the eye. To live in the style he lives, he told himself, on an island like this where opportunities must be limited, the man's got to be pretty much on the ball. He's a bit suave, even a mite too good to be true ... 'But I like the chap. He's there.' And he chuckled inwardly. Joseph Mordecai was there all right. All of him.

'And you fought your way through them?' said Joseph, genuinely impressed.

'I certainly did not,' responded Masterman. 'I crawled on my belly in a stinking ditch. And made sure everyone else did too. Twenty men with a couple of revolvers between them don't take on several hundred paratroops armed with machine-guns and hand-grenades.'

Had it been possible, it is conceivable that Joseph might at this point have called off his project. The man was altogether too knowledgeable about just those things he had hoped to rely upon. Firearms, parachutes, jungles—one did not expect a British Chancellor of the Exchequer to have been so briefed. But the arrangements were in hand and in any case just at that moment, Sydney, very smart in a gleaming shirt, black slacks and black bow tie, came out with the coffee.

'Thank you, Sydney,' Elaine, who had come out with him, said dismissively.

'Will that be all, Mistress?'

'Yes, Sydney.'

Sydney went back into the house.

'Do you take your coffee white, Mrs Masterman?' Elaine enquired.

'Black.'

'And you take black as well, Mr Masterman?'

'White,' said Sybil.

Elaine restrained herself and began dispensing coffee.

'A liqueur, Minister?' suggested Joseph, rising.

Masterman looked interested. 'What do you have to offer, Mordecai?' He had decided it was time to ease out of formality. 'I have to be a little careful.'

Joseph correctly supposed this to have been said in deference to his wife—men who led twenty others crawling through stinking ditches to avoid several hundred Japanese paratroopers and then a bit later took to the jungle to avoid being captured while all but a handful of the rest had accepted the situation were unlikely to be careful in their choice of drinks.

'My husband,' said Sybil, 'has an ulcer.'

The temptation was irresistible: 'We have just the thing,' Joseph said. 'Our own St Barbara liqueur. I'm told doctors often prescribe it for just your husband's ailment.'

Masterman grinned: 'And what do you call it?'

'Duckanoo. It's made from fermented star apples.'

'What's a star apple?' said Sybil with great suspicion.

'That fruit you had for dessert.' Joseph held out a hand towards a bottle on the trolley. 'Would you care to try it?' Elaine wondered exactly what Joseph would do if Mrs Masterman said she would.

But Sybil shuddered: 'No thank you.'

'A brandy then?' Joseph had turned back to Masterman.

'Nothing nicer.'

'Mrs Masterman?'

Sybil hesitated. 'It isn't local brandy, is it?'

'Actually,' said Joseph. 'It is Courvoisier Napoleon.'

'Courvoisier Napoleon!' exclaimed Masterman. Joseph nodded aimiably. 'Do you know, Mordecai'—his tone was of a man exchanging a happy confidence with an equal—'the last time I had Courvoisier Napoleon was with the P.M. ... With the Prime Minister.'

'Really! And when was that, if I may ask, Minister?'

'Well,' chuckled Masterman, 'as a matter of fact it was on the day we moved into Number Ten. It was the only thing to drink on such a day.'

'And you've never felt the occasion has arisen since?'

Masterman only smiled. 'Tell me,' he said, 'how did you come by it, Mordecai?'

'Oh,' said Joseph casually. 'I was able to render a little service to the French Government. A trifling matter to do with the removal of certain import restrictions on French wines and brandies into St Barbara. They gave me half a dozen cases.'

'Cases!'

'Cases,' said Joseph equably, already busy pouring. And then pausing for a moment to say to Elaine:

'Darling, when Mr and Mrs Masterman leave, you must remind me to give them a bottle of Courvoisier Napoleon to speed them on their way.' And although it was imprudent, added: 'Who knows, the day may come when you may ... I mean should the Prime Minister ...'

Sybil rose like a trout to the very first hatch of mayfly: 'The question does not arise, Mr Mordecai. The Prime Minister will be in Number Ten for many years to come with the unqualified support of every colleague.'

'No doubt,' teased Joseph, in whose agile mind a new idea, or rather a refinement of the original idea, had begun to burgeon. There were, after all, he told himself, people, particularly women, who, when they took a dislike to someone, automatically started disagreeing with them. 'Still it's not a bad thing to be prepared, is it? After all, in politics the most unexpected things are always happening.'

'One way and another,' interposed Masterman, 'I think it might be better if we changed the subject.' He was beginning to like his host very much indeed—the man was so obviously a rascal.

'Of course,' said Joseph graciously. 'Your brandy, Mrs Masterman ... Yours, Minister. And for you, my dear? A little Duckanoo, perhaps?'

'Nothing, thank you, Joseph,' Elaine said firmly—although not as firmly as normally she might. Where was the advantage in charming the husband and aggravating the wife?

She sat down to await events. Joseph meanwhile collected cigars, which he offered to Masterman, who took one appreciatively, remarking dryly: 'Havana, I see.'

Joseph shrugged gently: 'Cuba is so near.'

'You seem to be very public-spirited.'

'We try.'

'And your efforts do not seem to go unrewarded.'

'One reaps where one sows. A little kindness done here and there is not unnoticed.'

'It is a pity,' snapped Sybil, 'that kindness is such a rare commodity, Mr Mordecai.'

'It is indeed,' he agreed urbanely, regarding the cigar he had taken for himself with great attention. 'It is indeed, Mrs Masterman.'

'I noticed,' Sybil went on with a determination not to be checked, 'when we were on the way here from Government House that there were many who could do with a little kindness shown to them.'

Elaine did not like her tone at all.

'To what do you refer, Mrs Masterman?' she asked stiffly.

'To the natives, Mrs Mordecai.'

'The ... Oh, I'm sorry.' Elaine managed the pause brilliantly. 'We don't call them natives. We call them St Barbarans. Or Barbarans for short. Why did you think they needed kindness?'

'Well look at their conditions.' This was something of a hobby horse. 'Look at their houses!'

'Most people find them attractive.'

'Oh, I don't say they aren't attractive.' She managed to make the word sound sinful. 'But prettiness isn't everything. And I can tell you this. Something will have to be done about the way these poor people live.' And with a great sense of personal obligation welling up inside her. 'Something will be done.'

'What do you think?' said Joseph, delighted.

'New houses must be built, Mr Mordecai. Clean, strong, sanitary houses.'

'What,' beamed Joseph helpfully, 'would you suggest? Concrete?'

'Of course. It is the modern material.' And, with withering scorn: 'In the twentieth century, you can't go on building houses of mud and sticks and coconut leaves!'

'Wattle and daub and palm thatch, Mrs Masterman,' Elaine said quietly.

'Wattle and daub and palm thatch then.'

'They happen to be cooler ...'

'And cheaper,' added Joseph, getting in his first plug for St Barbara.

'So no doubt were wigwams in Americas! What sort of country do you think America would be now if they hadn't pulled down the wigwams and put up the skyscrapers?'

An interesting question, reflected Joseph.

Masterman, meanwhile, made no attempt to interrupt. He knew his wife too well. She could be a dangerous woman but, on the other hand, if she were left alone, not pushed too far, she would simmer down. There was a governor on her emotions which stopped them ever really running away with her. Mrs Masterman—and not unreasonably—was annoyed but in control; her husband, seemingly, quite enjoying it all.

'And it's not only houses,' Sybil was going on. 'Look at the way the children dress! No shoes on their feet, the babies naked below their navels ...'

'You think we should put them into Mother Hubbards?'

'I do not think, Mrs Mordecai, you understand what is happening in the world beyond your little island.' Masterman picked up the subtle change of tone; his wife's voice was more reasoned now, she was aware she had gone too far—so now she was speaking not as if to a novice, but as if to someone intelligent enough who, unluckily, had not been so blessed as to have had her own depth of experience. 'Everywhere in the industrialized world, Mrs Mordecai, there is progress and houses are an essential part of that progress. One visits an island such as yours and finds it delightful, enchanting even. But only on one side of the penny. And on the other? Let's be frank, Mrs Mordecai, what does one see? Men who might be doing something constructive lying fast asleep under banana trees, women gossiping on their doorsteps, children who ought to be at school ...'

'It does happen to be a Sunday.'

'But if it weren't?'

'Yes,' admitted Elaine. 'But the people of St Barbara ...'

'And then,' cut in Sybil, as if the people of St Barbara had had their fair share of the conversation, 'think of your infrastructure.

Houses, even delightful homes like yours, without telephones; roads so bumpy one can drive at only ...'

She broke off to slap her wrist. Masterman adeptly seized his chance:

'Talking of roads reminds me of something I meant to ask you, Mordecai.'

'Yes, Chancellor?'

'When we were on the way up here we passed a very curious group of people. In the way they were dressed, I mean. You know, it looked like ... well, actually it looked like fancy dress.'

Joseph showed interest. 'Where was this? Where you saw these people?'

'Well, I couldn't say. I don't know the island.'

'Of course.' Joseph thought about it. 'Ah!' he said. 'Was it on a corner?'

'On a corner? Yes, I believe it was.'

'Jemima's Corner! No doubt about it.' Joseph nodded sagely and turned to Elaine for confirmation. 'That would almost certainly be Jemima's Corner, darling, wouldn't it?'

'I expect so,' Elaine, annoyed by Sybil, baffled by Joseph, but loyal, agreed.

'Coptics, do you think?' pressed Joseph.

The penny began to drop. 'They could be,' Elaine said, more convincingly.

'Unless, of course, it was that new Orthodox lot. They're very active.'

'Tremendously keen,' Elaine confirmed.

'Did they,' Joseph asked of Masterman, 'have censers?'

Masterman found this rather difficult. 'Censers?' he enquired, smiling.

'Yes, you know, incense?' And, at Masterman's frown. 'How were they dressed?'

'Well,' Masterman began, 'they had the oddest hats ...'

'Very tall? The hats, I mean? Were they wearing tall hats?

'Yes, as a matter of fact ...'

'Ah!'

'And they all had beards.'

'Yes,' said Joseph, 'they would have.' He looked to Elaine for her concurrence. 'That would be the Washfoot Bretheren, wouldn't it darling? ... Or would it be the Schwenkefelders?'

'You have,' said Masterman, 'to be pulling my leg.'

'Certainly not, Minister,' said Joseph, a little hurt. 'The West Indies is a great place for religious sects and St Barbara is in particular.' He began to tick them off on his fat fingers, thus being able to glance at his watch and note to his satisfaction that it was all but nine fifteen. 'I've mentioned our Washfoot Bretheren and our Schwenkefelders. Then we have Zoroastrians and Two by Twos ...'

'Two by Twos!' echoed Masterman unbelievingly.

'Two by Twos.' Joseph frowned. 'You know, darling, I haven't seen any Two by Twos for ages.'

'Probably,' said Elaine dryly, 'become Pocomanians.'

'What's that?'

'You haven't heard of them, Minister?' Joseph was amazed. 'Surely? ... No? ... Comes from Pocomania. A little madness, you know. They get the spirit.'

'Really?'

Joseph nodded enthusiastically. 'It's a terribly noisy business. You can hear it going on from miles away. Groaning and drumming and all sorts of gibberish. They get quite carried away. You can stick pins into them and they don't even notice ...'

'I thought,' interrupted Sybil, 'you said there were no mosquitos on St Barbara.' She was examining a wrist she seemed to have slapped to some effect, for, after holding it towards the candle glow and examining it, she brushed something off with a quick, annoyed movement of her other hand whilst her face wore an expression of distaste.

'Well,' said Joseph largely, 'I wouldn't say never. But they're certainly very few and far between. And the ones we do have ... the few ... they're not dangerous, you know ... not the ... what's it called? ... the kind that carries malaria?'

When is that damn aeroplane coming? he was saying to himself. In a minute she's going to be insisting we all go inside and then all those arrangements will have been for nothing and there won't be time ...

'Darling, what's it called? The mosquito that carries malaria?'

'Anopheles,' said Masterman.

'Anopheles! Of course. And you'd know all about them, Chancellor, wouldn't you? I mean, after all, when you were in Java, in the jungle, trying not to be captured by the Japanese ...'

It was wasted, this prattling on. Sybil had risen to her feet and was reaching for her handbag. 'Mr Mordecai, if you don't mind, I wonder if we could go inside? I happen to be very susceptible to mosquito bites whether they be the anopheles or the other kind.'

'Oh, I'm sure, Mrs Masterman ...'

'I think,' said Elaine crisply, also rising to her feet, 'we should do as Mrs Masterman suggests.'

'Oh, very well,' said Joseph irritably, aware that any further attempt to prolong their stay outside would only arouse suspicion. 'But it does seem a pity on such a perfect night.'

'I agree,' said Masterman, standing as

well, brandy goblet in hand. 'But my wife is, as she says, very susceptible to mosquito bites.' He turned a little from them, in fact to take a last, lingering look at the velvety night—and the disloyalty of remembering on how many occasions he'd had to do the same sort of thing before because of Sybil's predilection for coming up in bumps, or her allergies, or something similar, did not escape him. But it was as Mordecai—and what an amusing character this Mordecai was turning out to be—as Mordecai had said, a perfect night. Or an all but perfect night. For such nights were not intended to be wasted—but were wasted unless they were shared. You could not hold such a night—scented, warm and languorous—alone; it was too big for that. Alone you could be commentator, watcher, onlooker—nothing more; only if you shared it could you be of it.

And Ernest Masterman, Her Majesty's Chancellor of the Exchequer, sixty years of age, would at that moment have exchanged all that the carefully plotted post-war years had given him to be back, getting on for forty of those years, to just such a night when he had for the first time taken in his arms a girl very much like Carole Mordecai. Disloyal it might be, but on such a night a man should not have for company a correct, dependable and dedicated wife, but a girl who did not give a damn about his career, whose skin was taut over a supple body, whose perfume rocked the room, who was, like the night itself, a mystery. He felt the emptiness, the bitter gut emptiness, which one day all men of the kind who, while they grow old in body, never really grow old in mind, must face.

And, because he felt this way, he paused, loath to go in, and for a moment longer stared into the darkness at the uncleared bush across from the broad swathe of parkland and then, raising his head, looked up into the sky—a sky so shivering with the stars as to make him catch his breath at the sheer wonder of it and the strength of his sense of *déjà vu*. He looked at the sky and was back to the time before politics crossed his mind, when all that mattered was the warmth of friends, the thrill of flying and the joy of women.

A snatch of doggerel came back to him—a bit of poetry, banal no doubt, but moving at the time, written in his prison camp about men who would never fly in the way they had flown again. 'Gone are the days of do or die, the days so young and free, when birds and I flew in the sky, on wings triumphantly.' He had stood in a concrete compound and watched the cumulus above the high enclosing prison walls and his frustration at captivity had been immeasurably more poignant than that of most of those about him because he had the comparison of a freedom such as they had never guessed, a freedom so encapsulated by that banal bit of doggerel. And now, nearly forty years on, he stood on Joseph Mordecai's terrace at Spoon Point on the Caribbean island of St Barbara remembering, regretting, looking into the blazing sky—and it was only because of this mood of unabashed sentimentality which few of his political friends or enemies would have imagined had a place in the make-up of Ernest Masterman, that Joseph Mordecai's preposterous scheme did not founder on the tiny obstacle of a mosquito bite. For as Masterman stared up into that brilliant sky, wishing the years away, as if in answer to his wishes he heard a sound quite unexpected but totally apt—the note of an approaching aircraft.

'Come on, Ernest,' Sybil chided him impatiently.

He shook his head, a little curtly, and made a gesture, rare to him—the gesture a man makes to silence someone swiftly. 'That's an aircraft,' he said, not turning to the others, searching the sky.

'Oh, no,' said Joseph, hiding his joy. 'Just cicadas.'

'If there is anyone,' snapped Sybil, for

the moment driven to forget her wish to go inside, 'who is likely to be able to distinguish between aeroplanes and cicadas, it is my husband.'

'Shh!' said Masterman. His eyes raked the sky—but he picked out nothing. 'D'you often get aircraft passing over, Mordecai?' he asked.

'Never,' said Joseph cheerfully. 'Do we, darling?'

'Never,' agreed Elaine, looking at him rather carefully.

'I'm sure you must be mistaken, Chancellor,' Joseph said confidently. 'In all the years we've owned Spoon Point, we've never seen an aeroplane. They don't head this way, you know. If they're coming up from Caracas ...'

'It's not that kind of aircraft,' Masterman interrupted. 'It's a small aircraft. Single-engined. Listen!'

And now there could be no argument. The peace of the night had been quite destroyed.

'In-line, you see,' went on Masterman, but offhandedly, the expert who can diagnose without thinking deeply, who does so instinctively. He stood, only his head moving, conveying certainty, an impressive figure. And suddenly. 'There! D'you see it?'

'No,' said Joseph.

'No,' said Elaine.

'It's much too dark,' said Sybil.

'No. Look. You can see the exhausts ... Look!'

And of a sudden, Elaine did see it, briefly, a swift dark shadow blotting out stars in its passage as it passed very low and just ahead of them, its roar at a climax. Then it was gone from sight, the sound of its engine still loud but fading.

'Well it's gone,' said Sybil with satisfaction and turned to go inside.

'I wouldn't be so sure,' said Masterman, still listening carefully. 'I think it's turning. Yes.'

'Isn't it fascinating, darling?' Joseph said.

'Fascinating,' agreed Elaine ironically.

'Look!' shouted Masterman.

'What? Is it coming back?'

'No. Straight ahead. In the bush.'

'In the bush?'

'There's someone there!'

'Oh, no. I assure you, Chancellor. No one would dare to go there at night. It's thick with duppies ...'

'There's someone there. Signalling.'

'Signalling?' Joseph sounded mystified. But then he laughed—a man who had solved a little mystery.

'Peeny weenies!' he announced.

'What are you talking about, man!' snapped Sybil, turning again. Had she been West Indian it would not have been rude and Elaine would not have been angry; but Sybil was not West Indian. And Elaine was very angry.

But Joseph was not angry.

'Peeny weenies,' he repeated. 'It's our name for fire-flies.'

'Ernest, where is the signalling?'

'It's stopped.'

'Peeny weenies,' Joseph insisted cheerfully. 'No doubt about it,' He became conversational. 'It's supposed to be a mating signal, you know. When I was a nipper I used to catch them and put them into bottles. Astonishing what light they give. Comes from the tail ... switches on and off all the time ...'

'There it is again!' There was a note of excitement in Masterman's voice. 'By God ... that's Morse!' He started to read it. 'A ... T ... T ... E ... N ... O ... Dammit, I can't see it for the trees ... He must have moved or something .... Blast! It's stopped again.'

'Why,' said Joseph, 'don't we sit down quietly ...'

'Mr Mordecai,' said Masterman. 'If you are about to suggest that I imagined ... I'm sorry. If you didn't see it ...'

'I saw it,' said Elaine—and Joseph wondered whose side she was on.

'And so did I,' said Sybil. 'But I don't

see why we have to bother with it. There may be any number of reasons why there should be a man out there ...'

'Crabs!' said Joseph. 'That's it. Crabs!'

'Really,' said Masterman, half laughing, half relaxing—for the sound of the aircraft was now very faint and there was, apart from the peeny weenies and the stars, once again only darkness ahead of him now. 'First you tell me it's fireflies and now you say it's crabs.'

'Land crabs,' Joseph explained.

'I suppose,' said Sybil with an irony quite to put Elaine's to shame, 'they carry torches in their pincers to find their way back to the sea!'

'You know,' said Joseph, as it were making a discovery whilst being blissfully unconscious of this irony: 'I never thought of that.' And to Elaine: 'Do you know, my love, whether land crabs go in the sea occasionally? After all, sea crabs come on the land.'

Elaine had no intention of responding but Masterman, whilst inclined to the view that Sybil was really getting no more than she deserved, felt in duty bound to protect her. 'I think,' he remarked drily, 'my wife was merely making the point that she could see no possible connection between crabs and torches.'

'Yes,' said Joseph eagerly. 'It's quite

105

obvious, my dear Chancellor, that Mrs Masterman quite misunderstood me.' He chuckled. 'I was not suggesting that crabs carried torches to find their way to the sea, but that people carried torches to see their way to the crabs.' Masterman laughed and Joseph, encouraged, went on. 'You know, they're quite remarkable creatures. About this time of the year they spawn in the sand and then go back to the woods and mountains—absolutely straight back to where they came from. They don't deviate an inch. If something's in their way they go right over it. And they're quite fearless. When I was a boy ...'

'I doubt,' said Elaine, 'if Mr and Mrs Masterman want to go on listening to your childhood reminiscences ...'

'Of course, how right you are. But you know'—he was talking to Sybil now—'they're extremely good to eat. A bit bony perhaps, but very good. Darling, we must get Gertrude to cook some tomorrow. You cook them in black pepper, Mrs Masterman, and then ...'

'It's very kind of you,' said Sybil, 'but my husband is not allowed shellfish of any kind.'

'Oh, isn't he? Oh, what a pity. Then ...' He broke off. 'Isn't that that aeroplane again?'

'It certainly is,' said Masterman. 'And,

106

what's more, he's being signalled to again!'

'Good Lord!' said Joseph, staring into the night ahead from which came stabbings of light which were unmistakably signals from an electric torch. 'How extraordinary. D'you see that, darling! There's someone out there flashing a light!'

'I wonder why,' said Elaine.

'Quiet, please,' said Masterman. 'Try to spot that aircraft if you can.'

He went to the edge of the terrace, with Joseph, a puzzled slightly affronted expression on his face, following to stand behind him—a tall straight man in black dinner-jacket and a very ample companion in a white tuxedo. The two women, in evening dresses, stayed at the back, picked out by the gentle glow escaping from inside the house. The flashes were continuous now while the sound of the approaching aircraft was growing louder with every moment.

'What's he signalling?' shouted Joseph.

'He isn't,' Masterman shouted back. 'It's just a series of flashes. He's ...'

But the rest of his words were drowned as the aircraft swept up out of nowhere, seemingly directly overhead, crossing the peninsula, shattering the night with its raucous discord yet, for all its loudness, not so loud as it had been earlier and its speed less urgent so that now there was time for all of them actually to see it, so close, and so comparatively slowly did it pass. And then, again, it was fading, seeming to pick up speed, heading out across the sea. And now, ahead, there was only darkness.

'Good Lord,' said Joseph, turning a low and massive head on a bulging neck to follow its course. 'What an extraordinary thing.'

'Very,' said Masterman—and there was that in his tone of voice which gave Joseph satisfaction. 'Very extraordinary indeed.'

Masterman continued to stare at the thick bush whose beginnings were clearly indicated by the irregular outlines of the topmost branches of trees against a sky which, by comparison, seemed almost light. And he listened—but he could hear nothing except the bullfrogs and cicadas, the shuff of the nearby sea and, from some way off, the sound of a barking dog. And at the base of his spine he felt a sensation which was half anxiety and half-excitement and again he was back all those years to Java, in a dark mysterious road which he, and a few fellow pilots, had been advised led them to the port where, perhaps, there was still a ship on which they might escape.

They had driven slowly down that road which soon became a lane, black as the night on either hand with bushes crowding in closer and closer, within which, for all he and his friends knew, were watching Japanese. And then the road became too narrow and too potholed and they knew they had been either misdirected or intentionally sent into an ambush—and they had left the car and carried on, revolvers in hand, edging along that track, ears pricked for the slightest sound, taut, hearts pounding in their chests. In the end the trepidation had been for nothing—there had been no Japanese in Tjilatjap nor any boat and the next day Masterman and one or two others had decided to take to the jungle because apart from prison camp there was nowhere else to go. But Masterman had never forgotten those few suspenseful minutes in the hot darkness of a tropical night—and he never remembered them so clearly as he did now.

'What *is* there, there?' he asked of Joseph, nodding his head in the direction from which the signalling had come.

'Well, nothing,' said Joseph. 'Just a lot of uncleared bush.'

'How much of it is there?'

'About six hundred acres.'

'As much as that.' And, after a pause, thoughtfully. 'That's a lot of land.'

'Oh, it's not much use,' said Joseph cheerfully. 'Very rocky, you know ...'

'Yet it supports a lot of trees.'

'Yes, it does, you know. But they aren't any use ...'

Sybil came to join them, leaving Elaine standing by the doorway.

'How do you account for it, Ernest?' she demanded.

'I don't know.' He spoke slowly. 'Let's sit down, shall we?'

'You don't think ...'

'I think, Sybil, we should sit down and discuss it. If you want to go inside ...'

'No, of course not.' And, as if concerned he might insist on it, Sybil went quickly to her chair.

'Mrs Mordecai,' Masterman said courteously. 'I wonder ... would you mind joining us?' And at her hesitation: 'I should be most grateful.'

Without a word, Elaine obeyed. Masterman indicated his old chair to Joseph—he might have been the host. Only when Joseph had taken it did Masterman sit. He still had his brandy and now he nursed it between both hands.

'We're hardly doing justice to this superb Courvoisier,' he remarked—but went on before anyone might have replied. 'Tell me, Mordecai, how do you normally use this property? Do you spend a lot of time in it?'

'No, not really. Just weekends, you know.' Joseph seemed unusually subdued.

110

'Just weekends.'

'Well occasionally we come for a week or so.'

'But usually just weekends. And how do you define a weekend? I mean ... do you come Friday nights and go back Monday morning?'

'Oh, no. Good Heavens! I couldn't do that, my dear fellow ...'

'You go back Sunday night so as to be in the office first thing Monday morning.' Masterman nodded his well groomed head. 'Because you start early in the tropics, don't you? Most offices are open by eight o'clock, aren't they? And no one wants to flog across the island first and arrive all hot and bothered.'

'What are you driving at, Ernest?' Sybil's voice was keen.

'That normally at this time of night on a Sunday evening the house would ... Mrs Mordecai? Your servants? Are they left here ... when you're back in Dukestown, I mean?'

'Just Sydney. We have a girl comes from the village for weekends. Hazel.'

'Ah, yes. Of course. But she normally wouldn't be here on a Sunday night. But Sydney would be ... I wonder. Would you mind very much asking him to come out here?'

Elaine hesitated. It was, she could see,

111

going the way Joseph had hoped. It was quite astonishing, and even more absurd, but there it was all the same—no doubt of it. Masterman was taking that ridiculous torch-flashing and that damn 'plane ... Carole! It was suddenly crystal-clear. Carole! she'd cajoled that damn Norwegian, Jodestal, into joining in on this ridiculous ... this ridiculous *spoof*— there was no other word for it.

She looked at Joseph. Oh, yes, she told herself, none of the banter now, none of the confident geniality, none of the playful chat ... for the moment that had served its purpose. Now it was another Joseph, a Joseph taking second place, playing second fiddle to Her Majesty's Chancellor of the Exchequer, former wartime hero, experienced pilot and all the rest! This infuriating Mrs Masterman ... she'd already written him off as a perfect fool who talked too much. Now she'd be happy. Now he would see how men who mattered, men who had stiffer competition to face than that which a drivelling little island had to offer, dealt with unexpected and potentially dangerous situations. She wouldn't know it, *Sybil* Masterman, but soon she would be ranging herself behind him, as his strongest ally. What an incredible, what an absurd, what a ridiculous ... the ability to find words properly to define what

she was thinking eluded Elaine Mordecai.
There were just *no* words. It was just
unimaginable that anyone could delude
a ... could *hoodwink* a knowledgeable,
mature, clear-thinking man of the calibre
Ernest Masterman had to be to have got
where he had got, into even considering
the possibility of unrest on St Barbara—yet
here was Joseph doing it! She looked at
Ernest Masterman, saw the sharpness in his
eyes—there was no wickedness now—this
was a man suddenly on his mettle, behind
that high forehead was an acute brain. Yes.
Well, for once at least, she told herself,
Joseph had gone too far, bitten off more
than he could chew, met his match. All
right. She'd have Sydney out. Why not?
It was the best thing. This nonsense had
to be stopped before it had gone too far!

'Of course not, Chancellor,' she said.
'I'll go and fetch him.'

'Oh, darling, there's no need for that,'
said Joseph hastily. And for a moment
Elaine felt a guilt-ridden stab of satisfaction. But she was at once disabused.
'Just ring the bell, my love,' Joseph
went on. 'We mustn't miss anything the
Chancellor has to say to us. It's a very
serious business when people start using
your property for ... for whatever they're
using it for.'

She looked at him steadily, massive,

mopping his brow with a handkerchief pulled from somewhere, worry in his eyes. My God, Joseph Mordecai, she thought, you're the biggest scoundrel in the Caribbean. But she picked up the little bell and tinkled it.

'Thank you,' said Masterman.

'I don't see ...' began Sybil. But she checked herself. She might nag her husband on his diet, worry him on the tie he ought to wear, go through draft speeches and mark them up, check him whenever she observed the least tendency to depart from whatever (at the particular moment) was the party line ... but never, never, never, would she in public criticize him on anything touching politics. This had been a golden rule—she had never wavered from it.

But as Ernest Masterman had been married to Sybil for even longer than Joseph had been married to Elaine, he too had that ability of knowing what she was about to say even before she said it. And he answered willingly enough:

'Our hosts ...' He repeated it. 'Our hosts are not normally here on Sunday nights. There's six hundred acres of uncleared bush out there, on a peninsula jutting out into the sea. Suppose ... well let's say, suppose you were a smuggler, could you think of a better place?'

'But,' objected Elaine, seeing, as she

thought, a marvellous chance of putting a spoke in Joseph's wheel and in fact achieving no more than putting a little more air into his tyres, 'He'd have seen we were here. That pilot. When he flew over ...'

But Masterman was shaking his head.

'Mrs Mordecai,' he said, 'there's a lot of misunderstanding about what a pilot can see from his cockpit and what he can't. And what he can do in the thing. We watch all these James Bond films ... and I love watching them. But it's a lot of nonsense, you know. This business of men in aeroplanes chasing people round fields like dogs let loose amongst a lot of sheep and finally gunning them down. Quite absurd. It came from over there ...' He indicated the direction from which the plane had come. 'Over those trees. By the time he cleared them ... look, it's rather dull and I'm not sure how much time we have to spare ... Just believe me. He could have seen that signalling but he couldn't have seen us. How much light have we on this terrace anyway? And why shouldn't there be light? With Sydney here?'

'Well the man signalling then? He'd have seen us?'

'Agreed. More of a possibility. But even then ...' He stood and went to the terrace edge. 'I don't know. It's lower ... the line of sight ... the screen of trees. Remember ... it was the beam we saw, not necessarily the end of the torch ... but, I agree, it's a possibility. Only I wouldn't want to bet on it.'

'Do you think it was someone smuggling?' said Sybil, who didn't imagine this for a moment.

'No,' said Masterman, seriously. 'No, I don't. I wouldn't want to ...' He broke off. 'Ah,' he said.

'Mr Masterman wants to ask you some questions, I believe,' said Elaine to Sydney, who had just come out from the house.

'Yes, Mistress.'

'Sydney,' said Masterman—and one could see him a Senior Cabinet Minister greeting a minor civil servant entering his office, or a young, yet incisive, Royal Air Force Officer questioning another rank, 'you live here, I understand, while Mr and Mrs Mordecai are away in Dukestown in the week.'

'Yes, Sir,' said Sydney. 'I always been here since Mr Mordecai done bought the place from Mr Lightbourne. Mr Lightbourne ...'

'Never mind Mr Lightbourne,' said Masterman quietly but firmly. 'You heard that aeroplane tonight?'

The question had the most extraordinary effect on Sydney. He appeared physically to back away from it. His eyes, large at any time, grew larger and flashed even in the modest terrace light.

'That ain't no aeroplane, Mr Chancellor,' he declared. 'That a duppy.'

'What?!'

'A duppy,' said Joseph helpfully, 'is a ghost. If you remember, a little earlier on ...'

He was waved to silence.

'That wasn't a duppy.' It was impressive the way Masterman could pick up a word never heard before that evening and use it in the conversation as if it were not new to him. 'That, Sydney, was an aeroplane.'

'No, Sir. That a duppy.'

'What nonsense,' snapped Sybil, exasperated.

'That not nonsense, ma'am. That the real trooth.' In his excited nervousness, Sydney slipped more into local patois. 'I reckon dat de ghost of de aeroplane dat done crashed in the sea twelve year back las' January. An' when them die in sea you can't put rum on them.'

'What is he talking about?'

Elaine noted that Sydney was managing not to catch her eye. All the same, she had to be impressed. He was doing it remarkably well for one who couldn't have had much time for rehearsals.

'Duppies,' she said curtly. She did *not*

like Sybil Masterman ... how such an attractive man ... but one saw it all the time. *And* the other way round. 'There is an old superstition in St Barbara. When someone dies you sprinkle rum on the grave to keep the duppies away.'

Sybil was scandalized: 'I never heard such nonsense!'

'Did you not, Mrs Masterman?' Elaine said easily. 'Well it happens to be true. And not only here. They do it in Jamaica and half the other islands ...'

'Never mind.' Masterman was quiet patience. 'About these duppies, Sydney. Do they come often?'

'No, Sir,' said Sydney. 'I never done heard that duppy come before.'

'You're quite sure?'

'Yes, Sir.'

'So,' said Masterman, 'we can take it that that is the first time you have heard an aeroplane flying over Spoon Point on a Sunday night?'

'On any night, Sir.'

'I see. Now, Sydney, one more question. Can you think of any reason why anyone should be walking around out there ...', he indicated the distant bush, 'at night?'

'No, *Sir!*' He was emphatic.

Masterman smiled faintly. 'More duppies?'

'That right, Sir.'

'If I were to ask you to come out there with me ... would you come?'

'No, Sir.'

Masterman nodded, seemingly satisfied. 'Thank you, Sydney. That's all.' He smiled pleasantly and Sydney went back into the house. Masterman waited until he had gone from their sight and then, coming back to the others, said:

'It may be nothing of importance at all. But ... Mordecai, tell me. This talk of unrest in Christiana. What d'you think of it?'

'Nonsense,' said Joseph promptly. 'Stuff and nonsense.'

'It's what ... three hundred miles away?'

'A little more.'

'And in between ... there's really nowhere. I mean ... of significance.' He was thinking aloud. 'Six hundred miles. That's a fair range for a single-engined aircraft. Not outlandish ... but a fair way.'

'You're thinking there might be a connection with what may be happening in Christiana and what happened here tonight, Ernest?'

'I'm not dismissing the possibility. Tell me, Mordecai ... it's a bit of a way-out idea, I know, but are there any islands in between here and Christiana from which a light aircraft could take off?'

This was, to Joseph, a quite unexpected bonus.

'My dear Chancellor, how should I know?' he protested. 'The only thing I know about the things is what I see from inside the cabin or whatever it's called.'

'Well let me try to help you. The runway at ... Siparia Field?'

'Yes?'

'A light aircraft like the one which just flew over could probably take off, land and take off again quite comfortably.'

'Really,' said Joseph, displaying little interest and in any case knowing this perfectly well from watching Jodestal taking off and landing from it.

'So, all we'd need would be an island fairly flat—it's surprising what you can unstick a light aircraft from once you've got rid of loose rocks and things—fairly flat, or with a bit of land that was fairly flat that was half the length, or even a little less, than, say, Siparia Field. Would you say that was possible?'

'Well, I daresay. But my dear fellow ... I mean, my dear Minister, it's quite absurd. No one lives on them. Except a few fishermen now and again perhaps.'

'Exactly,' said Masterman coolly. 'There are hundreds of islands ranging all the way from tiny specks to quite respectable ones like Bequia and Carriacou. It would be perfectly possible for someone to be using one as a base for flying to Christiana ... or here.'

'But what for?'

'Well,' said Masterman quietly. 'For example ... gun-running?'

Elaine heard Sybil catch her breath. And, incredible though it was, she even found her own heart beating faster than it had business to.

'Gun-running. My dear fellow ... how absurd!'

'Is it?'

Masterman was not at all so sure. In fact, again because of old associations, the idea of gun-running rather appealed to him. There had been another night ... not in Java, but in the Straits of Gibraltar. The *Ark Royal* had been sunk and so they couldn't fly off her to do tank-busting in the desert. They had to wait for a replacement aircraft carrier. Or for the War Office to think what to do with a squadron of pilots stuck on a rock with aircraft without the range to fly anywhere useful. And in the meantime they had to occupy themselves as best they could while waiting for something to happen—waiting in fact for Pearl Harbour to happen—and one of the things they had done was go as watchers for submarines on M.T.B.s patrolling the Straits at night. And the one Ernest Masterman, or rather Ernie Masterman, had always done his watching on had had as its skipper a remarkable character who had done gun-running for both sides in the Spanish Civil War. And Masterman could well imagine Red Hussey doing gun-running to Christiana and St Barbara from some uninhabited, or all but uninhabited, coral atoll in the Caribbean Sea. That would have appealed to him—that was real James Bond stuff. And Red had been of the stuff which made James Bonds creatable.

'Suppose,' he said, 'there was something in this Christiana business after all ... and don't forget if anyone had suggested there was going to be a revolution in Grenada they'd have been laughed out of court ...'

This was getting out of hand. 'You're surely not suggesting,' said Elaine, for once interrupting a guest in the middle of a statement, 'that what happened in Grenada is going to happen here?'

'Good Lord, no,' replied Masterman with a light laugh, 'but what I'm saying is that we don't have to discount the possibility that someone might be using St Barbara in general and Spoon Point in particular as a very useful place for landing something which could, just possibly, be arms. I'm quite sure it's happened before on other islands and I'm quite sure it's going to happen again. And let's face it, Mrs Mordecai, that *was* an aeroplane and that *was* someone signalling to it.'

And Elaine had to admit that, looked at in that way, it certainly did seem plausible.

'Tell me,' went on Masterman, easily now, relaxed, sitting in his chair, legs thrust out, 'apart from landing shall we say contraband on Spoon Point, is there anywhere they could store it? Somewhere out of sight? Any old buildings? Mills? Water-towers? That sort of thing?'

Joseph shook his head. 'Not that I can think of. Can you, my love?'

Elaine wished fervently that at least he wouldn't try to incriminate her as well. The sooner she got him into the bedroom and talked some sense into him the better.

'No,' she said shortly, and convincingly. 'There isn't anywhere.'

'There is a cave of course ... quite a few caves in fact,' Joseph said offhandedly. He put a hand towards the now empty brandy-goblet Masterman had put down on the table beside him. 'Can I ...'

Masterman shook his head.

'No, thank you. Caves, you said.'

'Yes,' agreed Joseph innocently. 'There's the big one where this fellow Cicurel used to keep his boat ...'

'Cicurel? Boat? What sort of boat?'

'Oh, one of these island-hopping things. The fellow turned up one morning at my office and asked me if he could park it in my cave for a few months while he went off somewhere ...'

'He just turned up at your office?'

'That's right.'

'How long ago?'

'Well, I don't know ... Darling, how long would it be since Cicurel bowled up?'

'Nearly a year,' said Elaine between her teeth.

'Nearly a year! And all that time his boat's been in your cave?'

'I really don't know.'

'You don't know.'

'My dear fellow, I don't go in the cave from one year to another. Nasty smelly place. Filled with bats. Snakes too for all I know. He's welcome to it.'

'Did he tell you what he was going to do while his boat was holed up in your cave?'

'Oh, yes. Said he was keen to get into the import-export business.'

Masterman looked meaningly at his wife. 'I'll bet he was,' he said. 'Tell me. D'you ever see him?'

'Oh, yes. Calls in the office occasionally. In fact I've put a little business his way now and then. But he's away a lot of the time. In the States, mostly.'

'What nationality is he?'

'American.'

Masterman fell silent, looking at Joseph. Incredible, he was thinking. The man has to be what Sybil's made it patently clear she thinks he is—a fool. A man arrives from nowhere with an ocean-going boat and gets permission to put it in the cave of a peninsula covered with uncleared bush. There's rumours, maybe quite unjustified, but rumours all the same, of unrest in an island which in Caribbean terms is almost next door. An aircraft flies low, without lights, over a bit of land which even on a dark night an experienced pilot could pick out and someone's waiting with a torch, signalling ... at a time when if it hadn't been for our arriving unexpectedly the house would be empty but for a superstitious West Indian who's too frightened of his so-called duppies to investigate even if he did see something. All these things together and there he sits, puffing his cigar and helping himself to a second brandy as if there's nothing to talk about but land crabs and peeny weenies!

He got to his feet with a sudden compulsion to do something.

'Mordecai,' he said. 'Do you have a torch? A good, powerful torch?'

'Oh, yes. But, my dear chap, you're not

thinking ... at this time of night ...'

'I certainly am.'

'What are you going to do?' cried Sybil in some alarm. 'Where are you going?'

'I am going,' said Masterman, quite grimly, 'to take a good look round in the place where I saw that signalling.'

'Oh, my dear fellow, don't be absurd,' said Joseph comfortably. 'You'll trip on a tree root and break your neck or something. No, I can't allow it. I really can't allow it. You are my guest. I would never forgive myself if anything happened to you.'

'And after that,' said Masterman, taking absolutely no notice of any of this, 'if you don't mind showing me the way, I would like to investigate your cave. I presume there's a path to it?'

'Oh, far too dangerous. Far too dangerous. There's cliffs, you know, and the path skirts quite a few of them. You might fall off ... or a landslip. We've had a lot of rain. I wouldn't ... No, no.'

'Very well,' said Masterman. 'I'm prepared to leave the cave until daylight but not the other.'

'I'll come with you,' Sybil said.

'You certainly will not. If Mr Mordecai cares to come with me, I shall be glad if his assistance. But ...'

'My dear fellow, why not leave it till the morning? You must be very tired after

126

your long flight. And all that bombing and shooting you've had to put up with in Santiago ... Leave it till the morning.'

'If I leave it till the morning,' said Masterman, 'if there is any evidence I have little doubt it will all have been cleared away ...'

'Evidence?' said Elaine. 'Really, with all due respect, Mr Masterman, this is beginning to verge on the absurd ...'

She broke off. She was speaking in exactly the way she would have spoken had Joseph coached her—she could almost hear his voice in her ears. 'Oh, no, you mustn't try to persuade him. Nothing like that. You must deny it. We must both deny it. The very last thing we must ever do is go along with any idea he may have that a revolution's about to break out. Not, that is, until we've got past the critical stage.' The critical stage. Yes, But when would that stage be reached? What else had Joseph up his sleeve? Wasn't it possible that if she didn't speak now, she would for ever after have to hold her peace? Because by not denying she had assented? Damn, damn, damn, damn, *damn* the man! Because she knew she couldn't do it—she couldn't let Masterman know this was nothing but a ridiculous deception. She couldn't let Joseph down. And she saw quite clearly what that meant—that if it went much farther she would, just by her silence, have become a party to it. She would be as culpable as Joseph.

'Mrs Mordecai.' Masterman's tone was considered and understanding, yet with that inflexion in it which it is difficult for a man of power and experience to avoid when speaking to someone, particularly a woman, who he feels has been sheltered from such realities as he has had to face. 'If,' he said, 'anyone had ever suggested the British Government would one day have to send policemen because of a revolution on a tiny Caribbean island, that Government would have been laughed out of office. But it happened in Anguilla. If, before Eric Gairy left for a visit to the States, anyone had suggested that in his absence a party calling itself the New Jewel Movement would have seized power, that person would have been derided as a driveller. But it happened in Grenada ...'

'My dear fellow, you're not suggesting that anything like that's going to happen here?!' Joseph interrupted, consternation and disbelief superbly mixed.

'No,' said Masterman. 'I'm not. In fact there may be a very simple explanation for the whole business. But what we do have to consider as a possibility is that these rumours about what is about to happen in Christiana, which I as much as anyone have been pooh-poohing up to now, may after all have some foundation and that those behind it find St Barbara a very useful base for their operations. This is an ideal place for such a base. Hundreds of acres of uncleared bush on an isolated peninsula which has a local reputation for being haunted, which is normally unvisited and possesses caves of which one at least is large enough to take an ocean-going cruiser. I think you have to admit they don't come much better to a potential revolutionary than that.'

'Well, yes, put that way,' responded Joseph grudgingly. 'But really it's all a bit far-fetched, you know. I mean, speaking plainly, you have, we all know, been under considerable stress in the last few days over this Chile business ...'

'How dare you!' Sybil was scandalized. She had kept silent under a good deal of provocation, but really this was too much.

'Sybil!'

'No, Ernest.' Nevertheless, she muted her anger. 'My husband, Mr Mordecai, happens to be the Chancellor of the British Exchequer. I can assure you no one rises to a position of such eminence without possessing the power of calm and reasoned judgement. My husband, also, has experienced something which very few on this island, I imagine, can match. I refer, of course, to his wartime experiences ...'

'All right, all right,' cut in Masterman tersely. 'And we're wasting time ... Do you have a torch? Or, better still, two torches?'

'You want me to come with you?' Joseph, for one who did not credit Masterman's possibilities, sounded anything but enthusiastic.

'I would *like* you to. But I don't insist, of course.'

'Oh, very well. Very well. I'm sure we have some torches. We do have torches, don't we, darling? Yes, of course we do. I'll go and see what I can find.'

And Joseph, heaving himself to his feet, mopped his brow and set off into the house, his eyebrows cocked in a pained and most expressive way.

FOUR

'They're not gonna come,' said Henry.

'Of course they'll come,' responded Carole. 'When Daddy says something's going to happen, it happens.'

She was wearing what she had dubbed, when coming out to join Henry in the bush, her battledress, which was a jeans suit and a piece of material which she had fashioned into a head madras.

Her coming to join him had been to Henry one of the magical moments of his life. Here there was a different darkness from that of the Mordecais and their guests upon the terrace. Here were breadfruit trees, trumpet trees, mangoes and all manner of others whose clawing roots thrust relentlessly between the rocks with which the ground was strewn, searching out the good rich soil, ignorant of drought or frost. And beneath and between was a wild tangle of ground creepers, brambles, minor bushes. Wherever there was any light by day, something grew, and where there was no light it was because of the leaves above. And so it was very dark and the fireflies here cast a different light—they no longer floated in the darkness but to a degree they banished it momentarily to render it more intense. It was hot and humid, sheltered from the night breeze, heavy with the smell of rich, damp earth mingled with the odour of rotting trees and vegetation; and there was that curious mixture of clamour and silence which laces a tropical night in such a place—the endless croak of frogs, the chatter of cicadas, strange piercing whistles, the call of night birds and other sounds which are unnerving because they cannot be identified.

Never before had Henry Cicurel been alone in such an atmosphere and Carole's coming to join him by way of a path she had known since childhood brought relief as well as joy. Of a sudden there had been silence with every cicada stilled and then he had heard the crackle of twigs snapped underfoot and she was on him, emerging from the night, her face gleaming faintly like the petals of some flower, her perfume putting all the other scents to flight and her nearness making his heartbeats so wild that he could scarcely breathe.

'Hallo, Cy,' she whispered and, magic of magics, touched his hand. 'Hi!' he answered—he could manage nothing more.

Their meeting-place was beneath a massive mango tree from which, as if caught by a projecting branch, hung an opened parachute. The tree was only a comparatively short distance in from the manicured parkland but separated from it by a screen of growth which needed to be parted to allow a view of the distant house. Henry had been waiting here since dusk: in the dark he could never have found his way. But to Carole, equipped only with a tiny flashlight, moving with an ease born both of natural instinct and knowledge of the few paths in this wilderness, there had been no problem.

Henry's mind, restless before, was now in ferment. So many conflicting emotions fought for precedence. The night itself, the hours of waiting and the contemplation of being involved in an absurd and dangerous adventure had built in him a sense of great confusion which was now overlaid by the mental presence and the physical nearness of Carole, who stayed so close that now and then her body brushed his own.

Moreover he was conscious that here, at last, was a wonderful opportunity in which to declare his love. Yet, like all timid lovers at such moments, he feared to destroy the magic by presumption whilst being racked by the anguish of minutes racing by unused.

It was, of course, foolish of him not to have seized his opportunity. Carole was not unaffected by the night and circumstances and she was, in any case, as Elaine at least understood, secretly taken with Henry Cicurel. He might not, it is true, have the looks to match many of the young men who courted her but none of them had arrived out of the blue by sea-going motor-cruiser, given by a doting father as an earnest of the dimensions of life being boss of an organisation such as Cicurels could bring. And it was certainly not every man who, having so arrived, proceeded to tie up his boat and determinedly unaided, set about proving he could carve out his own career.

Henry Cicurel had quite a lot going for him in the eyes of Carole Mordecai.

The trouble was that, brought up in the shadow of a successful and domineering father, he had developed into a modest young man who, not daring to believe he could ever win this dazzling creature, became gauche and tongue-tied in her presence. She could not, but, even now, compare him with Ernest Masterman. Had Masterman been ten years younger (and certainly had he been twenty years younger), Carole would have fallen for him—not because he was a successful man (daughters of men as successful as Joseph Mordecai take such things for granted) and not because of his wartime exploits for, so far as Carole was concerned, the war was just a bit of history put away years and years before she was even born. No, what Masterman had (which Henry, and most of the young men through whom Carole cut a path like a scythe through standing corn, lacked) was certainty. Had Masterman, not Henry, been standing here beside her now, there would have been none of the painful gaps in their whispered conversation—perhaps they would have spoken even less, but each word would have told; and instead of the nervous, unsure and half-stifled laugh of poor struggling Henry there would have been that quiet, assured chuckle from somewhere in the chest she had found delightful. In a word he would have been in control and in the heart of the beautiful, lissom Carole Mordecai, who rampaged so ruthlessly through the ranks of the young men of St Barbara, was a yearning to be mastered. She was a Guinevere surrounded by minor Lucans waiting for an Arthur to come along and, meanwhile, hopeful for a Lancelot—and, but for being so very old, even older than her father, Masterman might have done very well.

So Henry in a way suffered by comparison as he let the precious minutes slip by unused, but really in a kindly way and he did have on his side that quality which Masterman had so wryly reflected on that evening. Henry was young, well made and, for all his superficial uncertainty, an adventurer. If he had found the courage to seize the moment and take Carole in his arms she would not have snubbed him.

'It's all very well,' protested Joseph, 'but even if there is something—which I'm quite sure there isn't!—how can we possibly find it? There's more than six hundred acres!'

He was not exactly whispering—it was not in Joseph's nature to whisper—but he was talking in a tone appropriately low enough for conversation between two men approaching the parachute drop of a gang of revolutionaries.

They were making their way across the open parkland. They were equipped with powerful torches but as yet there was no need to use them with the sky above a vast bowl filled with blazing stars so huge, so many and seeming so near it was as if they could have been reached for and plucked. Only here and there as they passed beneath a coconut palm, with which the parkland was liberally studded, did they have to pick their way with care.

'Exactly,' responded Masterman cryptically.

'What *do* you mean.'

'That you don't drop things from the air into the middle of a jungle if you can help it—you do it in a clearing.'

'There aren't any. Or if there are, I don't know *where* they are. And I'm certainly not ruining my clothes and risking my neck searching for one in that lot. My dear fellow, why don't we leave it until morning? Sydney can rustle up a few men to help us. Or we can just hand it over to the police.'

Masterman was patient, although to be truthful he was feeling less well disposed towards his host than he had been earlier; he had taken Mordecai for an intelligent man even if something of an eccentric; now, disappointed, he was beginning to wonder if Sybil's judgement hadn't after all been the better one.

'I haven't,' he said, 'the least intention of searching through six hundred acres of jungle with a torch. I even doubt if it would be worthwhile by day. If there aren't any clearings, and you should know if anybody does, then what they would try to do would be drop their stuff in this open ground as near to the bush as possible. Which ties up with that signalling we saw. It wasn't far in ...'

'Then they'll hear us coming!' interrupted Joseph with commendable logic.

'Wherever they are, they'll hear us coming. I didn't spend four months in a Javanese jungle without learning that you can't move around in it without giving yourself away. The insects see to that. They stop.'

'Then they'll *hear* us coming!' said Joseph with surprising alarm for one denying all the possibilities.

'If there's anyone still there, they'll *see* us coming.'

'It's all very well ... but how do you know there aren't half a dozen of them waiting with machetes at the ready!' Joseph put a nervous hand to his fleshy throat as if he felt the cutlass cut already.

'I thought,' said Masterman dryly, 'this was all nonsense.'

'Well it is, of course ... I've never heard anything so far-fetched in my life ... But all the same ...' Joseph came to a halt. They had covered perhaps half the distance from the house to the line of bush.

Masterman stopped as well.

'You'd better go back to the house,' he said.

'Why don't we both go back? We can come out first thing in the morning ...'

'Off you go.'

'Well don't you agree? ... That really it's ... I mean ...'

'I don't agree.' Deliberately Masterman

138

switched on his torch and directed its probing beam towards the bush.

'Don't do that!'

Masterman jerked up his wrist and now the beam caught Joseph full face, showing his small blue eyes anxious and indignant, his forehead puckered, his eyebrows raised.

'What are you doing that for?!' he cried agonisingly.

'I think you'd better go back to the house.'

'I can't ... well I can't let you go on by ... My dear fellow, do shine that thing somewhere else. I'm quite blinded. Now I can't see anything ...' It was quite true. For the moment Masterman had vanished—there was only blackness.

'Listen to me,' he heard the Chancellor say. 'In my opinion there isn't any risk and for two reasons. The first is that anything dropped will have been taken away already, we've been so long getting here. And the second is that if anything is happening it's intended to be kept secret—and you don't keep something secret by murdering out of hand the occupants of a house you imagined weren't there, who decide to take a stroll through their garden on a pleasant night because they've perhaps seen your aircraft and maybe your man signalling. You just melt away and keep your fingers crossed they won't find anything. And frankly, Mordecai, I very much doubt if we will. In all probability if there was something dropped it's already safely stashed away in one of those caves of yours.'

'I still don't see why you have to ... well make a target of me!'

'I wanted to make sure that if there is anybody there, they know who you are—for the reasons I've just given you. There's a much greater risk in my opinion if they know a couple of people are heading for them but aren't sure who they are. But I'm not going to pretend, Mordecai, there isn't any risk at all because obviously there is. And there's no reason on earth why you should take it if you don't choose to.'

'It's very ... well you're making it very difficult.'

'Not at all. I'm going on. You can come with me or not entirely as you choose. If you do come the best thing's for both of us to use our torches and try to think of something to talk about which would be natural for the owner of a house and his guest taking a stroll around the grounds.'

'Natural! How can I possibly think of something natural ...'

'You are going to come then?'

'Yes ... Yes ... Yes. What else can I do?! ... But it's either foolish or foolhardy. As for chatting ...'

'You can tell me about those land crabs,' Masterman interrupted brusquely and with no more ado set off. After pausing for a moment. Joseph followed him.

'Here they come,' whispered Carole, quite unnecessarily with her father and Masterman now scarcely a hundred yards away and heading along the edge of the bush towards them.

'Yeah,' responded Henry inadequately.

But who could blame him? He and Carole were at the very boundary of their clearing, Henry holding apart some growth in an attempt to get a better view and Carole leaning against him, her arm around his back to steady herself. He could quite distinctly feel the firm pressure of her breast and the length of her leg, and her perfume swamped him. Sweat was pouring from him, his thudding heart was echoing in his ears and his legs were weak. There was a swimming in his head. It was no good telling himself that this was nothing but a spoof and in reality he was merely a few feet in from the edge of Joseph Mordecai's garden and that the physical closeness of his daughter was a simple matter of necessity. A cool pragmatist might have reasoned in such a way but Henry was no cool pragmatist but a young romantic with the blood running hotly in

141

his veins. He was as excited and as tense as if he *were* a revolutionary in grave danger of being caught if he mishandled the job in hand, and, worse, despised by the girl he loved so hopelessly.

He watched the darting beams of the pair of torches flickering in and out of the undergrowth threatening to expose them both at any moment and he listened, unbelievingly, to the chat of the two approaching men.

'They're talking about crabs!' he whispered.

'Well they've got to talk about something, haven't they?' He could feel her warm breath on his neck, even the vibration of her speech passing through her body, softly, into his. He was amazed she could be so calm.

'Maybe they won't see it.' There was anguish in his voice.

'Don't be so damn foolish, man.'

It *was* rather a foolish remark considering that it had been Joseph who had selected the tree from which the parachute would hang—but all that had been years ago and in another world. Henry could hardly relate the two.

'We'd better be ready.'

Henry felt the withdrawal of Carole's firm yet yielding body from his own as a positive thing. A moment had passed.

He stood erect, taut, his heart's thudding making it almost impossible to breathe. Joseph and Masterman were nearing them all the time. Their voices were louder, their voices, still about land crabs, easily listened to. The torch beams were stabbing the darkness, now on the ground at their feet, now probing the undergrowth, now raking through the trees. Any instant, surely, they must see the parachute. He glanced at Carole—as arranged she had turned away so that if the torchlight shone on her, it would not be on her face; even now, used to the darkness, he saw her in her denim hardly more than a shadow—but a firefly passing by, glowing suddenly yellow phospherescent, gave sufficient light for him to see the madras on her head which, cunning, gave her an extra inch or two of height. Instinctively he reached out a hand for hers but their fingers never touched ...

'Look!' Masterman's monosyllabic cutting, across the nervous flow of Joseph's peroration on land crabs said, more of the man than another could have got into a paragraph. It held satisfaction without triumph and was entirely calm; it was the utterance of a man who had never doubted, proved correct. And the hand which held the torch showed Masterman, even if the adrenalin was flowing faster, fully in control—for the beam lighting the swag of parachute, brilliant white against layered shadows of the mango leaves, was steady.

'Good Lord!' There was the one disbelieving cry from Joseph, superbly done, and then Carole, breaking cover, was crashing through the thin shield of vegetation out on to the open parkland and racing away, her back to her father and to Masterman.

'What's that!' Even Masterman was startled. He wheeled round, his torch carving a sweeping arc in the night, his free arm striking the soft, massive body of Joseph close beside him. The spread of light caught both the back of the blue-trousered Carole racing off and the white face of Henry peering at them from the undergrowth. 'Good God!' he shouted. 'Mordecai, look out!'

There was no time for more. Henry was breaking cover too, not with his back as Carole had done to avoid the risk of scratches, but over-zealously, making a business of it, aware almost with glee of a sharpness somewhere on his hand where thorns had ripped it. Then he was through, turning, running, seeing his shadow cast ahead of him, hearing the shouts behind.

Joseph watched with satisfaction, yet alert for the part, and not an easy part, he had to play. He was to be the larger than life yet rather stupid man brought down to earth, terrified out of his wits yet still unable to credit what was happening before his eyes.

He decided not to speak. Speaking he might give himself away. Instead he stood, mouth fallen open, wide-eyed, his torch falling from his hand to roll a few brief inches and lie carving a swathe uselessly in the sky. He felt Masterman brush past him, blotting from sight the fleeing Carole and Henry as he made to set off in pursuit. But almost at once he stopped.

'Aren't you going after them?' Joseph cried.

'No.'

'But they'll get away!'

'They've got away. I couldn't catch them anyway.'

'D'you think there's any more?'

Masterman turned to see Joseph gazing fearfully into the deep black shadows from which the two forms had emerged.

'There could be,' he said calmly. 'But I doubt it.'

'You didn't think there'd be anyone anyway,' Joseph cried accusingly. 'We might have been killed!' And for good measure: 'Shot out of hand!'

'Well we weren't,' said Masterman

briskly. 'That first one was a girl, wasn't it?'

'Was it? I didn't think so.'

'I'm sure it was. And the man was in some sort of uniform.' Masterman explored the night with his torch. But the parkland was empty, his beam picked up only the mottled trunks of coconut palms and, once, the bright eyes of some animal.

'Looked like a British bush jacket,' he observed. 'He was a white man, so that made sense.' He was thinking aloud. 'The other? The girl? I never saw her face, did you?'

'No.' Joseph spoke impatiently. 'My dear fellow, this is hardly the place to chat ... I mean ... it's all very well ...' He was looking nervously at the bush and turning to look behind him 'For all we know ...'

'Pick up your torch.'

Joseph did so.

'Stay here.'

'Where are you going?'

'To investigate.'

'But ...'

'Keep your eyes skinned.' Careless of his dinner-jacket, Masterman plunged through into the clearing below the mango tree, shining his torch all around him, exploring the enclosing vegetation.

'It's all right,' he called. 'You can come in under here. There isn't anyone.'

146

'Why don't we go back to the house?'

'For God's sake, Mordecai!'

The impatience of tone warned Joseph not to overdo it. He pushed his way, grumbling nervously, into the deeper darkness. His face, glazed with sweat, managed to reflect what little light there was, his huge upper torso, clad in white, was weirdly disembodied, a mid-air blur.

Masterman was standing underneath the tree, his torch focused on the parachute. 'Damn clever, these Chinese,' he observed.

'Chinese?'

'Just an expression.' Masterman spoke in the offhand tone of one to another he can hardly be bothered with but to whom he feels obliged to say something. 'If it hadn't been for the land breeze ...'

'What are you talking about?'

'I'm talking about that drop. Another twenty or thirty yards and it'd have been bang on.'

'Does it matter, man?'

'No, I suppose not.' But the respect in his tone still lingered.

'What are you doing?' Masterman was examining the ends of the parachute strings which hung like white liana, swaying very gently in the light airs under the mango's shade.

'It's very interesting. Look, Mordecai.'

Joseph came unwillingly to join him.

'You see? Cut! And this one. And this one ... but this one? Broken.' He cocked his head to the billowing silk a few feet out of reach. 'I'd say what happened was that whatever was attached was hanging and so they had to cut the cords to get it down and when they'd cut too many for the others to take its weight, they snapped. So ...' He started to flash his torch on the ground.

'So?' said Joseph. 'So what?'

'So the container would have tipped. Maybe ... Ah!' The beam caught something glinting in the trampled mess of old decaying branches and many years of leaves. With a quick step, Masterman was over to it, picking it up, holding it between thumb and forefinger.

'What have you got there, man?'

'I'd say ... a .45. That's a big calibre. They must mean business.'

'What are you talking about?'

'It's a bullet to fit a .45 calibre revolver.'

'Good Heavens!'

'I expect we'll find plenty if we look for them.' He scuffed with his foot amongst the leaves. 'The container tipped, smashed on that rock ... see, that's new wood, isn't it ...' He shone the torch on a splintered piece of packing case. 'Smashed on that and the lid flew open scattering bullets everywhere. And in this stuff ... at night

... There you are!' He picked up a second bullet. 'Maybe that's why they were here so long. Collecting the obvious ones. And then they saw us coming ...' He was thinking aloud again. 'Which means ...' he went on. 'That there had to be others.'

'Oh,' said Joseph. 'How do you know?'

'Someone had to take the container away. Those two certainly didn't have it.'

Joseph congratulated himself on his decision not to leave the packing-crate lest it be traced back to him—it had not occurred to him how much verisimilitude its absence might add by increasing the numbers theoretically involved.

'Have you seen everything you want?' He made his voice uneasily impatient.

Masterman nodded.

'Yes, I think so. I don't think there's anything more we can do here tonight.'

'So what do we do now?'

'Now?' Masterman chuckled. 'Now, we go back to the house to think it over ... over another of your Courvoisier Napoleons. I didn't really show proper appreciation of the last one, did I?'

FIVE

'This nonsense,' said Elaine, 'has gone on long enough.'

They were in their bedroom—a room which had the curiously austere feeling of most modern West Indian bedrooms which comes from an absence of carpets on cold tile floors and the use of the flimsiest of drapes.

'There isn't,' said Joseph complacently, 'any way of stopping it, my love.'

He started to take off his tuxedo.

'You've ruined that, of course,' said Elaine, not without satisfaction. 'It's got green all over the back of it.'

Joseph took off the jacket and examined it. 'How right you are. Now how did I do that? I thought I had been most careful.'

'I think you've gone mad.'

Joseph accepted this diagnosis with equanimity.

'Everyone is more or less mad,' he observed. 'Kipling said so. He also said the English were especially mad. So did Shakespeare for that matter.'

'It isn't funny, man,' expostulated Elaine. 'It's damn unfunny.'

151

He looked at her, scarlet cummerbund in his hand. 'Whoever,' he responded, 'suggested that trying to winkle several million pounds out of the British Government was funny?'

'Oh, that!' She dismissed the possibility. But as promptly came back to it. 'What's the next foolishness on the list? A submarine in the bay? Or is someone going to throw bombs at us?'

'Nothing so crude.' Joseph threw his shirt to the floor, this being his normal method of undressing, to throw everything into a heap and then gather it up in one bundle and dump it in the bathroom's Ali Baba basket.

'What did you mean there's no way of stopping it?' demanded Elaine suspiciously.

'It's like a ball rolling down a hill.'

'Do you mind not talking in riddles?'

'I'm not. It *is* like a ball rolling down a hill. It won't stop until it gets to the bottom. There's nothing the man who threw it can do at all. If it's going to be stopped, it has to be stopped by someone else. And the Mastermans certainly aren't going to try.' He took off his trousers and threw them on a chair and, sitting down on the other single bed, on the outside of it so that his back was to Elaine, attacked his shoes and socks. She was forced to swivel to speak to him.

152

'What are you saying, man?'

'That Masterman's never had such fun since he got surrounded by those Japanese paratroops in Sumatra. He's loving every minute of it. And so far as his wife's concerned, she's smelt a short cut to Number Ten. Ah!' He took off the second shoe and wiggled his toes. 'That's better.' He set about his socks.

'Even if that was true,' protested Elaine, but with a feeling of helplessness creeping over her, 'and I don't for a moment think it is, it won't last until the morning.'

'It will, you know,' said Joseph.

He picked up his second sock and adding it to the first crossed with them to throw them on the pile. Dressed he was huge—in vest and underpants, colossal.

I'm taking this seriously, Elaine said to herself. How does he manage it? I mustn't take this seriously. It isn't serious. It's ridiculous, absurd, it's ... it's asinine! She nearly said as much but managed to resist it. It would get her nowhere. She decided to treat it all with sovereign contempt.

'You'll see in the morning,' she said.

She got off the bed and started to undress. Joseph went into the bathroom and took a shower knowing perfectly well they hadn't come to the end of it. When he came out of the bathroom in dressing-gown, Elaine said:

'All right, man, you win.'

It was, of course, her best approach. Joseph adored her. He had no wish to make her small. But so long as she resisted him he felt obliged to defend himself and he had his own particular methods. But so soon as Elaine gave him best, he invariably crumbled. He sat on the end of the bed, massive, a huge overgrown schoolboy, looking at her reflection in the mirror.

'My love,' he said. 'I need your help.' In fact he didn't need her help—all he needed was her neutrality. But he was wise enough to know that neutrality from women has the briefest of lives.

'I'm not helping you.'

'But my love ... that woman!'

'You're a damn fool, Mordecai, if you think you can get round me that way.'

'It's very serious, you know,' he said.

'What?'

He didn't answer. There was no need to answer. She understood that however outlandish what Joseph had in hand might be, the losses of contract after contract were a very serious matter. She had the terrible difficulty of reconciling nonsense with reality—the method might be zany, the aim was factual. And she *had* thoroughly disliked Sybil Masterman. She watched him going round the room,

154

closing the jalousies, ramming home the pins. By the time he was done, the room would be so dark with the lights turned off, one could sleep till noon. She got up from the dressing-table and went into the bathroom. When she came back, her mosquito net had been organised and the air-conditioner was purring smoothly. Joseph was in bed, his mosquito net tucked in; she slipped, with the deftness of a lifetime's experience, under her own and with no more ado, said:

'All right then. As it's quite obvious any views I may have aren't going to make the slightest difference and as you know damn well I'm not going to let you down, you'd better tell me what's going to happen next.'

'That,' said Joseph, 'depends on Masterman.'

'Oh you don't have any bombs or submarines then?' She was sorry to have said this and went on quickly. 'Joe, just for once could you be serious? You and Carole may find this amusing. I don't. It's not only absolutely childish but so far as I can see can get us into all sorts of trouble.'

'Someone shining a torch? An aeroplane flying low? A parachute in a tree? A few revolver bullets scattered in the grounds?'

'It's not these things happening. It's why

they're happening. To make Masterman, and that awful wife he's got, think something dreadful's going to happen.'

'We haven't tried to persuade him. We've tried to dissuade him.'

'Well what about Henry then? Lurking in the bush dressed up as a ... a soldier? And Carole ... what on earth are they supposed to be doing ...?' She broke off at the obvious answer. 'You should have been christened Esau not Joseph!' she said with spleen.

'That part of it,' objected Joseph, 'was her own idea.'

'Oh what a brilliant man you are. Whatever happens, none of it can be your fault.'

'I would have thought,' said Joseph chuckling, 'that the one person you wouldn't have worried about was Carole.'

'What did you mean,' demanded Elaine, shying away from this, 'that whatever is going to happen next depends on Masterman?'

'That you never get a man to go down the road you want him to by trying to put him in a harness and cracking a whip. At least, not a man like Masterman.'

'What do you do?'

'You point him in the right direction and then just nudge him whenever he looks like veering off.'

'You don't really,' said Elaine amazed, 'believe that by doing what you've done so far, you're actually going to get him to hand over several million pounds of British taxpayers' money?'

'More or less,' said Joseph comfortably. 'It'll need a few more touches here and there.'

'Ridiculous!'

'My love,' said Joseph, 'the trouble is that you're looking at it from your point of view, not theirs. Just think about it for a moment. The man's just arrived from Santiago where there's been a revolution. He's been headed off from Christiana where there's talk of there being a revolution ...'

'Which is nonsense ...'

'Agreed. But he doesn't know. So far as he's concerned Christiana might be only a repeat of Grenada where no one imagined there was going to be a revolution. So he arrives ... what shall we say? Primed for revolution? He sees a man signalling to an aeroplane, goes to investigate, finds a parachute hanging from a tree, ammunition scattered on the ground and a man and a woman making their getaway from a place where normally smugglers, gun-runners or revolutionaries could expect to do what they wanted undisturbed. Now he can't, as you could, relate this to anything. So far as he's concerned St Barbara's a mystery.

All he's seen of it is a shabby airstrip, an even shabbier Government House, a few miles of road that's mostly through banana or sugar plantation, or just plain bush, and a peninsula, a bit of land, most of which isn't cleared, sticking out into the sea. Just imagine you are him, sitting on our terrace. Just a house behind—otherwise darkness. No idea what's to left, to right, or before him. No idea what sort of people St Barbarans are. It can't feel all that different from sitting in the middle of darkest Africa. So what does he do? What would anyone in his position do? He'd try, so far as he could, to relate to the nearest thing in his own experience. We live by comparisons after all. And it so happens that he's had a pretty damn traumatic time in Java and Sumatra which can't feel all that different. So when something happens like what's happened tonight ... Bingo! He's back again. Back in the middle of the war when parachutes dropping and aeroplanes flying all over the place and guns and ammunition and people disappearing into the jungle were like coconuts falling off trees are to us.'

'What you're saying of course,' said Elaine, 'is that you're just damn lucky, as you usually are, because he happened to have the wartime experiences he's had.'

'I'm saying nothing of the sort,' responded Joseph with slight protest. 'We all get an equal share of luck—it's just that some of us have the knack of using it. My love, I'm trying to explain Masterman to you, to show how he's going to do our work for us from now on. If he hadn't been a fighter pilot but ... well a pacifist, or in the Army, or there hadn't ever been a war, he'd have reacted in a different way—but how he reacted would have been conditioned just the same and we'd have had to find the way to use that conditioning.'

'You,' said Elaine. 'Not we. And I don't believe what you're telling me. That amounts to saying you could have ... and you haven't yet, and you won't ... you could have pulled the wool over anyone's eyes whatever kind of man they were.'

'Yes,' agreed Joseph, 'that's exactly what I'm saying. Given these particular circumstances. And maybe you don't even need to have had any revolutions, maybe any old Chancellor of the Exchequer who didn't know St Barbara from Timbuctoo could be talked into forking out a few million. It's not his money after all. But of course it would be more difficult. Maybe one would *have* to have a bomb or two. But let's keep to fact rather than speculation or we won't get any sleep. And we're going to need clear heads in the morning. The slightest slip ...'

'All he's got to do is to talk to that

159

sergeant of police ...'

'What can *he* tell him? Only what we have. That the whole idea of an uprising in St Barbara is absurd. Anyway it doesn't have to be an incipient revolution. Christiana *could* be using us merely as base ... old Gairy *might* be trying to arm a force to retake Grenada. There could be all sorts of reasons ...'

'Which will be going through his mind anyway ...'

'Which will be going through his mind anyway, as you so rightly say. No, we haven't got to our revolution yet. But it's in his mind ...'

'How do you know it's in his mind?'

'Because he *didn't* go to see the sergeant of police. Now, my love, just work that out. Why didn't he do what, on the face of it, is the obvious thing? ... I'll tell you ... Because he's loving it. He's never had such a splendid time since he was crawling through ditches being eaten alive by centipedes, and whatever else lives in ditches in Sumatra, leading twenty men to safety under the noses of the Japanese; or since he spent four months avoiding them and a lot of fifth-columnist Indonesians in Javanese jungles. I'd bet if you'd asked him to tell you what has meant more to him in life ... what's happened in the House of Commons or what happened in the Dutch

160

East Indies, it'd be the Dutch East Indies he'd plump for. So!'

'So? So what?'

'So revolution's in his mind. The wish is fathering the thought. He'd throw it all up, being Chancellor—to be twenty again, flying Hurricanes and all the rest ... You know something? If he hadn't married that woman, he'd never have thought of going into politics.'

'I don't see him as an airlines pilot ...'

'No. Too dull altogether. Too unimaginative. He'd have wanted something challenging. That's the only reason she talked him into politics, because she put it across as challenging. All the same, for all the talk, it's not exactly a heroic business, politics, is it? You don't get awarded medals, do you? You might get a peerage or half a dozen dummy directorships—but no medals. And he's the sort of fellow given the chance'd have more medals on his chest than a dentist has letters on his notepaper. You should have seen him down there with us. Absolutely in his element.'

Elaine followed with her eyes the tiny neon light of a firefly until it switched off, to reappear moments later somewhere else and she listened to the thud of a June bug which for all Joseph's precautions had somehow found its way into the room and was flying madly around, thumping against walls, falling to the floor, righting itself and setting off again on its absurd career. Her mind gave little thought to these things—they were part of the background to every night before one fell asleep, as was the purr of the air-conditioner, the distant barking of dogs, the sounds of frogs and cicadas, the faint feeling of enclosure wrought by a mosquito net. Her mind was much more filled with what Joseph had said to her. It was, she was forced to admit, convincing. She would have changed Joseph for no one, her life was full and satisfying. But one remembered all the same. One looked at one's daughter with her unblemished skin, heard her laughter—and one remembered. And was a little sad. There had been an occasion ... and not so many years ago. Joseph would have been astonished had he known. And, admit it, she had been tempted. Not by the man—she knew that now. But because she had been offered the chance of delaying for a little while something slipping inexorably away. Even of clawing a few years back. It would have been absurd, of course. She'd have bitterly regretted it. And the man?—Now when she met him she wondered how on earth she could have considered him in the same league as Joseph. But it had been very real, very tempting at the time. And so, although it was very different, she could imagine how Ernest Masterman had felt that evening. Joseph was going on, but now Elaine was only half listening to him. She was thinking of Masterman ... and of Sybil. How could a man like him have married a woman like that? And, having married her, how stayed with her? Because of his career, presumably. Would have had affairs? Somehow she doubted it. He had noticed Carole—but then all men noticed Carole. She was too damn beautiful altogether. But the look which had passed through his eyes had expressed exactly the feeling which sometimes passed, guiltily, through her own mind when she looked at Carole, perhaps standing by the pool, the sun gleaming on wet skin, her hand behind her head in that pose she used too often, half a dozen idiots of young men dancing attendance on her—a feeling of regret, not sharp, she had had her share before Joseph swept her off her feet—no, not sharp, but very real, very lasting. Masterman's eyes had held something of that—mingled acceptance and regret. Not the look of a man alert for a possible on the side affair but the look of a man who has come to terms with his situation. Who has rationalized his life and accepted that while there may still be new horizons, loyalty and common sense and rueful admittance of one's age inhibit doing anything about yearnings which have yet to ebb away entirely. But then, suddenly, an incident occurs which brings memories flooding back and temptation to believe is very real—in her case ... well never mind her case, her case was one to be looked back on, seen in perspective. But Masterman ... in the darkness she shook her head. How clever Joseph was, she thought, how good at reading people and, while reading them, convincing them, almost convincing himself. Here he was, under cover of near farce, engaged on a very serious project indeed, conveying the impression of a somewhat overblown and slightly dulled pudding-head while beneath it all alert, watchful, scheming; noting every point, every weakness. Playing on characteristics and emotions.

'What about her?' she demanded suddenly.

'Sybil?'

'Sybil.'

'No trouble,' Joseph said.

'I should have thought she was going to be your greatest danger.'

'On the contrary,' said Joseph, 'she's going to prove my greatest ally.'

Elaine, and Joseph, had got some way towards understanding how it was that the relationship between the Mastermans had endured when they were so obviously unsuited to each other. What they did not understand, and what few people without Ernest Masterman's experience could have understood, was the effect of his having been a Japanese prisoner of war.

Sybil Capel-Davies had been to Ernest Masterman at the time he left Scotland for what was intended to be the Middle East, a cool, attractive WAAF officer who stood out from amongst her contemporaries because of the air of inaccessibility she so well conveyed. She had a style most of the other WAAF officers lacked, a reserve which gave her a touch of mystery and an ability to make Masterman feel he was rather more of a personage than it had ever occurred to him to imagine he was. But he was not in love with her, had absolutely no plans for spending the rest of his life with her and was not under the smallest sense of obligation.

But before he went abroad she spent a night with him at the Regent Palace Hotel in Piccadilly, London, which was the wartime haunt of fighter pilots. It was not, perhaps, the most exciting of nights Ernie Masterman had spent with a girl, but it had a rather special quality. It was, Ernie had admitted to himself, rather like sipping China tea out of Minton, as distinct, say, from gutsy Indian in chipped cups in a lorry-driver's pull-in. He was left with a sense of rather having let things down by not having arranged a suite in Claridges and the certain belief it would not have happened at all but for the fact he was going overseas and Sybil felt such sacrifice was therefore just acceptable. Even so, there would have been no sequel had it not been that as a parting gift Sybil pressed on him a photograph just small enough for him to carry around through all the vicissitudes of the next few months. He lost kit in Signapore, replacement kit in Sumatra and further replacement kit in Java. But one thing he didn't lose was Sybil's photograph, which basically forgotten in his wallet, stayed with him through the jungle and into POW camp.

Anyone who has been a prisoner of war will be aware of the power of the only photograph of a girl a man happens to find himself still owning. Over the months, whenever things are too depressing he turns to it for solace and encouragement, for a reminder that another way of life exists and, with luck, will come again. When food is short he thinks of meals, of tea on a lawn and, of course, of a pretty girl in a pretty frock. And at once gets out his wallet and takes from it the dog-eared photograph. She, who was perhaps merely one of many, becomes the one girl in the world and it is not too long before he has convinced himself he is in love with her. A little sentimentality rounds the sharp edges of life in a prison camp. He begins to toy with ideas which probably never crossed his mind before and soon these ideas, being agreeable, harden to plans which, after a further passage of time, become not merely as it were decisions of late but decisions ante-dating his incarceration. When it's over, when the boat's rolled on, they will marry. Of course. Perhaps it was never spoken of—but it was understood. The number of marriages which have taken place which would not have but for photographs pored over in prisoner-of-war camps must be quite remarkable.

Something of this sort happened to Ernie Masterman so that when the time came to send the only card he was allowed to send, it went to Sybil, who felt entitled to regard this as significant. She waited. She wrote him many letters. On his escape (he had been the only prisoner to escape from a prison camp in Jampan, having done so in a seaplane conveniently moored and left unguarded near his camp), she telegraphed him in India. And when he finally got back to England, she was waiting. The question of their not marrying did not arise.

Before their wedding day, Masterman had realised his mistake but although he had the courage to break off their engagement, he lacked the cruelty. The girl had waited for him and had been given reason to wait.

So they married.

Thereafter it was simple. Sybil had achieved the first step in her plan; Ernest, aware as he stood beside her in the church of what he was doing, was without extravagant expectations. If not, in fact, a marriage of convenience, it was fairly close.

A frequent result of such marriages is an absence of serious discord; when emotions are not stirred, passions are not aroused. When, additionally, there is shared ambition and respect, a workable partnership can result. With behind him a glittering wartime record underlined by the glamour of his dramatic escape, a career in politics for which Ernest Masterman had the equipment and Sybil the influence, made sense and held together what otherwise would have been an empty marriage—many other politicians have found the same.

'I don't think,' said Sybil, 'you should rule

out anyone. Not even the police.'

They were in a room very much a twin of Joseph and Elaine's except that it lacked the air-conditioning. Masterman had left the jalousies open so there was not one solitary June bug but at least a dozen, all bumping against the walls and hissing helplessly on their backs where they had fallen. There were as well several fireflies and not a few mosquitos. Sybil, having examined her net with scrupulous care and rechecked Ernest's tucking-in, had grudgingly agreed to a state of siege rather than spend the night tossing and turning because of heat.

'That's quite true,' he responded. 'As often as not the police are amongst the first to go over to the other side. They certainly were in Grenada. I remember reading they ran up white flags everywhere.'

'So what are you going to do?'

'Well ...' Masterman's voice was thoughtful. 'I want to take a look at that cave and see if it's been used lately. I want to get that 'chute hauled down and see where it came from and check what that ammunition is. And then I think I'll get Mordecai to run me into ... what's it? ... Dukestown ... And I'll have a word with the P.M. on Jeffery-Smith's telephone.'

'It could be tapped.'

'It could. But I doubt it. I don't imagine

they're all that sophisticated. And in any case, I don't see that it matters too much. Those two were obviously left behind to watch whether or not that 'chute was spotted and now they know it was, the thing ... if it is a thing ... is pretty well blown anyway.'

'Do you really think something is going to happen here?'

'That we're sitting on a powder-keg?' He chuckled. 'No, Sybil, actually I don't. It doesn't feel like it.'

'I thought Jeffery-Smith's wife was a bit jumpy.'

'I thought that was just the kind of woman she was. Anyway it's no joke having a Chancellor of the Exchequer and his wife chucked at you when you're got your roof off is it? No, I don't think anything's going to happen here. What I think's more likely is that there really is something in this Christiana business and St Barbara's a useful ...'

'I simply don't see,' Sybil muttered, 'how you can draw that conclusion. If it can happen in Christiana, why can't it happen here?'

'It just doesn't feel like it. We drove to Dukestown from that airstrip and to here from Dukestown ...'

'And saw a lot of people sitting around in their Sunday best looking as if butter wouldn't melt in their mouths. Don't you think that's exactly what we'd have seen if we'd driven into whatever the capital of Grenada's called ...'

'St George's.'

'St George's. The day before Bishop made his move?'

'Quite possibly.'

'And don't forget *this* Chief Minister's just gone to America!'

'I don't rule it out. But I'm not making any snap assumptions either. There may be any number of reasons ...'

'Such as?'

'Well, I must admit I can't at the moment think of any good reason for dropping arms by parachute except someone intends to use them ...'

'And,' interrupted Sybil, pressing her point at this sign of modification in her husband's attitude, 'for all we know, or the Mordecais know, last Sunday may have been rifles ...'

'And the week before hand grenades! Perfectly possible, Sybil. But it's equally possible tonight's drop was nothing more than someone indulging in a little illicit gun-running ...' But, after a pause, Masterman added reluctantly: 'Although if that's *all* it is, I can't see why they can't simply bring them in by boat.' He thought about it. 'It certainly does look as if something might be imminent ... somewhere, anyway.'

'I suppose,' suggested Sybil bluntly, 'it isn't possible the Mordecais are involved in this themselves?'

'For about half a dozen good reasons, no. Why accept us here if there's going to be a drop? Why have coffee outside on the terrace? Why, anyway? The style they live in ...'

'Frankly,' said Sybil, 'I think it's remarkable they *can* live in such a style. In such a limited island. He's not the brightest of men ...'

'He's brighter than he makes himself out to be.' And, ruefully: 'Certainly too bright to queer his pitch, which judging by his brandy and cigars is pretty plumb!'

'How,' said Sybil, momentarily nudged off course, *'could* you have accepted that second brandy?!'

'I didn't accept it. I suggested it.'

'You're absolutely hopeless. I do my best, God knows, but the moment ...'

'Sybil, I'm fine.'

'What about tomorrow? It's not a one-sided thing, you know.'

'When was the last time I had a bad attack?'

'Only because of the trouble I take and the constant reminders you call nagging.'

You can't win this sort of argument so

where's the sense in fighting it, thought Masterman. 'Well, I drank it,' he said. 'And by God it was good. Can we get back to our revolution?'

'It isn't funny, Ernest!'

'It might,' he agreed, 'be far from funny. Suppose ... All right, let's suppose the worst. That St Barbara's booked to be a second Grenada. You and I are part of the group arranging an arms drop. Our parachute catches on a tree for anyone to see next morning. So we're detailed to keep guard on it until it's light enough to get it down, or Harry comes back with a ladder and a saw ... While we're waiting a couple of men come down from the house with torches and spot the damn thing hanging. We go back and report ... there have to be others because what was dropped had already been shifted apart from a few bullets which got scattered when the crate containing them broke open ... We go back and report the whole thing's blown. That tomorrow it'll be all over the island something's cooking ... So. What do we do?'

'We bring it forward.'

Masterman nodded. 'Possibly. On the other hand ... Think of it this way. The only people who know so far are those in the house because there isn't a telephone ...'

'But there is a radio transmitting set.'

There was a touch of triumph in Sybil's voice to which Masterman, whose main concern had been to reassure his wife, was obliged to yield. 'True,' he said.

'There is, of course,' said Sybil, as it were pressing her advantage, 'something very simple they could do.'

Yes, agreed Masterman inwardly, there isn't any blinking that. Aloud, he said: 'If only we knew how imminent this damn thing was.'

He stared through the open jalousies. If they came, he was thinking, where would they come from? Not from the bush—there'd be too much open parkland for them to cross. They'd come from there, from behind those casuarinas. It's narrow there ... what? Thirty, forty yards? He felt a prickling on his skin and found himself listening hard and hearing sounds which up to now he hadn't noticed. I wonder, he mused, what time it gets light here. Six? Half past five? What was it now? Getting on for one. Four and a half ... five hours. That's a long time.

'I don't think,' he said easily, 'we have anything to worry about tonight, if at all.'

If only, he was thinking, I were on my own; if only Sybil hadn't come with me on this trip. He was not afraid—he was one of that very rare breed of men who

174

do not know fear. When the Japanese had strafed the airfield at Palembang he had stood on the end of the runway aiming at them with his revolver, not because it was a brave thing to do or because anyone was watching and marvelling, but because the Japanese were strafing and he had a gun and it was worth a try. But there hadn't been any Sybil with him—all the Sybils had been where they should have been, safe in U.K. Not that Sybil lacked courage. Palembang was not the only airfield he'd known attacked. Hawkinge had been attacked in company with most of the other fighter airfields in 11 Group. And when it had been attacked, Flight Officer Sybil Capel-Davies had been about her business, shepherding the WAAF other ranks down into the shelters, setting a good example, prepared to be blown to bits rather than admit she was every bit as scared as they were. What a frustrating woman she was—the moment she almost drove you to distraction some splendid quality reared its head and sent your bad intentions sprawling. Not for the first time the humour of the situation struck him. All because of a bloody photograph!

And the recollection, and the night filled with danger, with the real possibility that close at hand there could be a bunch of men getting ready to rush the house and murder them all out of hand, took him back through many years and forced comparisons. He was Chancellor of the Exchequer. He walked with lords and dukes and earls and even, sometimes, with royalty. The problems of life were swept away. There was inbuilt dignity and respect, there were no financial problems, his future was assured and there was even the distinct possibility that the one glittering prize yet to be won, the premiership, could one day be his. Could one ask for more? And, just as Joseph had forecast to Elaine, he ruefully admitted one could. What more?

Well, for a start, a beautiful young girl with coffee-coloured skin and such massive conceit in the power of her lithe and sexual body and such indifference to power when it was bracketed with age, that neither Chancellorships nor Dukedoms nor wealth nor fame were qualities yet to be bothered with, where a man was a man because it was as a man you wanted him. Yes, that would be a start, a girl like Carole Mordecai, a girl like Julie. And he remembered, vividly, Julie Venema lying naked beside him in a room not so unlike this room, on a night not so unlike this night, his awareness, as tonight, brought to a fine pitch by the danger of his situation ... Yes ... but what was it Osler had said?

... about the uselessness of men above sixty years of age ... 'the incalculable benefit' if men of his age stopped work? Well it didn't matter ... not the actual words, only the reality of them. A start? He laughed softly at himself. He was too far past the start ... the start had been back in Java and Sumatra and he had left it there when the door of a native gaol had slammed on him and a crowd of haggard, unshaven men had raised their heads to inspect another with a thin face and a damaged belly, in tattered shirt and shorts ... and in one pocket a wallet with a photograph!

So he laughed softly to himself without even realising he was doing so—and Sybil heard, misunderstood and was irritated.

'If,' she protested, 'you find it amusing to be marooned on a peninsula on an island hundreds of miles from anywhere having just got away from one revolution by the skin of your teeth only to drop promptly in on another one, I don't. If you want to know, I'm bloody scared. And if you think that you're making me feel less frightened by making light of it ...'

'I'm sorry,' Masterman said. 'I was thinking of something else.'

'There'll be plenty of time for day-dreaming tomorrow. I should have thought the thing to concentrate on was how to make sure we get through tonight!'

'Well,' he said, 'the safest place to be has to be in the house because if they wanted to do us in, nothing would suit them better than our leaving it.' And, he thought, 'then cut our throats, chuck us into those six hundred acres and leave it to the vultures to clean us up.'

'In here, d'you think?' said Sybil.

'It's as good as anywhere.' He explained his thinking. 'They couldn't cross this side without our seeing them. And Mordecai locked up the house before we went to bed.'

'Nothing to stop one of the servants unlocking it. I didn't trust that Sydney. He kept looking at us in the most peculiar way.'

'Yes,' admitted Masterman. 'He did.'

'As if he knew something no one else did. In fact I thought he was a bit odd right from the time he picked us up from Government House.'

'And he didn't come here the quickest way.'

'What d'you mean?'

'That was quite a loop he did. I'm sure to get here from Dukestown there has to be a quicker way.'

'You didn't say anything at the time.'

'Didn't think anything at the time. It's only when you start ...'

'There's something else that's odd. That

178

girl taking herself off to bed like that. It isn't every day your parents put up the Chancellor of the Exchequer.'

'I wouldn't make too much of that ...'

'Her mother did. She was quite mystified. I suppose she couldn't have been that girl you saw?'

'You don't think that's a bit far-fetched?'

'A daughter holding exaggerated political views? In this day and age?'

'She didn't look like an Enid Kroll to me.'

'I don't suppose Enid Kroll looked like *an* Enid Kroll. I don't trust anyone these days. It's all hijacking and car-bombs and God knows what by people who when you catch them often look as if butter wouldn't melt in their mouths!'

'Anyway,' argued Masterman. 'If it was her, that would make our position safer—with her own parents in the house.'

But secretly he was reflecting on Carole's manner over dinner, admitting to himself that the girl had undoubtedly been tense, keyed up, expectant. Her eyes had been over-lively her gestures exaggerated, her speech not quite convincing. At the time he had dismissed it as youthful exuberance. Now, reflecting on it, he was not so sure.

'Perhaps we ought to tackle them,' Sybil suggested staunchly.

'You mean *now?* Wake them up?'

'Why not?'

'Because,' said Masterman, 'there could be a simple and logical explanation that just hasn't as yet occurred to us.'

This sobered Sybil. It didn't seem likely there could be a simple and logical explanation but if there were and they had done something dramatic ... That *would* be a pretty kettle of fish; they'd be at risk of being the laughing-stock of Westminster.

'Well *he* didn't have one!' she retorted defensively whilst abruptly abandoning the Mordecais to their fate. 'They'll have to look after themselves. It's their precious island, not ours. And I daresay if they ran it better there wouldn't be all these peculiar goings-on.' She shrugged. 'I suppose, assuming, that is, nothing else does happen tonight, the sensible thing's to tell Jeffery-Smith tomorrow what we've seen and heard and catch the next flight back.'

'That,' Masterman agreed, 'is the sensible thing. But it isn't what we're going to do.'

'Oh, for goodness sake, Ernest. You're Chancellor of the Exchequer not ...'

'A wartime fighter pilot! Right. I'm still not walking out on this one.' He softened. 'I think you ought to try to get some sleep.'

'You don't think ...'—she was half serious, half annoyed—'... it might be a good idea to get ... I don't know ... a cudgel or something?'

He laughed.

'The Chancellor of the Exchequer laying about a bunch of revolutionaries with a cudgel? How about that! Ought to put a bit of life into the P.M.'s Question Time, oughtn't it?' He put a reassuring hand upon her substantial shoulder. 'Don't worry, Sybil. I'll give them the good old knees up! There's nothing more effective in the dark!'

SIX

Whether at their home in the foothills above Dukestown or at Spoon Point, the Mordecais invariably breakfasted out of doors unless, as was seldom, it rained. Normally they rose no later than six to enjoy the magic of tropical morning when the air is fresh and filled with birdsong, when every blade of grass and every leaf sparkles with dew, when it is blissfully cool and the day is filled with promise.

Their bedroom, like that of the Mastermans, faced the bay to catch the morning sun but be protected from it at siesta time. It boasted its own small patio for privacy, an area of paving which died into the grass which ran down towards the low cliffs overlooking the bay and the myriad islands beyond.

Joseph was aware of a sense of holiday. For all his easy-going manner he was, so far as business was concerned, a strict disciplinarian, normally being at his desk by eight. It was rare to be at Spoon Point on a Monday morning so he breakfasted well on paw paw drenched with lime juice and eskovitch fish of the heat of an

Indian curry, dressed still in pyjamas and dressing-gown as was his usual custom.

'We must,' he said, pouring himself another cup of coffee, 'make sure the paper isn't delivered. It'll be full of Carnival.'

'That matters?'

'Very much. I have arranged that the Port Lucea Carnival entry use the cricket pitch for practising this morning.'

Elaine's eyes sharpened.

'They're calling themselves the Ninth Battalion this year, aren't they?' she observed. 'And you tell me, man, you don't have all the luck?!'

'They were the Eighth Battalion last year and the Seventh the year before,' Joseph pointed out.

'That's not what I meant as you know damn well. What I mean is you should be so lucky the local entry is Marines!'

'My love,' said Joseph, 'there is nothing in the least remarkable about the Port Lucea band being Marines. It usually is and at Carnival in Trinidad about every fifth band is Marines.'

'Don't avoid the issue, man! The fact we just happen to have a local band of Marines'—the irony was crushing—'isn't something you just happened to remember last night, is it? You remembered it when you talked poor Henry into all this nonsense.'

184

'It crossed my mind,' Joseph admitted.

'It crossed your mind. Where is he, by the way?'

'Henry? Back in the gazebo, I imagine.'

'What do you mean: "Back in the gazebo, I imagine?"'

'He had to move his boat and ours.'

'You had Henry shift two boats! In the middle of the night!'

'They've got good lights ...'

'Where's he put them?'

'Port Lucea wharf. A perfectly natural thing to do for varnishing and that sort of thing ...'

'Drive his boat from the cave! Walk back! Drive your boat! Walk back again! In the middle of the night! Sleep in the gazebo! He'll be an absolute wreck, poor boy! As for you ... well if it's any comfort, so will you before the day is through.'

Joseph's eyebrows raised. 'Me? Why should I be a wreck?'

'Because you may be able to stop the paper being delivered, but there's no way you can stop the radio. And it's nothing but Carnival preparations!'

Elaine's satisfaction was almost gleeful ... but short-lived.

'Oh,' said Joseph cheerfully, 'that was another of Henry's little tasks I forgot to mention. He broke into the house last night and stole them all. And I'd removed the one the Mastermans had in their room. I didn't imagine they'd be interested in island gossip.'

Elaine shook her head, impressed in spite of everything. 'Man,' she said. 'I've got to hand it to you. You're the biggest scoundrel on St Barbara but you're thorough.'

He stood and came round the table to put an arm around her slim shoulders. She looked up at him, made tiny by his enormous size, but very protected by his cradling arm. 'Why was I such a fool,' she said, 'as to marry an idiot like you?' She pushed his arm away. 'Go and drink your coffee,' she ordered, 'and tell me what I've got to do.'

He didn't sit, he paced, softly, in bedroom slippers.

'You must do nothing,' he told her. 'Just go on maintaining it's a lot of nonsense.'

'Not difficult.'

He shook a wise head. 'It may be. You're going to be asked your opinion. By Sybil Masterman particularly. She's going to ask how, if you disbelieve what they think, you explain all the things that are going on ...'

'I thought you said nothing else was going to happen.'

'Nor is it. Or at least very little. But they will think that many things are happening. They will be presented with a series of perfectly normal occurrences all of which have simple explanations into which, because of the way they will look at them, they will read something sinister. They will go down to where we found the parachute and it'll be gone; into the cave and find traces of its being used very recently. Sydney will report ... no, Gertrude would be better—I rather think they're suspicious of Sydney already. We must be careful not to over use him. Gertrude would be better—or even Hazel. Yes, Hazel, I think. Gertrude can be so voluble when she gets going. Hazel will report her radio stolen and when we look round we'll find the others have gone as well. Masterman will want to use my transmitter to contact Dukestown and when he does we'll find the transformer's missing.'

'Henry?'

'Henry. With all these things against the background of last night and the fact they'll have lain awake for most of it, wondering if some gang isn't going to break into the house and murder us all out of hand, they'll be seeing revolutionaries under every bush.'

'Or in every Marine of the Ninth Battalion?'

'Precisely.'

Elaine shook her head very slowly. 'I must admit ... it's damn clever. You might even get away with it. But how ...'

'Do we translate all this into a grant-in-aid? I have yet to work that out. But I'll think of something when the time comes.'

Elaine gazed at a yellow banana quit perched on the side of the sugar bowl helping himself unhurriedly. She could not but draw a parallel of Joseph helping himself to several million pounds of British taxpayers' money. But just then a small breeze caught their bedroom door left ajar and slammed it. The banana quit flew off in alarm.

'That's what's going to happen, you know,' she said.

'What, my love?'

'Something unexpected—that you didn't take into account.'

Joseph was unperturbed. 'Probably several things,' he said. 'But we will meet them as they come.'

It was almost ten when Masterman put in an appearance.

'Good morning, Chancellor,' said Joseph. 'Sleep well?'

'Frankly, very little.'

'Oh, I'm so sorry. And Mrs Masterman?'

'Not too much either. As a matter of fact she's still in bed. She took a couple of Mogadons.'

'Have you had breakfast?'

'I wouldn't mind some coffee.'

'Of course.' Joseph tinkled the handbell. Sydney might have been waiting, so quick was he. 'Bring the Chancellor some coffee, Sydney, will you?' Joseph said.

As Sydney turned to go, Masterman stopped him. 'One moment.' He turned to his host. 'If it isn't too much trouble, I wonder whether Sydney might run me into Dukestown? In about an hour?'

'Bring the car round at eleven, Sydney,' Joseph said.

'Yes, Sir.' Masterman detected a gleam in Sydney's eye which had no business being there, and, when he had gone, said:

'How long has Sydney been with you, Mordecai?'

'Sydney? About fifteen years. Why? My dear fellow, you don't think ... I assure you ...'

'Has he ever,' Masterman interrupted, 'showed interest in politics?'

'Sydney? Good heavens, no! Ha. Ha.'

'You're absolutely certain?'

Joseph raised his eyebrows.

'You haven't noticed any change in him, then? In the last few months?'

'My dear fellow.' Joseph looked challenging, and affronted. 'What *are* you saying?'

'I'm saying,' responded Masterman,

'nothing. I'm merely considering every possibility. Did you walk down to where we found that parachute last night?'

'Yes. It's gone.'

'I know. I took a walk as well. Not only has it gone but there are no more bullets. And it's quite inconceivable that with a torch we found the only two which were scattered around when they cut those cords.' He was at the opened doorway, staring at the distant bush.

'You think that's serious?'

'On the contrary,' said Masterman, 'I'm rather pleased. It means that almost certainly they don't know that we found *any*. They know we've seen the parachute and that man and girl running off. But that's all they do know. I take it you haven't discussed this business any further with your staff?'

'Good heavens, no!'

'And have you reached any conclusions as to what it might be all about?' And when Joseph did not at once answer. 'You must have thought about it. Talked about it to your wife.'

'Well not really. I mean, not all that much. You see ... She thinks there must be some simple explanation. Someone playing a game or something.'

'A game!' said Masterman with an ironic laugh.

'You don't think ... that it could be that? Just a game?' There was masterly dying hope in Joseph's tone.

Just then Sydney came in with the coffee, followed closely by Elaine.

'Good morning, Chancellor,' she said.

'Good morning, Mrs Mordecai.'

'Sleep well?'

'I fear he did not,' said Joseph with a warning look at Sydney.

'I'll deal with it,' Elaine said. Sydney withdrew. Elaine began pouring coffee. At this moment, I'm an innocent party, she was telling herself; by the next, I won't be.

She handed Masterman his cup and at once launched into the usual courtesies as to Mrs Masterman and breakfast. These done, she said: 'If you'll excuse me, I have to do the flowers.' She crossed to an interesting table, a palette-shaped piece of plate glass nestling around a baulk of driftwood. On it lay a mass of flowers: wild banana, anthurium lilies, scarlet hibiscus, others.

Masterman put down his coffee. 'Mrs Mordecai?' he said.

'Yes?' She turned, long-stemmed flower in hand. She wore lemon-coloured slacks and busy shirt.

'I wonder if I might interrupt you?'

'Of course.' With beating heart Elaine

191

laid down the flower.

'I gather,' Masterman said, 'you think what happened last night was nonsense. A game or something?'

'Something like that. What else could it be?' She was doing her best to regard him in the way any sensible woman would have regarded a Chancellor of the Exchequer possessed of the strange notion a revolution was about to break out on her island. 'I think,' she said, 'everyone got rather excited last night.'

'Mrs Mordecai,' he responded. 'With respect, I think you have to be running away from reality persuading yourself someone is playing a game on us.' He listed Joseph's reasons. 'All these things,' he said, 'taken together point to the inescapable conclusion that something nefarious is going on. It may be no more than someone smuggling arms. But when I thought it over I was inclined to discount that because it seemed to me that could more easily be done by boat. And, incidentally,' turning to Joseph, 'I was sure I heard one last night. A boat, I mean. It seemed to be coming and going.'

'The Government launch,' said Joseph happily. 'P.J ... Sir Peter, said he'd arrange to have it on patrol.'

'He didn't mention it to me.'

'I expect he didn't want to worry you.'

192

'Worry me?'

'Well ... you know ... with all that happened in Santiago ... and this talk of Christiana ...'

'I haven't seen any Government launch this morning.'

'Neither,' admitted Joseph, 'have I. Perhaps it's gone into Port Lucea to refuel.'

'What's more,' said Masterman, 'I heard someone sneaking around the house last night.'

'A pity you didn't call us,' said Elaine.

'No. The fellow could quite easily have been a decoy hoping to lure us outside.'

Elaine took a long, deep, mental breath.

'Mr Masterman,' she said.

'Yes?'

'The man you heard last night was not,' she even managed a touch of irony, 'exactly what you imagined.'

'You are saying, Mrs Mordecai?'

'That the man you heard was nothing more than a common or garden tief ... thief. We were broken into last night. They took three radios ...' She turned to a delighted Joseph. 'Hazel's has gone as well.'

'Oh, dear,' said Joseph. 'How unfortunate.'

'Where did they break in?' said Masterman quietly.

'It's a bit of a mystery,' said Elaine finding the going astonishingly easy now she had taken the plunge. 'I suppose Sydney or one of the girls must have forgotten to lock the kitchen door.'

'Unless someone else inside unlocked it?'

'Oh, really, Chancellor!'

'Is there anything *else* missing?'

'Not so far as I can see.'

'A thief breaks in ... and with all the things there are to steal takes just .. three radios?'

'Mr Masterman,' said Elaine, on surer ground, 'you obviously do not understand petty *tieving* as we call it on St Barbara. I can assure you that to break in and then take three radios and nothing but three radios is not in the least abnormal. They are often very simple people. They take things they understand and which are easy for them to sell. I could leave all my jewellery in a pile and as likely as not they wouldn't touch it.'

'I stand corrected,' Masterman said deferentially. 'All the same ... it doesn't strike you as an odd coincidence?'

'Frankly, no, Mr Masterman.'

'But then,' he ended for her with a disarming smile, 'you don't believe in any of this revolution nonsense.' He spoke to Joseph. 'Would I be right in thinking that

194

with three radios stolen there's none left in the house?'

'Well there's one in the gazebo.'

'I imagine,' said Masterman dryly, 'you will find there *was* one in the gazebo.' And, as Joseph made to rise. 'No, don't bother. You'll only be wasting shoe leather. The important thing is not that the radios have gone but why they have. And I suggest the answer is that there is something being talked about, or about to be talked about, which whoever stole these radios didn't, or doesn't, want us to listen to. I suppose you don't happen to have a local paper delivered here when you aren't in residence?'

'We do,' said Joseph, constructing a meaningful frown. 'Sydney's here all the time.'

'And has it come this morning?' Masterman's question was an answer in itself.

'Well, no ... no. Actually it hasn't.'

Surprise, surprise, said Masterman's faint smile. 'Odd, isn't it? How far's ... what was it? Port Lucea?'

'Three miles.' Joseph waved a massive hand. 'Other side of the bay.'

'So we could walk in if we wanted. To listen to the radio or buy a paper?'

'Well, it's very hilly ...'

'I don't think,' Masterman responded, 'a few hills would really present an obstacle.

195

So why does someone go to the trouble of stealing radios and intercepting newspapers when all we have to do is walk, or drive, three miles?' And now his tone changed.

'I will tell you why,' he said. 'Because, Mrs Mordecai, this is anything but a game. This is a very serious business and we could very well be in danger if we do the wrong thing. By the quite unforeseeable accident of my wife and me being diverted here, we have stumbled on to something. Those involved know we have an inkling of whatever it is but they don't necessarily know how much we know. But almost certainly we've forced them either to abandon what they're up to or bring it forward and the evidence of the radios being stolen and the newspaper not being delivered ...'

'Mean they've brought it forward!' Joseph interrupted excitedly.

'Not necessarily although quite possibly,' said Masterman. 'In fact I'd say, probably. But it could just be what they want is for one of us to do something very ordinary such as drive into Port Lucea for another newspaper.'

'You mean,' said Joseph, horrified. 'To kidnap one of us?!'

'Well it is,' said Masterman, 'very much in the fashion nowadays.'

'But you've asked Sydney to run you into

Dukestown. Chancellor, my dear fellow, you mustn't go ...' Joseph's hand was on Masterman's arm, his eyes wide with alarm.

'It's all right,' Masterman said reassuringly. 'It's only a faint possibility. And a risk I'm prepared to take. But there are two things I must do first. Get a radio message through to Jeffery-Smith; and take a look at that cave of yours. If that *was* the Government launch I heard last night, then unless I'm very much mistaken,'—he brought revolver bullets from his pocket—'we shall find a lot more of these and the things they fit. If it wasn't the launch ... then we shall find nothing but,' he smiled, 'snakes and bats.'

'That's all very well,' protested Joseph in an impressive amalgam of disquiet and indignation. 'I mean ... well it's all very far-fetched, of course ... I mean this isn't somewhere like Chile, just a peaceful little island ... but if you were right ... well it's a long way to the cave and the path ... well I mean, anyone could be ... well, waiting. Why don't we just leave it to getting a message through to Dukestown?'

'I have not the least intention,' Masterman interrupted, 'of contacting Dukestown ahead of taking a look at that cave. How exactly do I find it?'

'You're going by yourself?'

'Unless you, or someone else, is going to show me how to get there, I don't seem to have an option.'

'But supposing ...' Joseph didn't finish it.

'If I'm not back within a reasonable time, you get on to Dukestown, don't you?'

'Darling!' Joseph said. 'Can't *you* dissuade the man? We'd never forgive ourselves if anything should happen to him.'

'Nothing,' said Elaine, 'is going to happen to either of you.'

'You mean ... you think that I ...'

'No,' Elaine cut in crisply. 'Carole can show him the way. I don't know why she isn't down anyway.'

And before anyone could have objected she had left them.

'Mordecai,' said Masterman. 'While your wife isn't with us ... I suppose that couldn't have been your daughter we saw last night?'

'My daughter!' spluttered Joseph.

'Or the man ... Cicurel?'

Joseph was silent.

'Your daughter had met him?'

'Well, yes, once or twice ... but ...'

Joseph recovered poise, remembered who he was.

'My dear Chancellor,' he said, 'you go too far. And in doing so prove the point my wife is continually trying to make. It's very strange what is going on. I quite agree. But to dream up an ... an uprising or something with which my daughter is connected ...' He seemed to become even more massive. 'If you choose to go trudging through the bush to that nasty, dirty, smelly cave, do so by all means. But don't expect me to come with you. I haven't been near the damn place in years and I don't intend to now. There's not just snakes, you know, there's scorpions! No, and I don't see why Carole should have to either, particularly now you've started accusing *her*.'

'I haven't.'

'You have as near as Robert is to Bob.'

'It's very easy for a young girl to be swayed,' Masterman said comfortably. 'Particularly so, I should have thought, on a small island like St Barbara where there can't be all that much which is exciting for her to do.' And he had a mental picture of Carole Mordecai taking London by storm. 'You should think of it very seriously, you know. You may be a very important man in St Barbara ...'

'Are you threatening me, Chancellor?' Joseph was all dignity and amazement.

'My dear chap,' Masterman responded easily. 'Let's not quarrel. No, I'm not threatening you. Merely giving you what seems to me to be good advice.'

Joseph was not quite sure how to go on from this point but fortunately at that moment the subject which had triggered off the argument presented herself, looking extremely fetching in mauve corduroy slacks and a suspiciously yielding loose lilac sweat shirt. She came swiftly up to them, tossing her head. 'Morning,' she said to Masterman. 'Mummy tells me you want me to take you to the cave.'

'If you've no objection.'

'Let's go, man.'

Masterman was taken by surprise. 'By all means,' he said. 'How long will it take?'

Carole shrugged prettily. 'Ten ... fifteen minutes each way. Depends on how fast we walk.'

'Any cigarettes on you?'

They had just emerged from the gloom of bush into blazing sunshine. Ahead the ground was open, a wide uneven path strewn with huge boulders whose presence defied imagination, on one side shaded by breadfruit trees, on the other thickly overgrown, falling steeply towards the sea.

'Yes,' said Masterman.

He lit one for her, cupping his hand

around it expertly against the cooling breeze. He found her posed—one foot on a boulder and one hand on that knee, other hand behind her head as if holding her hair to stop it blowing round her face. She was looking out to sea. The twist of her body thrust her breasts through the sweatshirt, her head was turned just so much as to show the perfect profile, the slightly open, full, moist, inviting mouth.

'Your cigarette,' Masterman said.

'Oh.' It was as if she had forgotten. 'Isn't it beautiful?'

'Very.'

'All those islands. thank you.' She took the cigarette.

'Shall we go on?' Masterman suggested.

'Oh it's such a waste of time. And too damn hot.'

She had taken her hand off her knee to accept the cigarette and was now facing him, leaning back against a higher boulder. Her other hand was still behind her head, her dark eyes were unsmiling.

'There's a path just round the corner leads down to a little beach,' she said. 'Why don't we go down there and swim? Much more better.'

'We're hardly equipped for swimming.'

'No one could see us.' She brought her hand down and moved deliberately towards him. 'Why don't we do that?'

201

It was not the first time a young girl had offered herself to Masterman but seldom had it been done with such blatant assurance and so much out of context. He didn't believe it for a moment. He went to the edge of the cliff.

'I can't see a beach,' he said peering down.

'It's undercut. There's just enough sand for two.'

An intriguing image. A man of sixty and a girl of twenty both nude on a sand beach just big enough for two.

'I hardly think,' he said, 'we've time both to go swimming and inspect the cave.'

'Damn the cave!'

He turned. The cigarette was to her mouth, the smoke wreathing from it whipped off by the breeze.

'Miss Mordecai ...'

'Carole!'

'Yes, my dear, if you like. Carole. I'm very sorry, Carole, but pleasant though it would be to go swimming on such a perfect morning in such a beautiful place in the company of such a delightful companion, I intend to inspect that cave.'

There were gratifying nuances in his tone; Carole decided to push her luck.

'You can't be such a fool as that, man!' she said. 'I don't believe it. How often you get such a chance, eh?' And when he didn't answer. 'I saw you looking at me las' night.'

'You're a lovely creature. But you know that.'

She brought her hand down from her head at last (the muscle was in any case beginning to ache) and put it, and the other hand, with the burning cigarette held between two fingers, to her hips.

'No one will know,' she said. 'We can go down and have twenty minutes on the beach and then go back and they'll think we've been to the cave.'

'Why d'you want to stop me going to the cave?'

'I don't give a damn about the cave.' She tossed the cigarette away and came up close to him. 'I'm hot for you,' she said. 'You know that.' She put a hand up to the single button of her shirt.

'Stop that!' said Masterman.

She laughed as if she was going to get her way—and undid the button. 'It's all right,' she said. 'It doesn't do anything. You can't see any more of me.'

This was not quite true for the shirt fell away sufficiently to show the swelling of firm, enticing, naked breasts.

'If you want to see more of me, you'll have to take it off,' she said. And, as if her own words had excited her, her breathing came more quickly. 'Come on,' she said, 'we don't have too much time. Let's not waste it.'

She grasped his arm.

And Masterman realised that both of them were very close to danger. There were pulses beating in him which had no right to be beating, especially as this had all been so patently planned merely to keep him from the cave. He did not think she had intended to do more than get him down to the beach, use up that twenty minutes fooling around, then change her mind and maintain there was no time left. Recollection of Julie Venema were hammering in his mind. The blood in her had flowed so violently that once started there had never been any stopping her. He suspected that Carole was much the same. And if he was right, any lingering compunction she might have could be assuaged by the knowledge that when it was over she would hold the cards. Masterman saw this very clearly ... and he saw something else, that here was the final watershed. She was quite right. He'd never get such a chance again.

He hesitated ... And Carole read him.

Afterwards she could not have said why she did it. Whether it was just gilding the lily, underlining the conviction in his mind she wanted to keep him from the cave—or whether it was something else. Something quite different.

At all events in one swift movement she put both hands to the hem of her shirt and pulled it up and off, shaking out her hair instinctively.

'All right!' she said. 'Let's do it here!'

'Carole ...'

She threw her shirt away, stood proud and beautiful, naked to her slacks, black eyes blazing at him.

'Give it to me, man!' she cried.

Ernest Masterman felt a terrible dryness in his mouth. He knew, even if Carole did not, that she was now his for the taking. He had but to touch her and sex would follow. And he knew something else, an ineffable sadness ... because he had the strength to resist, the strength to admit that he was too old to allow this to happen.

'Don't be such a silly girl,' he said. 'Put that shirt on again and take me to the cave.'

The immediate effect was as if he had slapped her face.

'You think I don't mean it, man?' she called at him.

'No,' he lied. 'You didn't mean it. You just wanted to find a way of keeping me from looking at that cave.'

'You damn, bloody fool,' she said.

But the spell was broken. She bent for

her shirt and put it on again, again shook out her hair.

'You won't get the chance again,' she said.

'I know.' He spoke very quietly. With regret.

'What d'you want to go to the cave for anyway?'

'Your mother didn't explain?'

'Only some damn foolishness that you thought it was being used for smuggling.'

'You think that's foolish?'

It was all very deliberate on Masterman's part, jockeying her back to their initial relationship, aiding her recovery from chagrin or embarrassment. For her part Carole was not so clear of mind. If nothing else, her body was in revolt. It had been the nearest thing.

'Crazy!' she said.

'You must have heard about the parachute drop.'

'Parachute drop?'

There was still dullness in her responses. Masterman gave her time.

'Last night,' he said. 'Just after you had gone to bed.' He explained what had happened. 'You must have heard that 'plane,' he said.

She shook her head. 'I just don't know,' she said, 'what you are talking about.'

Masterman breathed more easily. That

was better. She was recovering. The eyes half closed, even the furrow of her brow.

'You must be a very heavy sleeper, Carole,' he said. 'You went to your bedroom just after nine, fell asleep within ten minutes and didn't come down to talk to anyone until your mother came to tell you to show me the cave?'

'Right.'

'And why,' he said, 'did you pretend just now to want to have sex with me? When I'm nearly three times your age?'

'Who says I was pretending?'

'I do.' He ignored her offer of sex on the path as if it had not been made. 'You wanted to get me to go down to your beach on the pretext of having sex with me, change your mind and by the time we got up here again have a good enough reason for not showing me the cave.'

He paused to give her time to reply. When she did not, he said:

'That was you and Cicurel your father and I saw last night, wasn't it?'

'I don't know what you're talking about.'

'You're playing a very dangerous game, Carole,' Masterman said. 'I only hope for your parents' sake you don't come to regret it.'

'I thought,' she replied very coolly, quite recovered now, 'you wanted me to show you to the cave.'

'That's right,' said Masterman. 'Do that, will you?'

So Carole took him to the cave. And in the cave Masterman found exactly what he had expected to find and exactly what had been prepared for him. There was no boat but there were oil traces on the water; there were no bullets, but there were broken pieces of a packing-crate; the sand behind the ledge which served as a landing stage was scuffed by footmarks.

There was even the butt of a recently smoked cigarette.

SEVEN

It took Sybil quite a little time to work out where she was. Every jalousie blade was firmly shut against the glare but at each corner there was a tiny orifice enabling them to work so that the walls were a regular pattern of minute points of light which, in her bemused state, reminded her of the dots put on a clean sheet of paper as a child before beginning a game of boxes. Also there were sounds difficult to place: one like that of brushing one's fingers against one's palm; another like the regular stroking of a woollen sweater; and a third, the most perplexing, a curious, hasty, running scratch of a sound. Then too there was a scent of cedar and a feeling of security, of being cocooned like a child in muslin.

'Good God!' Sybil sat bolt upright, reaching out both hands to test the realisation and all but ripping the mosquito net in the process. 'Ernest!' she called. 'Ernest! Are you in the bathroom?'

There being no reply she negotiated her way clear of the mosquito net and crossing to the jalousies began to pull out their pins. Bang! each went. Bang! Bang! Bang! And with each bang, bars of sunlight of crucifying brilliance flowed into the room. Now she could see the coconut palms and the sea which had made the first two sounds, and now the several small lizards hunting the jalousie crevices and making the third, hastily decamped.

Sybil Masterman was conscious of numerous conflicting affections and emotions. There was heaviness from the Mogadon tablets. There was a sense of returned apprehension which vied with the rueful feeling known by those who have been taut through a night which seemed so filled with danger but daylight has shown to have been one of perfect peace. There was impatience to be involved with all that must be happening outside the room. There was plain, ordinary annoyance at having wasted so much of a day already.

So she dressed with unusual haste, not giving careful thought as to what out of her enforcedly limited wardrobe she should choose but grabbing at almost the first thing which came to hand. Everything she had to do—the showering, the making up of her face, the arranging of her hair—was a confounded nuisance, taking too long, holding her back. But at last she was done. She opened the bedroom door and ventured along a cool, white corridor which led eventually into the sitting-room, an odd-shaped room with its front wall a battery of glass sliding doors and its roof of curiously folded shape.

There was no one about. The cool green and white sofas were undimpled; the cool green and white Casa Pupo rugs lay correctly on the cool cream terrazzo floor. The magnificent view of manicured grass leading towards the scattered myriad of islands, poured into the room. But there was no one about. And, apart from the indifferent creaking of palms and rustling of leaves, no sound. Or at least no sound connected with human activity.

A very distinct sense of foreboding overtook Sybil Masterman and all the night's apprehensions came flooding back. The silence, the lack of activity, were portentous and put her in mind of Ernest's story of being on that deserted Sumatran airfield and Japanese paratroopers all around in what they called the 'rubber'. She wanted to call out but yet was uneasy of doing so; she yearned for human contact yet was unwilling to draw attention to her presence. Various hob-goblins of possibilities crossed her mind the most pungent of which were that Ernest had been kidnapped and all the other inhabitants of Spoon Point put to the cutlass blade.

Cautiously she went out through the open doors on to the terrace. It was quite deserted. Ahead the bush. To her left the empty pool and beyond it, some way away, the sea glittering through the line of casuarinas. To the right the bay. Not a fishing boat in sight, not a human being. Only the birds. And lizards.

With much trepidation she inched her way towards the swimming-pool and, passing this, reached the end of the house so that now she was able to look along the side of it and across the sweep of drive towards the gate-house where, Jeffery-Smith had told them, there would always be police on duty. But there were none in sight. Inside, perhaps, she tried to reassure herself. She made her nervous way along the side of the house, red-spattered high by rainstorms bouncing off the soil, through stiff, thick-leaved grass which made a rustle she could well have done without, and when at last she reached the corner suddenly saw something which made her blood run cold.

Ahead was movement. Beyond the roadway leading past the property was a piece of land bounded by magnificent flame of the forest trees. But it was not the spectacular orange-red fire of their blossoms which caught the shocked eyes of Sybil Masterman—it was the soldiers!

There must have been upwards of twenty of them—it was difficult to tell how many because of the intervening tree trunks and other vegetation but there had to have been at least a score. They were clad in a uniform such as Sybil travelling the world with her husband had seen in more than one place in the world—in heavily camouflaged khaki battledress. She stared aghast. The men, all black, were drawn up in a double line with rifles on their shoulders and were being addressed by a speaker she couldn't see. Perhaps, had she been calm, for all the West Indian lilt, she might have deciphered what was being said. But by now the adrenalin was being pumped into her veins as never before in her whole life, not even in the days when Hawkinge had been bombed and strafed. Her heart was pounding, her pulses racing and she was aware, more even than of fear, of a desperate sense of loneliness.

If only, it flashed across her mind, if only Ernest were here beside her. Oh God, she thought, they've killed him! They've killed them all! Only she had escaped the wholesale slaughter because it hadn't occurred to them to go searching through bedrooms in the middle of the morning! But the police! Where were the police? Why weren't they at their posts? Had they been murdered too? Or was Ernest right?

Had they thrown in their lot with these ... these rebels! Even acted as decoys! Anything was possible.

What to do? Terrifying helplessness overcame her. What *could* she do? Alone on this peninsula? Not even a telephone in the house. Only a radio transmitting and receiving set. Ernest knew all about radio transmitting and receiving sets. He'd had to know. It had been part of the equipment essential in the jungle. But Ernest was dead. Or captured. What then? No telephone. Only a transmitting set she couldn't operate. It came to her. The bush! There were six hundred acres. No one ventured into it. Why should these men? It was in the open now. Ernest had been right. Their unforeseen arrival had precipitated things. All had been secrecy. But the cover had been blown. Now there was no point in secrecy. Now it was in the open. So they wouldn't have need of those six hundred acres. She turned her head. It was a long way to the bush. Open all the way. It was impossible to cross the parkland unseen. Wait! Could she get to the casuarinas? If she could get to them ... What was it? Forty, fifty yards. A no-man's-land! But if she could get to them ... then she could go down behind them, using them as cover. And where they ended, there the bush began.

Yes, but Ernest? Shouldn't she ... What could she do? No! Into the bush! It was the only place. If she could get there then she'd have time to think. To plan. Wait until dark ...

She pulled herself together and sufficiently so to realise of a sudden that she was bathed in sweat. What am I *doing* she strictured herself, standing like this in the open? If I can see them, they can see me. If it weren't that they were all looking at the man addressing them they'd have seen me already! She glanced quickly round for immediate cover. There was a bush of some sort a few yards to her right. She looked quickly back to the rebels, to the line of shining black faces, the green berets, the sloped rifles, the jungle uniforms ... and found herself looking directly at a policeman who had emerged from somewhere and seemed to be about to move to the gate-house. She could so easily have missed seeing him for he darted back at once from whence he had come and was gone from sight.

Oh my God! thought Sybil Masterman, he's seen me! He's gone to tell them I'm alive. There isn't time to steal away. They know I'm here. There's only one thing to do. Run! Run! Run! Run for the bush!

And she turned and ran as fast as her middle-aged legs would take her, flying past the house, caution thrown entirely to the winds, heading for the bush which had seemed so threatening and was now so welcoming, her heart pounding and thumping in her breast, her lungs gasping for air, she ran and ran and ran! And ran full tilt into Joseph and Elaine coming round the corner from talking to Henry in the gazebo.

And any woman would have done the same. How could it have occurred to her that a policeman who leaves his post to sneak a preview of the local entry for Carnival will do all he can to get back to it unnoticed?

Joseph Mordecai's judgement had been correct. On the evidence presented to her and thrown off balance by the anguish of the night, Sybil Masterman had needed only the sight of a few local villagers dressed up as Marines to be utterly convinced—and the normal happening of a policeman trying to keep out of being reported to his Sergeant was more than sinister in her eyes. It was the final proof. A revolution was imminent on St Barbara!

'My dear lady!' Joseph gasped.
She had knocked all the breath out of him. And his panama had fallen sideways

on his head giving him a rather drunken look. His eyebrows were at their highest and his eyes especially brilliant with the shock of it.

'Oh!' said Sybil 'Oh!' And then, grasping at Joseph's arm. 'Where have you come from?'

'Taking a stroll in the garden,' said Elaine.

'Taking a stroll!' Sybil turned her head. But from here she could no longer see the soldiers. Only that she was not pursued. 'But ... don't you realise? ... Where's my husband?'

'Gone with my daughter to the cave.'

'To the ... cave?' Sybil was terribly short of breath, her words coming spasmodically. She was still clinging to Joseph's arm, its enormous girth giving her subconscious comfort.

'Yes—Joseph! Put your hat straight! You look like a damn racecourse bookmaker.' Elaine turned back to Sybil. 'Is something the matter, Mrs Masterman?'

'Is ... something ... Yes! ... Yes ... You haven't ... seen them?'

'Seen who, Mrs Masterman?'

'We must go inside ... At ... once! No ... not inside ...' She was terribly unsure, in a state of mind rare to her. Instinct still urged her to seek cover, reason told her she had misjudged the urgency of the situation, pride that she looked foolish. Reason and pride together triumphed. She released Joseph. She turned and, more deliberately, looked back the way she had come. There was nothing to see of any account. Only the side of the house, the driveway, the deserted gate-house. From the new angle from which she was now looking she could no longer see any men in uniform, nor any men at all.

She made a great effort. Her heart was still pounding but her breathing was a little easier.

'I ... I'm sorry if I ... I startled you.'

Joseph had put his hat straight. He was looking at her with his head slightly cocked and jogging up and down a little. He gave no impression of being about to speak. He had been very badly winded.

Elaine also gave no impression of being about to speak—but for different reasons. She was the perfect hostess with the self-control not to make an embarrassing situation worse.

'There are,' said Sybil, 'soldiers just outside your property.'

'Soldiers,' said Elaine factually.

'S ... s ... soldiers?' said Joseph exaggerating his shortage of breath disgracefully to cover up his delight.

'Well men in ... in uniform,' said Sybil, realising that 'soldiers' was really hardly the word and how much off balance she must have been to have used it. She was recovering her nerve fast and in the process gathering irritation. 'Rebels,' she snapped, 'might be a ... a better word.'

'Mrs Masterman ...' began Elaine with patent concern.

'I am,' interrupted Sybil, 'feeling perfectly well. Mrs Mordecai—if that was what you were about to ask. I have just seen upwards of twenty men, fully armed, lined up and taking instructions in that field just outside your property.'

'On my cricket pitch!' said Joseph indignantly, forgetting his breathlessness.

'If that is what it is, they are certainly not intending to play cricket. They are fully armed and dressed in some kind of uniform ...'

'But, my dear lady ...'

'Please do not interrupt me, Mr Mordecai. There isn't time for any of your ... well never mind. There just isn't time. We may very well be in imminent danger of being massacred. How long do you think my husband is likely to be?' She was looking anxiously in the general direction of the cave.

'Oh, any minute now,' said Joseph consulting his watch. 'Any minute.'

'Thank God for that. Now listen to me, both of you. It isn't only that there's a bunch of villains ...'

'One moment.' Joseph held up a powerful hand. He could be very impressive when he chose. He chose to be impressive now. It was essential to cover their position for the future. He was prepared to chance his arm to do so. 'How do you know if these men you say were there ...'

'Were there? Are there!'

'Are there. That they aren't there for some perfectly innocent purpose?'

'Do you think perhaps the St Barbaran Army is carrying out a military exercise on your cricket pitch?!'

'We don't have a St Barbaran Army,' said Elaine icily. 'We have a police force which is quite adequate for our needs.'

Sybil wheeled on her.

'Is it? Then I've got news for you, Mrs Mordecai. Your police force has thrown in its lot with them.'

'Exactly what are you talking about? Really, Mrs Masterman!' Elaine began to appeal to Joseph. 'Joe ...'

'My love,' said Joseph. 'It is quite clear Mrs Masterman believes she has seen something. I do think we should give her the opportunity to explain.'

'Explain!' almost screeched Sybil. 'My God! Talk about Nero fiddling!' She was becoming so angry as almost to forget alarm. 'With my own eyes I saw one of

220

the police you put so much confidence in watching these men. And as soon as he saw me watching him he darted back in the hope I wouldn't see him.' She bit her lip. She must not lose control like this. This, if ever, was a time for a cool clear head. Emotion must be subdued. With a tremendous effort she calmed herself. In the absence of Ernest she had a huge responsibility. Not just to herself, not just towards these hopeless Mordecais, but to St Barbara, to the British Government itself.

'Now listen to me, both of you,' she said, as if she too were back in time, to Hawkinge, addressing a file of WAAFs. 'Whether you care to believe me or not, we are all in great danger. It is patently obvious an uprising such as happened in Grenada, and there are rumours—and it seems to me well-founded rumours—of happening in Christiana, is about to break out. Up to now it has all been kept secret. Your property has obviously been considered a suitable base for training and preparation. Now, possibly because we stumbled on last night's arms drop, it is in the open. They are flaunting themselves just across the road. It is not impossible, and I am not whatever you may think being over-melodramatic, it is not impossible that what I stumbled on was a briefing to invest this property with the intention of at best taking us all hostages and at worst slaughtering us out of hand.'

'Good Lord!' said Joseph, a picture of alarm. 'You don't really think so?'

'I do.' Sybil was a trifle mollified by this reaction. At last the fools were beginning to listen to her. 'When I ran into you I was ... and I'm not ashamed to admit it ... running for the bush because that seemed to me the safest place. I don't mind telling you, I thought you, and my husband, and your staff ... any that are loyal, that is ... had already been ... dealt with.' Joseph's mouth dropped open at the last two words. 'It was a reasonable assumption. The house was quite deserted.' She whipped round on Elaine. 'Where are your staff?'

'I've no idea. In the house, I suppose.'

'They are not.'

'Well they ought to be.' This was accurate enough, but Elaine had a shrewd suspicion where they were. Watching the Ninth Battalion.

Joseph was now holding his panama in one hand and mopping his forehead with a handkerchief with the other.

'My love,' he said. 'Don't you think ... I mean ...' He cast uneasy glances around him. 'If Mrs Masterman ... well ... well don't you think we ought ... well at least to go into the house or something?'

'Are you telling me, man,' snapped Elaine, 'you're beginning to believe all this damn foolishness?'

'Well, no ... that is ... not exactly ... but, my love ...'

'Never mind!' There was sudden triumph in Sybil's tone. She was looking away from them. Towards Ernest and Carole who had just come into view and were heading out of the bush from which they had just emerged across the open land towards them. She straightened herself and there was much in her stance that was probably in that of Baden-Powell at Mafeking at the sight of Lord Roberts of Kandahar arriving to raise the siege.

Ernest Masterman knew at once that something of great importance had occurred whilst he had been inspecting the cave and that there was an on-going crisis. In her wild dash Sybil's blouse had come adrift from her skirt and had yet to be tucked in again; in all their years of marriage Masterman had never known his wife's dress awry. He watched her walking swiftly to meet him followed, at a more leisurely pace, by an alarmed-looking Joseph and a calm, long-suffering Elaine.

When almost within earshot, he instructed Carole: 'Wait here a minute.' Ignoring any possible reaction by not even looking at her, he strode faster to meet his wife.

'Ernest ...' she began, calling from quite a distance.

'Wait!' The authority in his tone silenced her. When he had come up to her, he said: 'Whatever it is, however important—don't say anything.'

'You mean ...' gasped Sybil, staring over his shoulder at Carole standing fetchingly some way away.

'Yes.' His voice was curt. 'We have to talk to the Mordecais.'

He waited for them to come up, Joseph still puffing and holding his handkerchief in his hand, his face gleaming in the sun.

'Mordecai, Mrs Mordecai,' Masterman's voice was low but unhurried. 'I think it would be wise if you were immediately to confine your daughter to her room.'

'I beg your pardon,' said Elaine.

'For her own good.'

'I have never ...'

'Heard anything so ridiculous?' He shook his head, briefly, smiling faintly. 'I'm sure you have not. But I must ask you to do it just the same.'

'You are not suggesting that ... my daughter is in league with these ... these villains?' expostulated Joseph.

'Yes. That is exactly what I am suggesting.'

'If she were,' said Elaine, 'you don't seriously think, man, do you ...' (this was the first time she had addressed the Chancellor in such a manner) 'that she would stay there? This is hardly the age for standing girls in corners.'

'Surprisingly enough, I think she will. And I have to tell you that if you do not, I shall have to ask the police to take her into protective custody.'

'But, my dear fellow ...'

'I'm sorry, Mordecai, but I don't have the time to argue. Mrs Mordecai will you, or will you not, do as I say? You shall have a full explanation later. But in the meantime please take your daughter to her room and lock her in.'

'My dear,' said Joseph. 'I think ...'

'Oh, very well!' snapped Elaine (in the tone of a woman who finds the rest of the world gone mad), and headed for her daughter.

'Ernest,' Sybil began at once. 'I ...'

'Just a minute!'

Masterman stood watching Elaine go up to Carole. For all the stress of the moment he could not put from his mind the astonishing thought that not half an hour before she had stood in front of him half naked inciting him to have sex with her. That he had very nearly succumbed. That had he done so, not merely the course of history in St Barbara, but his own life story, even his future career perhaps, might have been very different. The superb self-confidence which had until that episode characterized her had been, temporarily at least, clearly dented. Her expression was sudden petulance mingled with unease. She hardly seemed to listen to what her mother said softly to her and certainly did not reply. She merely tossed her head and made her way quickly towards the house, looking the other way as she passed, followed by Elaine, who allowed herself one withering glance at Joseph as she went by.

Sybil, meanwhile, was in a plethora of impatience which barely allowed the two to go out of earshot before she launched into a full but controlled account of her startling news.

Masterman listened in silence, asked her a question or two of detail and then, turning to Joseph, said:

'That boat I heard last night was not, as you not unreasonably assumed, the Government launch; it was Cicurel taking all the arms that have been dropped here. And he made at least two trips.'

'What boat?' said Sybil.

Masterman explained and went on: 'The cave is quite empty but has obviously been used in the last few hours. There are even cigarette ends still to disintegrate.'

'I daresay ...' Joseph began to object but Masterman cut him short.

'In that atmosphere they would disintegrate in no time. That cave has been used within the last few hours. Anyway there's other evidence.'

'Ernest ...'

'I don't think,' said Masterman, over-riding his wife, 'we are in any immediate danger.'

'But those men ... and the police ...'

'The way I read it is this. They don't know what we know and they obviously aren't quite ready.'

'Ready?' prompted Joseph. 'Ready for what?'

'To do,' said Masterman, 'what Bishop did in Grenada and this man St John Bosworth may very well have in mind for Christiana—to take the island over. These things have to be carefully timed and properly liaised. And it would have been just *too* much of a coincidence for my wife and me to arrive the very day they were going to make their move.' He was quietly convincing. 'They realise we know about that drop which means they'll have to speed up their plans as is underlined by Cicurel taking his boat and those arms away last night. But they can't be fools. They must know that a motor cruiser can't get far these days before it can be picked up. So either it's been taken to another safe anchorage where it can't be easily seen or it's going to distribute the arms it's carrying. We don't know how much time they need but it probably isn't all that much on a small island like this one. So, providing they can stop us being in contact with the outside world, we may be no more than a damn nuisance to them. After all there's no reason to think whoever's running this show wants violence. Bishop certainly didn't. There *were* one or two policemen killed in Grenada but I'm sure he regrets it. Once a coup's successful, those who've stage-managed it have to get on with the rest of the world, and never more so than when we're talking about a small place like St Barbara. So where's the profit in doing away with us? Or even taking us as hostages? We can't get off the Peninsula unless we swim for it.'

'Too risky,' Joseph interjected hastily. 'The currents are terrible.'

'Really?' said Masterman dryly, recalling Carole's invitation.

'On the other hand,' he continued, 'it would be plain stupid to make out there's *no* danger. Policemen *were* killed in Grenada and this lot may be perfectly prepared to kill *us* if they feel they have to. So, as I see it, what we have to do is have them believe we think it's no more than someone smuggling arms which, Mordecai, is where your daughter comes into it. I'm not going to give you all my reasons but I'm now utterly convinced it was Carole and Cicurel we saw last night. That doesn't mean she has to be deeply involved and we must hope she isn't; it may be no more than infatuation for this Cicurel fellow. Let's hope that's all it is, or else she's going to be in *serious* trouble ...' He hoped he was convincing but was privately unsure; Carole's recent actions hardly spoke of an infatuation so deep as to make her willing for that reason only to throw in her lot with revolution. 'If this thing can be put down peacefully, obviously it'll be a lot better for her. So that's what we've got to aim for. Putting it down peacefully. I think I've convinced her we believe it's no more than simple arms-running and the best thing's for her to pass that on to them.'

'But how can she locked up in her bedroom?'

Masterman smiled grimly: 'You know your daughter better than I do, Mordecai, but I'd give odds she won't be there long.'

'So what do we do?' asked Sybil who had been much comforted by this calm logic.

'Sit tight on the peninsula and—' to Joseph—'get through to Dukestown on that set of yours.' He broke off at the expression on Joseph's face—then said quietly but without surprise: 'What's happened then?'

'The transformer's gone.'

'What!' said Sybil. 'You didn't tell me.'

Joseph refrained from pointing out that he'd had all the breath knocked from him when they met and there'd been no opportunity since he'd got it back.

'Just the transformer?' Masterman, much less put out than Joseph had imagined he would be, said meantime.

'Well it doesn't work without it,' Joseph objected. 'And that's a damn nuisance. I can't get through to my office ...'

'If we can't get through to Dukestown, you may very well soon not have an office to get through to,' Masterman pointed out. 'Tell me about your set.'

'Man, I don't know the first thing about it. I just turn switches on and tap things ...'

But Masterman was paying small attention. He was deep in thought, his fingers playing vaguely with the end of his moustache. 'I wonder ...' he said.

'What?'

'A ferrite collar ... yes.' He was thinking aloud. 'Have to be pretty high permeability iron of course "E"s and "I"s. Or "T"s and "U"s ...'

'You don't mean,' gasped Joseph, trying desperately to sound pleased, 'that ...'

'You cannot,' interrupted Sybil who simply could not resist it, 'buy spare parts in the jungle.'

'You can make one?' Joseph was incredulous.

'Oh, yes,' said Masterman. 'It isn't difficult. One has to have the right materials of course. But you're bound to on a property like this.'

Joseph thought hard; it would be risky pretending not to have what was wanted if it was something he would be expected to have; it might be straining credulity too hard. And once *he* was suspect ...

'What d'you need?' he asked.

'Oh just some wire and bits of metal. And scissors to cut them with. Sort of thing we'll find in your garage most likely. I'll come with you and look.'

That settled it; Joseph abandoned any idea of denying Masterman his requirements.

'How long will it take you to make it?' he enquired.

'Oh,' said Masterman. 'Couple of hours. Maybe less.'

Joseph thought of the banana quit which had flown off because of a slamming door; and of Elaine's prophecy shown justified.

Sybil was thinking too. 'Ernest,' she said, laying a hand on him to detain him.

He looked at her, dishevelled, her dress awry, her make-up carelessly applied. He felt peculiarly sympathetic. The encounter with Carole had underlined home truths.

'Yes, Sybil?' he said quietly.

'That policeman saw me.'

He nodded encouragingly. 'Perhaps. But he doesn't necessarily know you saw those men. And even if he suspects you did, so long as the people running this thing believe we can't get a message out and know we're still all on the premises ...'

'You won't speak to the Sergeant?'

He shook his head, wisely.

'The very last thing I'd do. No, what we have to do is just go on as if nothing is happening. Stroll round the grounds openly, take a swim perhaps, enjoy a cool drink or two on the terrace ... And all the time *one* of us winding that ferrite collar as fast as he or she can go.'

'You've abandoned the idea of driving into Dukestown then?' said Joseph.

Masterman favoured him with his attractive smile.

'Do you really think,' he said, 'that if these people go to the trouble of stealing radios and making off with your transformer, they aren't going to take good care your cars are all u/s?'

'I never thought of that,' said Joseph.

'I think,' said Masterman, 'that when we get to the house we'll find a very puzzled Sydney waiting to tell us they won't start or something. That the tyres are slashed ... No, that would be too blatant. What would you do, Mordecai, to make sure someone didn't try to drive out of here and thus perhaps oblige you to kill or capture him?'

'I ... I ...' He had to say something. 'I'd let out all the oil. Would that do, do you think?'

'I should think,' said Masterman, 'it would do very well indeed.'

In fact Joseph had done something even better. He'd poured sugar, of which in St Barbara there was never the least shortage, into the petrol tanks.

EIGHT

'Where are they?' said Elaine.

'In the radio room.'

'But you said it didn't work.'

Joseph chuckled: 'He's winding his ferrite collar.'

'He's doing his what?'

'Winding his ferrite collar.'

'I once,' said Elaine, 'lived a sane and sensible existence. Now I've got my daughter locked up in her bedroom and a Chancellor of the Exchequer and his wife in your radio room winding his ferrite collar. I've got a posse of policemen at the gate and two dozen so-called revolutionaries marching up and down across the road. I've got an American who needs a shave, dressed up as a colonel, armed to the teeth, in possession of the gazebo; two cars neither of which I can drive because they're all gummed up with sugar; and a staff who've found they're employed by a practical joker and are likely, if they've got any damn sense, to give notice before the day is out. What exactly is a ferrite collar?'

Joseph explained.

'How long's it going to take him?'

'An hour or so.'

'So that's all the time you've got. An hour or so. Or do you intend to cut off the electricity or something?'

'Sadly, my love, it works on batteries.'

'Is it too early for a drink.'

Joseph raised his eyebrows.

'I have never,' Elaine explained, 'needed a drink so badly in my life.'

'It's only half past eleven, you know.'

'I don't care if it's only halfway through breakfast. Get me a drink.'

Joseph did so—and got one for himself while he was about it. Elaine was lying on a chaise-longue in the sunshine. Joseph sat beside her in one of the basket-weave chairs. To Joseph chaise-longues presented avoidable problems.

'It all,' he observed, 'seems to be going very well, don't you think?'

'If you mean by that, have you persuaded them a bloody revolution may break out any moment? yes. But once you've broken eggs into a frying-pan, you can't put them back in the shell, you know.'

'Ah,' said Joseph, 'but think of the things you can do with them, my love.'

'Has it occurred to you that at any time someone might call in?'

'Unlikely. We aren't usually here on Mondays.'

'Your office manager might telephone Roy Mahfood.' (Mahfood was Joseph's local manager in Port Lucea.)

'I had Carole call on him yesterday afternoon.'

'You didn't tell me.'

'Yesterday you weren't on my side.'

'Man,' said Elaine, 'if you think I'm on your side right now, you'd better start rethinking. But anyone might call ...'

'Again unlikely.'

Elaine put down her well prepared gin and tonic which tinkled pleasantly and sparkled gaily in the brilliant sunlight.

'What else have you been doing?' she demanded.

'I hear,' said Joseph innocently, 'there is a tree down on the road. That ceiba just this side of Port Lucea ...'

'Which will take longer to shift than it'll take them—' Elaine nodded her head towards the house, 'to wind their ferrite collar.'

'Hopefully.'

'And the other way?'

'One of those cane carts has broken its axle. I always warned Dudley against overloading them. I should think that'll be there most of the day. There isn't much traffic that way, is there?'

Elaine shook her head—half in disbelief, half with grudging respect.

'So what next?'

'We release Carole. I wonder if you'd mind ... I'll top up while you're off doing it.'

'What's General Masterman going to say?'

'Group Captain Masterman actually. What's he going to say? Oh, he's expecting it.'

'You don't think it would be more convincing to have Sydney chop down her door? Or kick out a set of jalousies?'

'My love, do curb your enthusiasm—these things cost money. And there really isn't any reason why Carole couldn't have provided herself with a spare key against just such an emergency.'

'You think of everything, don't you?'

'It's really the Chancellor's idea, you know.'

'He's discussed it with you, of course.'

'As a matter of fact he has.' He explained. 'While he's quite convinced,' he ended, 'that she's thrown in her lot with the revolutionaries, he's hopeful he's convinced her he thinks she's no more than one of a gun-running gang.'

'The thing that amazes me,' said Elaine, 'is that we're starting to discuss these things as if they were normal everyday conversation.'

'Yes, I must admit, it is surprising how

quickly one adapts. Anyway, to continue. He's quite sure she's going to get out of her room to report to Henry and then I suppose he imagines she'll slip back to her room unnoticed.'

'And that's what she's to do?'

'That is what she is not to do. She is to lead us to Henry's hiding place. Or rather lead Masterman.'

'And?'

'In the nick of time Henry will see him coming ...'

'And shoot him dead?'

'And escape from the gazebo. Or rather try to escape.'

'Oh, I see. The Group Captain is going to capture him.'

Joseph beamed.

'Go on,' Elaine said coldly.

'Henry will try to escape because as the Chancellor has already explained—and very well, I thought—the revolutionaries neither wish to spill unnecessary blood nor have their plans rumbled before they are ready to make their move. Henry, being the leader of the local force ...'

'Oh, really?'

'Didn't I mention that? How remiss of me. Yes, Henry's the leader of the local force. A mercenary with political sympathies—they're very much the fashion these days. And being who he is he has certain papers on him from the co-ordinating committee, or whatever it is these people who arrange revolutions call themselves. The worst thing would be for these to fall into anyone else's hands and so he will try to escape. Unfortunately he will trip up on a tree root and Masterman, being a man of great resource, will catch and disarm him and bring him back to us in triumph.'

'Man ... you have to be pulling my leg!'

'I was never,' said Joseph cheerfully, 'more serious in my life.'

'All right. All right.' Elaine put her hands palm outwards upright in the gesture of one who had finally given up a struggle. 'Masterman has brought Henry back at gunpoint ...'

'Correct.'

'Why not throw in Sydney while we're about it?'

'Because Sydney has other things to do.'

'And you're not going to tell me what things, are you?' Elaine fixed the jovial Joseph Mordecai with an eye which would have made many a man quail but had not the least effect upon him.

'My love,' he responded apologetically, 'if you don't mind, no. I think ...'

'It would be altogether more convincing

if I go on disbelieving all this nonsense and am continually showing surprise at all the absurd things which keep on happening.'

'Quite,' said Joseph.

The gazebo was a clever piece of architectural nonsense. Octagonal in shape with its shingle roof surmounted by a tall gay finial, its sides were white painted louvres which, like its door, could be raised to the horizontal and kept there by iron stays giving the whole the effect of a spaceship with its power panels extended and suspended some seven or eight feet above the ground. This curious floating effect was enhanced by the paving's running uninterruptedly through the gazebo and being broken up by cunningly located pockets out of which grew crotons, succulents and the like. Sited as it was on a small knoll close by the cliff which overlooked the bay with its scattering of brilliant islands, out of sight of the house itself but connected to it by a path between a high double hibiscus hedge whose aimless wandering was intended to make the statement that here was hardly a route for those who found time pressing, the gazebo was a *fun* place. It was not, however, intended for sleeping in.

Henry, after a dreadful night in which

he had been plagued by insects, with a body aching fearfully from having to be contorted to fit between the plant pockets, exhibited a weariness which, combining with his unshaven face and dusty uniform, added much colour to the part which he was playing. He wore bush jacket, long shorts and socks and had colonel's insignia on his shoulder tabs. At his hips were two holstered Colt .45s and around his waist a belt stuffed with bullets. On his head was a cap of greenish hue not exactly in keeping with the rest but (as Joseph had misquoted) we not only live but sometimes dress as best we can.

Carole, who had approached the gazebo by a circuitous route as if to avoid being seen—whilst knowing perfectly well that Masterman was following at a distance—eyed Henry with feelings which were, for her, unusually confused.

She was badly shaken. What had been an intended mock seduction of the British Chancellor of the Exchequer had come perilously close to the real thing. She had read in Masterman's eyes what her own body had been telling her; with the least encouragement she *would* have had sex with him then and there. It had been touch and go. Had it happened it would have been disaster—she saw that clearly. But that didn't help overmuch. It did not dispel the sense of disbelief that she had been so very near to losing self-control; it did not assuage the murmurings of a cheated body; and it did not remove the chagrin of rejection. Men did not reject Carole Mordecai; if rejection was the order of the day, it was meted out by her. So all in all she was not nearly as in control of the situation as she would otherwise have been. And, most curiously and irritatingly, she felt towards Henry a sense of guilt which vied with a small anger towards the man discreetly tracking her.

'I suppose you'll do,' she said to Henry shortly. 'A couple more days of beard would help. All the best revolutionaries have beards. Ever since Castro it's been the fashion.'

This was rehearsed stuff, intended to keep Henry in his place. But Carole was further to be surprised. Even the most lovelorn swain is not at his most gallant after a night with little sleep through which he has been devoured by ants and mosquitos.

'What d'you mean, "I'll do"?' he snapped belligerently.

Carole blinked.

'You're to be captured,' she snapped back.

'Captured?'

'Why do you always repeat everything I say to you?'

'Now you listen to me, Carole Mordecai ...'

'No, you listen to me. Daddy's decided you're to be captured. Here!' She thrust out a piece of paper. 'Put this in your pocket.'

Henry ignored the piece of paper.

'You know damn well why I'm doing all this ...' he began.

Carole didn't like this at all.

'There's no time for that sort of talk ...' she interrupted—only to be interrupted in her turn.

'There has to be time or there ain't gonna be a revolution!'

Henry did not speak triumphantly and it hadn't been planned—but he had played a joker.

'Say what you've got to say then, but make it quick, man,' Carole answered furiously.

'I'm crazy about you, that's why I'm doing all this,' Henry secretly amazed at his own effrontery, burst out. 'Crazy about you! That's why I'm all dressed up like a goof doing these crazy things!'

'You're doing it for the money.'

'Nuts to the money! If I wanted money all I've got to do is wire Dad!'

This statement was so undeniable as

to silence Carole. This was no mean achievement. Probably it had never happened before. Certainly Carole could remember no occasion. She was conscious of a bewildering sense of loss of power. First the business of Masterman—now this. For one brief moment she stood unsure.

And Henry, with the timing of a genius, seized his opportunity. He took one quick pace forward and before Carole realised what was about to happen, his strong hands pinned her biceps and she was being kissed. It was as if divine inspiration had been given Henry. He did not make the mistake of awaiting a response. He kissed Carole good and hard and then released her, in fact almost threw her away from him.

'Right!' he told her. 'Now it's in the open. Now you know what it's all about. And don't think we won't talk about it later because we will. Now what's the next crazy thing I've got to do?'

Confusion might have been redoubled in Carole Mordecai but at least she had been handed the bonus of restored self-respect. The marvellous defence mechanism of youth clicked into place. At least Henry was of her generation. She must have been mad! Moreover there *had* been something very masculine about the scratchiness of

Henry's beard; she could still feel the rasp of it upon her skin. In a word the kiss had not repelled her.

'I've told you,' she said, admitting nothing. 'You're to be captured.'

'Who by?'

'Masterman. Group Captain Masterman. No! ... Keep looking at me!'

'That's not hard.'

'Be serious, Henry!'

'I'm all shook up,' said Henry. 'Are you?'

'No,' lied Carole. 'Listen! I'm supposed to be locked up in my bedroom ...' She went on hastily seeing a gleam in Henry's tired eyes. 'But I've escaped and Masterman's followed me. He's somewhere out there. Behind me. Watching us. He's all set to capture you but it's going to be difficult unless we help him. There's not enough cover between the bush and here. When he's captured you he's got to find that piece of paper ... Where is it?'

Henry grinned.

'In your hand. You must be shook up too. Sor ... ry.' Henry was very much abreast of the situation.

He took the paper from her and read what was typed upon it:

'Ninth Battalion will rendezvous Bathsheba Halt twenty-third 0400 hours and await arrival Solitaires and Highland War- riors before marching into Dukestown. Rochambeau.'

'It's gobbledegook!' Henry declared. 'Plain gobbledegook!'

'Nothing of the sort,' said Carole, feeling better and hoicking a packet of cigarettes out from her back pocket and offering it. 'It's absolutely genuine. We didn't even type it. Daddy got it from Robbie Rose who's organising the Ninth Battalion.'

'The Ninth Battalion?'

'Carnival Band, man! Don't be so slow.' But this was said more as to an equal. 'The Solitaires and the Highland Warriors are other bands.'

'And Rochambeau?'

'The Mighty King!'

'Oh,' said Henry, catching on. The Mighty King was a calypso singer. He'd heard of The Mighty King—he hadn't heard his name was Vivien Rochambeau.

'Want one?' Carole was waving the packet.

'Yeah! Thanks! I'm out.' Henry did more than take a cigarette; he took the packet.

'Yes, you might as well keep it,' said Carole, making up a little ground. 'You'll need a few cigarettes where you are going.'

Henry cocked an unshaven head. His dress was curious but Carole found herself reflecting on the oddity that it rather suited him. Henry Cicurel had somehow gathered character.

'Where am I going?' he asked.

'You're going to be locked up in the pool-house.' She chuckled. Henry had never heard such a chuckle before; it was strangely intimate.

'Wouldn't it be better in the cellar?' he suggested.

'Much more better. Only you don't get cellars in modern houses.'

'Your father must be sorry.'

'Yes, I rather think he is. He's such a stickler for accuracy, you know.'

'Are you going to be locked up with me?' enquired Henry with put-on lecherousness.

Carole shook her head. 'I'm in my room. I've just slipped out to lead him to you and as soon as I've finished explaining, I'm going back to it. He thinks I'm there now and he'll think I never left it.'

'After following you here?'

'It's all double-think stuff. He knows I'm in with the revolutionaries but he's persuaded me that all he thinks is that I've thrown in my lot with a bunch of petty arms-smugglers. That way he can put a face on it. I'll stay in my room because Mummy's ordered me to, while believing I won't and will lead him to you. Got it?'

'I got it,' Henry said. 'It's crazy, but I got it. Just one thing I don't get. Why should he think you'd throw in your lot with some outfit running arms?'

'Not some outfit.'

Henry got it now. 'You mean ...' he said.

'Yes.' Carole tried to brush it aside. 'He thinks I'm in love with you. That that's why I'm doing all this. Obviously ...'

'Now how ...' Henry overrode her with mock irony '... could he be so stupid?'

And recalling what had taken place between herself and Masterman still within the last hour Carole appreciated how near she had been to wrecking everything.

'He doesn't think I'm in love with you,' she pointed out. 'That's what he wants me to think he thinks.'

'But why,' insisted Henry, 'shouldn't he think you're in love with me?'

This was getting difficult; when she did not reply, Henry made it more so.

'If,' he reasoned, 'Masterman doesn't think you're in love with me but wants you to think he thinks you are, then if he's to be convinced he's fooled you, we ought to be doing what we would be doing if you were what he wants you to think he thinks you are.'

'Henry ...' Carole, comprehending only

too cleverly the drift of Henry's thinking began to object ...

'Cy!' he corrected her. And went on: 'Here's me! I've been driving a couple of boats around the ocean in the dark. I've hoofed it miles on foot. I've broken into the house and stolen three radios and a transformer. I've spent what was left of the night twisted like a corkscrew and eaten up by mosquitos ... And you're nuts on me. Right?'

Carole sighed.

'Now,' said Henry logically. 'You've broken out of your room to hand me an important message which Masterman, once he's captured me, is going to read that's going to tell him the revolution's all set to break. And now you're going back. What do you do first?'

Carole smiled wanly.

'Okay, man. I kiss you.'

'Too darn right, you do. And you make a real good job of it. Like you might never get the chance of kissing me again. Okay?' Carole nodded; Henry saw in her eyes something quite lacking up to now. Respect.

'Okay?' he said.

'Just a minute, man!' She swayed back from the movement of Henry's arms. At least she would have her pound of flesh. 'Before we go through this ... this kissing routine.' She paused. 'Well,' she said, 'after we do that, I'd better have a good look round to give him the idea I'm taking care no one's watching me, then head back to the house the way I've come. This'll take me past him but of course he'll see I don't spot him and then, when I'm well out of the way, he'll be working out some way to capture you. But you've got to make it possible. So, *Cy*, what I suggest you do is this—go and stand on the edge of the cliff and look down on Daddy's jetty as if you're expecting someone to slip round the point or across the bay or something. While you're doing that, he'll sneak up behind and fell you with a karate chop or something ...'

'You don't,' said Henry, 'even look as if you think it's funny!'

'Well revolution is a serious business, man. It wouldn't do for him to see me smiling.'

'You're like your father. You've always got an answer.'

'Well then ... Cy?' She moved nearer.

'Just a minute!'

'Oh?' Her heart was a little faster than it should have been.

'What happens when I'm captured?'

'Oh.' She threw it away. 'Leave it to Daddy.'

'What do you mean by that?'

'Just don't say anything that'll wreck it.'

'You don't figure that's quite an order?'

'Oh,' said Carole largely, 'I shouldn't think it'll be too difficult. Anyway most of the time you'll be locked up in the pool-house. All right. Put that paper away.' She watched as Henry unbuttoned his tunic, folded the paper, put it in his pocket and did up the buttons.

She was conscious of impatience to be in Henry's arms.

'Outside, I think,' he said.

'Eh?'

'So he can get a proper view of us.'

'You usually kiss your girl friends in public?'

'I don't,' said Henry, 'have girl friends. Not any more. Remember that.'

In the Radio Room, which was nothing more than a small study furnished in a masculine way with desk, leather chairs and a bench top along one wall, on which was the equipment and under which were one or two filing-cabinets and the like, Sybil was busy winding. She had shifted her chair so as to be able to look out of the window towards the casuarinas. If she looked hard to her left she could see the drive and the gate-house now tenanted by two policemen. She was no longer nervous. The final touch of reassurance had come with the return of the policemen. So, she told herself, Ernest was right again. Everything was to appear as normal. St Barbara was just another peaceful, sleepy, backward little island where coconuts, bananas and sugar cane grew and the gentle trade winds ruffled a blue and turquoise sea.

In the kitchen an altercation which had nothing to do with the impending revolution was going on. Gertrude, sleeves rolled up, arms white with flour, was busy at an enormous bowl. Hazel, seated at a table, was leisurely shelling shrimps. Gertrude was a rolling mountain of a woman, Hazel wraith-like by comparison, but both were dressed alike in gingham of Monday's colour—which was yellow. Both wore a madras of matching material on their heads.

Gertrude, pausing in her work (which was being carried on at no tremendous pace), eyed Hazel inimically.

'By when you'm done, Hazel,' she observed, 'it the time for Sydney to take out the mornin' drinks.'

Hazel looked up, checking the points on Gertrude's madras. Like the Martinician women, Gertrude tied hers to express a state of being—but whereas in their case it was their availability for attention from the opposite sex, in Gertrude's it was to do with mood. When she awoke in a reasonable mood, she tied one point, normally it was two and if there were three even Elaine gave her the widest berth.

This morning there was just the single spike and Hazel was encouraged to respond:

'Now don't you rass me, Gertrude. I don't sleep a wink. Not a wink.'

'Huh!' snorted Gertrude. 'You don' sleep a wink? You sleep all the time. Even when you standing up and making like you workin'.'

Hazel was not put down.

'I don' sleep a wink an' when I do, I hear tiefs in yard an' can't get off again.'

'How come you can't get off again if you haven't even started? You talking like a fool. An' what you mean tiefs in yard?'

'Them take my radio.'

'Huh.'

'I tell you, Gertrude, there was tiefs. Just 'cos you sleep like you was dead, that ain't no cause to disbelieve when I tell you.'

'Now don' you speak to me, gal, like you was Queen of England just because I only got one point this morning,' Gertrude warned her. 'An' don' you try to read that paper while you peeling shrimps.'

The morning paper was lying on the table.

'What for Sydney not take them the paper, Gertrude?'

Gertrude fixed her with an angry eye 'You all what for these days. What for Mr Mordecai not go back to Dukestown? What for Miss Carole not go to work today? What for them p'licemen at the gate? What for that airplane buzzing roun' the house las' night? What for them niggers marching up an' down the cricket pitch? What for? What for? What for? I never heard so much what for.'

'An',' said Hazel, not without triumph, 'I never heard so much no reason why. You don' know either.'

Gertrude stayed comfortable. 'You'm wrong, Hazel. Mistress don' tell me why.' She hesitated. She had had her instructions. But in the end she could not resist.

'It's all a game,' she said.

'A game? What sort of game?'

'A game to make Exchequer laugh.'

'Oh,' said Hazel, trying to work this out. And then, as if this was relative: 'An' to make Mistress Exchequer laugh? I see him laugh a lot but I never done see her laugh ...'

Gertrude interrupted witheringly:

'Mistress Exchequer! What for you talking so damn stupid, gal? That not him name, Exchequer. That what him am. Him Mister Masterman. An' him Exchequer.'

'What that mean, Gertrude ... Exchequer?'

Gertrude sniffed. 'I ain't got time to waste talking to a gal what don' understand nothing unless it spell out like she was still at school!'

And she buried her black arms deep into the dough.

Jeffery-Smith had a problem—a fallen cotton tree. He had not got so far as the cotton tree, having been warned in advance by another driver forced to turn back because of it. Apparently arrangements were in hand for shifting it but the road was unlikely to be cleared for some time, if indeed at all that day.

So Jeffery-Smith sat in the back of the Government House Daimler and pondered.

He had tried to get through by radio, to check with Joseph that the Chancellor was comfortably settled in and had no messages or tasks for him. Failing in this he had decided against either having someone from Port Lucea call in at Spoon Point and telephone him back or sending his A.D.C. The first approach might have seemed an intrusion on Masterman's privacy and the second might have seemed discourteous—if anyone should call from Government House, surely it should be himself.

In the end he had decided to drive over. Yet all the way had been harried by doubts. For the Administrator to call in on the Mordecais on a Sunday morning was one thing, to call two days in succession quite another. And Masterman, he told himself, was here to rest after the most frightful experiences in Santiago. There wouldn't be much of a rest for him if it leaked out he was staying at Spoon Point. Perhaps it had been unwise to set out, perhaps he should turn back. Thus he was not displeased to hear about the road being blocked. Yet, even so, he asked himself, isn't it my business as I don't even have that radio contact at least to let him know I've been trying to get through? He found it difficult to decide. And then, as he sat there, under the welcome shade of a saman tree whose enormous spread entirely covered the road and well beyond its sides as well, it occurred to him that the demise of the cotton tree ahead had been an act of God. There were, after all, other ways of calling at Spoon Point without advertising his presence quite so openly. Mordecai, he recalled, had a small dock. He would call in on Willie Matthews in Port Lucea and Willie would run him in on his fishing cruiser. Willie was reliable. Willie would keep his mouth shut.

Much relieved Jeffery-Smith gave appropriate instructions to his chauffeur.

Sydney was in the bush. He too had been given appropriate instructions. By Joseph. And the better to carry them out he was properly equipped—with a loaded shotgun. He had also made certain preparations including a jug of sangaree in the refrigerator with an ample supply of ice beside it and a crisp white shirt ready to slip into the moment he got back.

Outside the gate-house Chisholm Swallow-field watched the departing Ninth Battalion. He didn't think they had a chance of carrying off the prize. His money was on the Solitaires. The Solitaires had a Tock-Tock and a Base-Bum. The Ninth Battalion had a Tock-Tock too but no one who could play it well enough since the Saracens had bribed Ewart Russell to come and join then. You couldn't win with just a lot of noise and a lot of pans. You had to have a Tock-Tock and someone who could make it sing! And how curious, he thought, that they should come and practise without pans. He couldn't remember hearing of such a thing so close to Carnival. But life, he reflected philosophically, was full of surprises—such as being driven up from Dukestown to mount guard on Mr Mordecai's place without being told the reason why. But not bad, not bad, man, really. Better than directing traffic. Much more better. He put his hand up to his peaked cap as if to make the point. When he directed traffic he had to wear a white pith helmet which was stiff and sore-making on his forehead. He chuckled to himself at the thought of Walter doing double duty. Be damn hot there, in Harbour Street. Sun right overhead. No shade. Damn hot. Much more better here. He looked up above him. Through the trees which lined the driveway the sun twinkled brilliantly. But only twinkled.

NINE

'Ah!' said Joseph.

Elaine looked up from her hemming, followed the direction of his eyes and then observed.

'You look like a well-fed cannibal watching his next meal being brought to him for inspection.'

'Oh,' said Joseph, with slight disappointment. 'You've seen.'

'The British Chancellor of the Exchequer delivering a revolutionary at pistol point? Yes, I've seen.'

She went back to her hemming.

'All in the normal course of a Monday morning at Spoon Point, eh?'

'I don't think,' said Elaine, not looking up, 'that anything in my life will ever be normal again. Hadn't you better go and tell Sybil?'

'What on earth for?'

'It's hardly cricket to let her miss such a moment of triumph, is it?'

'Don't tell me an affection is growing in your breast for her, my love.'

Elaine put down her hemming.

'She's just about,' she said, 'the most

infuriating woman I've ever met. But you have to hand it to her. She's well structured for a crisis. Most women, believing what she believes, would be terrified out of their wits. I know I would be.'

'No, my love,' said Joseph. 'Your behaviour would be as superb as it is now.' He stood. 'Come along.'

'Come along? Come along where?'

'To the end of the terrace. By the pool. We must greet the brave Ernest Masterman with excitement and respect.'

'I can greet him with excitement and respect just as well here as by the pool.'

'My love, I beg you.'

She looked at him sharply.

'What damn foolishness are you up to now?' she demanded.

'Sydney may not be the best of shots.'

'What are you talking about?'

'And in any case we shall be usefully near the pool-house.'

'I asked you what you were talking about.'

'It's where we're going to lock up Henry. In the pool-house.'

'Joseph!'

'Oh ... about Sydney? He's going to shoot a few louvres out. I thought it would be a good touch. Just as Masterman is covering the last few yards with his prize

... Bang! Crash! Very effective, don't you think?'

'Now listen to me ...'

'Oh, it's all right,' Joseph hastily interposed. 'He's not really going to break any. It's only going to look like that. Carole's going to do the breaking. I've told Sydney to fire into the air. Carole's standing by to knock over a chair or something as soon as she hears the first shot. It's all right ...' He became very reassuring. 'Only a few glass louvres. We've got plenty spare.'

'Joseph! This is going too far. This is getting ridiculous. I will not have it. You must stop him. You ...' Words failed her.

He put a huge, comforting arm around her.

'My love,' he said. 'There is nothing I can do. Sydney has his instructions and there is no way I can countermand them. When Masterman is almost safely back, he is to fire.'

'But as you've already convinced him ...'

'Sybil will hear the shots and come running out. Masterman will be trying to decide if he's being shot at, Henry's being shot at, or we're being shot at. There will be a great confusion and a sense of urgency a trifle lacking just now, don't you think?' While speaking he was benignly watching the progress of Henry and Masterman towards the house—Henry

263

in front, Masterman close behind. They were within perhaps a hundred yards. 'And the timing is so important,' he concluded.

'Why?'

'My love, there is really not the time to explain that to you.'

'And anyway it'll be all the more convincing if I'm surprised! I tell you, you should have been christened Esau! Only you wouldn't have stopped at just a brother—you'd have gone through the whole damn family tree right down to the last third cousin twice removed!'

'My love ...'

'All right. We'll go and stand by the pool and look amazed or whatever it is we're supposed to look ...'

'A little hurt, I think. After all I have been putting business Henry's way ...'

'But one thing you must tell me! One thing I have to know.'

'What's that, my love?'

'How you're going to use this ridiculous situation. How you're going to persuade the man to hand over several million pounds.'

'Oh,' said Joseph. 'I shan't do that. I shall leave that to Henry.'

'He knows, of course?'

'That I'm leaving it to him? Oh, no. But he's an intelligent boy. He'll pick it up as we go along.'

When they were on the pool deck, which was raised a little above the adjoining ground by a low stone wall off which was a rail of comfortable leaning height, Joseph, an expression of hurt disbelief on his face, called out:

'Good Lord! Darling ... it's Henry Cicurel!' And then, even more loudly, across the intervening fifty yards or less. 'Chancellor! Are you all right? D'you want some help? Shall I ...'

'Stay where you are!' Masterman's command was crisp. Henry, meanwhile, having little doubt that Carole would be watching him, was playing his part impressively. His head was down, his shoulders slumped in what he imagined to be the appropriate manner for a revolutionary who, while pretending to be cowed, was in reality only waiting an opportunity to turn the tables. Now, as if because of this speech, he slowed. At once Masterman jabbed him with a revolver and snapped: 'Keep moving!'

It was really, mused Elaine, exactly like something on the films.

And it became more so for, even as she was thinking this, Sydney, from the fastness of the bush, fired his gun and then again—and on the second shot Carole gleefully hurled the stool and as the shattering of glass rang out, there was a third and final shot from Sydney.

Masterman's reaction was commendable. He took a quick pace forward and knocked the astounded Henry to the ground by the simple expedient of thrusting one foot round an ankle and pushing him in the back. Henry fell like a skittle and Masterman down on one knee, jabbing a revolver in his back, called out, 'Don't move!' then shouted up to Joseph and Elaine: 'Get inside the house!'

'But, my dear fellow ...'

'Do as I say!' And as Sybil flung open the radio room door and came hastening out: 'Go back!'

'Ernest ...'

'Go back, I tell you!'

Hazel appeared to see what the commotion was. Masterman shouted: 'Mordecai, tell that woman of yours to go inside! All of you get inside!' Now he turned his head, quickly, to the direction from which the shots had come. But he could see nothing, only the distant wall of bush. In fact there was nothing to see—Sydney, having laid the gun down in a previously selected spot, was hurrying away towards his clean crisp shirt and his jug of sangaree.

Henry, nervous at having the muzzle of a loaded revolver grinding in his back, began a protest but a swift and menacing 'Shut up, you!' from his captor silenced him. On the pool deck, Joseph, the very *picture* of alarm, was calling: 'Come on, my love!' and hustling Elaine inside; Hazel with a squeaky: 'Lawks!' had vanished within to spread the news to Gertrude, who needed more than a few shots to draw her from her kitchen; Sybil, torn between being brave and following instructions, was hovering by her doorway; and Carole was returning the stool to its proper place in front of her dressing-table.

Masterman looked around him, sizing up the situation. Out in the open he was a sitting target, albeit by crouching down a lesser one than he had been. Between him and safety was, as it were, a no-man's-land of perhaps twenty yards with, as the nearest obvious protection, the pool-house, which looked a substantial structure. With that as cover he ought to be able to make the house.

'Now listen to me, you,' he instructed Henry, making the point by further bruising with a revolver muzzle. 'When I say move, we go behind that small building. The one beside the pool. Have you got that?'

'Yeah,' said Henry.

'You move quickly but you do not run. Have you ...' He broke off noticing Sybil still by her doorway. 'Get in!' he shouted at her. 'Get inside and stay inside!' Sybil did so. 'Have you got that, Cicurel?' he resumed.

'Yeah,' said Henry.

So he *was* Cicurel.

'If,' Masterman said, 'you make the slightest attempt to get away, I'll blow your brains out.' Joseph was quite right—he had not enjoyed himself so much in years. 'Have you got that?'

'Yeah,' said Henry.

'Then move,' said Masterman.

He stood, openly, facing the bush as if to challenge anyone there to give away his position by opening fire. But there was no movement. There was nothing but the line of bush under a cloudless sky. And recollection was very strong. The rubber around Seletar airfield in Singapore, the jungle thick with paratroops at Palembang in Sumatra, the rubber again around Tjillitan airfield in Java. It looked so innocent the rubber, the bush—so innocent and so threatening.

He turned towards the house, following Henry. He was conscious of the nakedness of his back but he was not afraid.

Once behind the pool-house, he said: 'Stay there!' and quickly crossed to the house and flung open a door which proved to lead into the kitchen, where he surprised Gertrude and Hazel, who had been peering at him through the louvres.

'Tell Mr Mordecai I want him,' he ordered. 'And don't stand by this door again—do you understand?'

Hazel backed away, huge-eyed at the extraordinary spectacle of a house-guest, revolver in either hand, standing sideways in the doorway of her kitchen, and of, beyond him, Mister Cicurel, queerly dressed, flattened against the wall of the pool-house. Gertrude stood solid; it took a lot to shift Gertrude from her calm. She merely eyed the Exchequer (as he would for the rest of her life be to her) with an indignant and disbelieving look—it was not so much that he should be armed with two revolvers and perhaps be about to shoot Mister Cicurel before her eyes, as that all this should be happening in or from her kitchen. Never, never before had anyone had such temerity; she would certainly have to speak to Mister Mordecai about it.

'Hurry!' called Masterman.

Hazel scurried away.

'You can go back to whatever you were doing,' said Masterman to Gertrude. 'There's nothing to worry about.'

Gertrude grunted. She hadn't been worried. The only things which worried Gertrude were things which affected Gertrude. The rest of the world went on in its own peculiar way with most of its happenings thoroughly disapproved of.

Preparing meals, eating meals and sleeping off meals represented the boundaries of Gertrude's life. She went back to her table, where a large red snapper awaited her attentions, and started to rub lime juice over it.

Joseph came in, followed by Hazel, who hovered at a distance.

'Have you anywhere safe we can lock this fellow up?' enquired Masterman, waving a revolver vaguely towards Henry.

'Aren't you going to question him?'

The unexpected uneasiness in Joseph's tone made even Gertrude pause momentarily; then she shook her head, just the once, and went on with massaging her fish.

'Oh, yes,' said Masterman. 'I'm going to question him.' He said this in a tone which gave Henry little pleasure. 'But the first thing I must do is alert London. Get things moving.'

'Will we ...'

'I hardly think,' observed Masterman dryly, 'that this is the proper place to discuss the problem.'

'Oh ... no ....' said Joseph. 'Of course not. But ... er ... this fellow.' And as if this brilliant idea had only at that moment occurred to him: 'Why not lock him in the pool-house?' His eyebrows were very high, his small eyes very bright. 'It'll be a bit of a squeeze for the fellow, of course ...'

'You haven't anywhere else?'

'Well not really ... These modern houses, you know, no cellars or anything of that sort. Why don't we just hand him over to the police?'

'I have already explained that. All right ... we'll put him in the pool-house. It does lock?'

Joseph nodded. 'I'll go and get the key. You're sure you'll be all right?'

'So long as I've only this one to deal with ...'

'But you don't think ...? My dear fellow ... You don't think they might rush us!'

'If they do ... Do you have any arms? Shotguns or anything?'

'Shotguns?' Joseph thought quickly. 'Yes, I believe we do. Yes ...' With great relief he saw the door open and Sydney, smart and crisp come in. 'Sydney!' he said. 'Where *have* you been?'

'Making the sangaree like you tol' me, Sir,' responded Sydney, affronted slightly, and then, seeing Henry through the open doorway: 'Why, Mister Cicurel ...'

Joseph was aware of deep concern. A *tête-à-tête* between Cicurel, Masterman, himself and all the Spoon Point staff had not been included in his plans. And he had noticed, dangerously obvious, the island's

271

daily newspaper, *The-Voice-of-St-Barbara*, lying open on a table.

'Sydney,' he said, moving to stand between Masterman and *The-Voice*. 'You know where the key to the padlock on the pool-house door is?'

'Why, yes, Mister Mordecai ...'

'Go and fetch it, Sydney.'

'Yes, Mr Mordecai. Yes, Sir.' Sydney withdrew. Joseph was very pleased with his performance.

'Get on with what you have to do, Hazel,' he commanded. 'It's all right.' He waved a podgy hand reassuringly. 'It's all a ... a sort of game.'

'A game?'

'A game, Hazel. Nothing to worry about.'

Gertrude looked up from her fish which she had now started to rub inside with salt and pepper. There was a look of triumph on her face, which puzzled Masterman.

'You heard what Mister Mordecai don' tol' you gal!' she snapped. 'Go peel them yampies!'

And she picked up a handful of mixed onions, breadcrumbs and parsley bound with lime juice and thrust it into the cavity of the snapper with the force of a woodman sawing a tree trunk.

'How many shotguns do you have?' enquired Masterman.

'Why two, I believe. That's right, two. I remember ...'

'Anything else?'

'Well I've one of those.' Joseph nodded his head at Masterman's revolvers. 'Against burglars, you know ... not that I ever had any ...'

'Go and get it and come back here. Don't leave any ammunition around. Bring it all. And hurry!'

Masterman turned while speaking, so as to keep a watchful eye on Henry—Joseph swiftly picked up the newspaper and departed, making his way through the dining-room and into the sitting-room. He was about to turn off into the hall and thence to the store-room to collect the two remaining shotguns when he notice Elaine standing just inside the opening to the terrace. She was looking through binoculars out towards the bay.

He stopped.

She heard him and turned.

'Is all going well?' she enquired.

He nodded.

'All according to plan?'

Again he nodded.

'Is William Matthews popping in on us for a drink part of that plan?'

'What!' Joseph took a pace or two until he was beside her. Now he could see what she had been looking at through the glasses.

Threading its way between two islands was a fishing cruiser, its outriggers swaying like the antennae of some enormous beetle. And it was clearly heading for his dock.

'Damn the man!' he said.

'Which one?' asked Elaine with disarming innocence.

'Which one? ... What are ...' He broke off. She was holding out the binoculars.

'I was looking at him before he turned,' she said. 'There's a passenger.' She chuckled. 'P.J!'

TEN

By the time Joseph has presented Master-man with his shotguns, revolver and ammunition and various other matters, such as hiding the newspaper and locking Henry in the pool-house, had been attended to, William Matthews' fishing cruiser was under the lee of the cliff and out of sight.

Simplistically the obvious stratagem was to shoo off Jeffery-Smith on the grounds that the Mastermans were resting but this, Joseph saw, would be only a short-term solution in that eventually the Chancellor would be sure to learn of the Administrator's visit. And outrageous though what he was doing might be, yet Joseph was planning it in such a way as to give him a total answer at the end.

He had told no lies and for every happening, however trivial, with which the *household* had been concerned there was a perfectly reasonable explanation. It was not Joseph Mordecai who had persuaded the British Chancellor that a revolution was about to break out on St Barbara, but, resisting the suggestion almost to the last, he had been finally overborne by the combination of one or two unusual happenings and the Chancellor's persuasion. This, at least, had been the scheme. All imaginable contingencies had been allowed for—but that P.J. should arrive by boat had not. Ergo there had to be a swift change of plan and yet, at the end, he must be as guiltless as he had been before.

'Well, man,' said Elaine. 'You decided what you're going to do?'

'Yes,' said Joseph mildly. 'I think we'll have Sydney bring out the sangaree as soon as P.J. pitches up. He's bound to be hot and sticky toiling up from there.'

Elaine looked at him in astonishment. He had left her rattled, been gone a mere five minutes and now was as calm, as imperturbable as ever.

'What have you been doing?' she demanded.

'Doing? Oh nothing, really. Chatting to poor old Masterman.'

There was a clue in this—but she was too irritated at seeing her rare victory torn up and thrown like confetti to the winds.

'You told him P.J. was here?' she said disbelievingly.

'P.J?' Joseph looked about him. He even looked at the bay. 'I can't see P.J,' he said. 'I haven't seen P.J. since he called here yesterday. Was it only yesterday? It does seem much longer ago than that. But then so many things have happened ...'

'You don't seriously think that P.J. having come all this way is going to be fobbed off with some feeble excuse and go back again without speaking to them?!'

'Good heavens, no. Anyway it's far too good an opportunity to waste.'

'You're telling me you *want* him to speak to Masterman!'

'My love,' said Joseph as if surprised it was necessary to explain, 'it's the best possible thing that could have happened. It makes for a much better solution than the one I had in mind. Don't you think?'

'I shall leave you!' Elaine said furiously. 'I really will. I shall walk out this minute and never come back if you don't tell me what you're up to ... if you don't stop treating me like ... like an imbecile ...'

Joseph chuckled. He put his great arm round her.

'Patience, my love,' he said. 'And be patient with me. The situation is very finely balanced and to succeed I need to get my timing absolutely right and for both of us to be in exactly the proper frame of mind when P.J. arrives.'

'You must want me damn mad then!'

'Precisely.'

He gave her a friendly squeeze and then,

releasing her, sat into his favourite chair with the sang-froid of a Francis Drake.

'Where,' he explained, 'it could have gone all wrong would have been if Masterman had decided to question Henry ahead of getting the radio working. But he's a sound fellow. Have to be, of course, to get where he has got. I often say the important thing in business is to get one's priorities in the right order ...'

'Keep to the point.'

'But I am. When I could see he wasn't going to, I suggested to Masterman that he ought to question Henry before he got a message out. But he pointed out that that would be only wasting time. That Henry, to use his own expression, would keep. That the important thing was to get a message through to London so as to get things started. He also felt he would get more out of Henry if he was able to tell him a gunboat was on its way ...'

'He actually said that?' interrupted Elaine, aghast.

'Well,' Joseph responded regretfully, 'not in so many words. But I suppose that's what they'll do. Unless they send paratroops like they did in Anguilla ... I think he'd prefer that, old Masterman. He'd feel at home with paratroops dropping all around him. Anyway ... where was I? Oh, yes. He felt that once Henry knew action to pre-empt his revolution, or quash it if it had begun, was already in hand, he'd be more likely to cave in and tell him everything he knew whereas asking him now would only delay getting the action started. And I think he's probably right ...' He broke off and rose to his feet, his eyebrows high with surprise, his blue eyes glistening with delight.

'Darling,' he said. 'Look who's coming! What a marvellous surprise! What a relief!'

Elaine's shoulders drooped. She was defeated. P.J. had come in sight. He was alone, walking unhurriedly towards them up the slight slope from the cliff.

'Do I,' she demanded, more to have *something* to say than anything else, 'fetch Masterman?'

'Not yet,' said Joseph, waving a cheerful hand towards Jeffery-Smith. 'What you do is instruct Sydney to hold up the sangaree for a few minutes, then go and chat up both of them in the radio room. I must have ten minutes with P.J. to prepare him.'

'To prepare him,' Elaine echoed dully.

'To prepare him. Off you go.' And, as Elaine turned helplessly away: 'Oh, just one thing. Remember that while all of us here at Spoon Point are in rather unusual frames of mind, P.J. is not. To him it is simply a pleasant Monday morning on the peaceful island of St Barbara and he is doing no more than the courtesies his office requires towards such distinguished visitors.' He smiled. 'Now off you go. And trust me. There is nothing to worry about. Nothing at all.'

And he left her and moved across the terrace to greet Jeffery-Smith.

'This *is* a surprise!' said Joseph, taking the Administrator's hand warmly in his own. 'But how did you get here?'

'There's a damn tree fallen down across the road. Be there all day, I should think, the way things get done in St Barbara. Got William Matthews to run me in from Port Lucea. Decent fellow.' Jeffery-Smith was a trifle puffed and this was causing him to speak in a somewhat military manner. There were, exceptionally, small beads of perspiration on his forehead. But he looked otherwise as neat and self-composed as ever.

'Where is he?'

'Willie Matthews? Tied up at your jetty. You don't mind, do you?'

'Good heavens, no. You should have asked him up.'

'No. No,' said Jeffery-Smith. 'Mustn't bother the Chancellor with strangers.' He accepted the chair Joseph offered with a gracious gesture. 'That's better. Damn steep that cliff of yours. The rest's all right. Well—how's it gone?'

Joseph hesitated—and he was particularly adept at conveying much by hesitations.

Jeffery-Smith misunderstood—as he was intended to.

'Bit of a heavyweight, isn't she?' he suggested with a rather boyish grin.

'No ...' said Joseph slowly. 'As a matter of fact, P.J. ... well she's been marvellous.'

'You mean ... *him?*' Joseph nodded and sat down. This was a very effective ploy. 'But ...' said Jeffery-Smith. 'Well I'm sorry, but he struck me as being a very decent fellow.'

'Oh, yes,' said Joseph. 'I'm sure he is. Normally.'

'Normally? ... What the devil are you saying, man?'

'He thinks,' said Joseph with something of a sigh, 'that a bloody revolution is about to break out on St Barbara.'

Jeffery-Smith absorbed this in silence for a moment or two, then said, quietly but expressively:

'Good God!'

Joseph stared at the bush ahead, as if remembering the previous night's exploits. It was tempting to speak—better to let P.J. do so. Even at the risk of wasted seconds.

'You should have been in touch with

me,' Jeffery-Smith said at length.

'We're not allowed to leave the property. None of us.'

'But you could have told the police to contact me.'

'He thinks they've thrown in their lot with them.'

'Thrown in their lot with who?'

'With the revolutionaries.'

'I don't believe it! I just don't believe it!'

'Yes,' agreed Joseph. 'It's difficult to get used to.'

'Where is he now?'

'In the radio room. He won't leave it. He's winding something he calls a ferrite collar. I think he's hopeful of getting through direct to London.'

'Five thousand miles! He must be off his rocker!'

'Oh, no,' said Joseph hastily. 'I wouldn't say that. But I suppose ... all that Santiago business. And the talk of Christiana ...' He left it there.

'Well it's incredible,' said Jeffery-Smith. But after a pause. 'Mind you ... we were warned he was in a pretty nervous state. Not that I believed it when I saw him. Thought it was all woman's talk. You know—that wife he's got ... But you say she's all right?'

'Just marvellous. And loyal. You know

'... I was wondering.'

'Wondering. Wondering what? Say what you mean, Mordecai. This is a damn serious business we've got on our hands.'

'Well I was wondering if it's something that's happened before. I mean, she's taking it so calmly. Even his locking up poor Cicurel.'

'You don't mean it!'

'In the pool-house. He thinks he's their leader. Henry Cicurel. Well you've met Henry ...'

'Certainly. Damn decent chap.' He was lost for words. 'Incredible,' he managed. 'It's just incredible.'

'No,' said Joseph, 'the really incredible thing is Sybil Masterman. That's what makes me wonder if this is something that happens from time to time ...'

'Cracks under the strain, you mean?'

'And she covers up for him. D'you know if she came out now and joined us it wouldn't surprise me if she even looked you in the eyes and told you about last night's arms drop.'

'Arms drop!'

'Yes. He thinks Carole was mixed up in that.' Joseph smiled wryly. 'We smoothed that one out by locking her in her bedroom.'

'Fantastic!' And, after a pause. 'What d'you think's the best thing to do? Fetch a doctor? Have old Oswald take a look at him?'

'I don't know,' said Joseph. 'Elaine ...'

'What's she making of all this nonsense?'

'Pretty damn angry.'

'I bet she is. And I don't blame her.'

'P.J?'

'Yes?'

'When you see Elaine ... I wonder if you could persuade her ... Look, I'm not a doctor. Nor a psychiatrist. But it seems to me the best thing to do is go along with Masterman's revolution ...'

'Humour him.'

'That's right. I mean ... as like as not he'll suddenly snap out of it and no harm done. But ... well you know Elaine. She just isn't prepared to humour either of them. So far as she's concerned it's just a lot of nonsense and every time they bring it up, she tells them so. And it worries me, P.J. I mean ... he seems all right. Locking up Henry was a bit extreme perhaps but otherwise ... well he's rather like a child playing cowboys and Indians.'

'You mean he's enjoying it!'

'He's never had so much fun since he was flying Hurricanes and being surrounded by paratroopers in Sumatra.'

'Was he?'

Joseph was wry. 'Oh, yes. We've had that all right. From both of them. But ...'

He became more serious. 'If he hadn't got those revolvers ...'

'He's armed!'

'Three revolvers and two shotguns. And every bullet we could find ...'

'And you think he might suddenly go berserk or something?'

'It's so difficult to know. I mean—in every other way he behaves absolutely normally. Just this fetish. I mean, given it were true, that there was a revolution about to break out here ... well, you know, you could only be impressed. He's cool, calm, collected, quite without fear. Matter of fact I've never met anyone I'd rather have beside me if we were about to be attacked ...'

'He thinks that as well?'

Joseph frowned—and rubbed his chins.

'Let's say,' he answered, 'that he doesn't dismiss it as a possibility.'

Jeffery-Smith got up from his chair and began to pace, hands in pockets, head down, not going very far—just a few paces and then returning.

'Only one thing,' he said, reaching a decision. 'We'll have to have old Oswald in.'

Joseph nodded gloomily.

'I suppose we have to. The only thing ...' Again the effective hesitation. 'It would be a pity for the whole thing to come out, wouldn't it? I mean he isn't doing any *harm* and its probably only a temporary reaction after Chile ...'

'That's all very well,' interrupted Jeffery-Smith who had made up his mind, 'but you don't have the damn Government and all that lot in Whitehall to deal with.'

Joseph sighed submissively.

'Oh, I suppose you're right. Only it seems such a pity—I rather like the man, you know. He's very warm. And I'd hate to feel I'd been responsible for maybe losing him his job. The more so as maybe by tomorrow he'll be as right as rain again ...' And, as Jeffery-Smith was again about to interrupt. 'Yes, I realise. One has to do these things even if doing them puts one at risk oneself.'

'Good Lord, I didn't think of that.' Jeffery-Smith stopped dead in his tracks.

'Didn't you?' said Joseph with raised eyebrows. 'Elaine and I have been worrying for you all the time.'

'The man's supposed to be staying at Government House.'

'Well, yes ... But you have got the builders in. I'm sure when you let them know ...'

Jeffery-Smith emitted an unusual sound, something of a cross between a laugh and a snort. 'You don't know 'em like I do, Mordecai! When they're looking for a scapegoat there's no one like the Foreign Office all the way from Setubal to Vladivostok. They'd have my balls for breakfast!' Then, after a pause, and with a tinge of hope, he went on:

'You really don't think he's dangerous?'

Joseph shook a thoughtful head. 'No,' he said. 'Not so long as we keep on humouring him. That's why I'd be so grateful if you'd ... you know, chat up Elaine. There's always the risk that if she tells him once too often he's making an ass of himself ...'

'That's all right.'

Of a sudden Jeffery-Smith was crisp; he was over the initial shock, accepting the situation and adjusting to it. Even seeing the amusing side of it.

'Know what we've got to do, Mordecai?' he said. 'Get the blighter on the first plane back we can. By the sound of it, he'll probably hijack it as like as not but that won't be our problem. Teach those idiots a lesson. Teach 'em not to dump their ailing Ministers on us without notice or as much as a by your leave. But I've got to keep my shirt-tails clean. So I'll tell you what I'm going to do. I'm going to get Oswald over here and certify the blighter's off his rocker even if it's only a temporary thing. If this gets out all hell's going to break loose and I'm not carrying the can for it. All I

287

want's a nice quiet couple of years before I retire and I'm damned if I'm jeopardising my pension because of someone else's shellshock. Where's Elaine?'

'She'll be out any moment, I should think.'

'Good. I'll tell her that if he thinks he's Fidel Castro she's got to go along with it.'

'Oh,' said Joseph hastily. 'It's nothing like that. He doesn't think he's anyone else ...'

'Quite! Quite! said Jeffery-Smith. 'I've got the picture. Now tell me ... what about the staff?'

'We've told them it's a sort of game the English play ...'

'They don't believe that?'

'It was the best that we could do. It was impossible to keep it from them. They saw him with Henry at pistol point. We had to tell them something.'

'And the police?'

'We've managed to keep it from them. So far.'

'Good. Try to make sure your staff don't speak to them.'

'Will do,' said Joseph.

'Now, listen. I don't suppose I'll be able to get Oswald over until this evening. Monday's his hospital afternoon. But I'll have him here before dark if I have to shanghai the blighter. In the meantime I'll fix a flight ... that'll probably be some time tomorrow. It won't be possible to arrange it earlier ... I wonder ...'

'What?'

'If it'd be best if I just slipped away. If he hasn't seen me arrive ...'

'But we don't know,' interrupted Joseph. It would have been one thing P.J. slipping away before the tale had been told—it was quite another now. 'He's pretty sharp, you know,' he went on. 'Might very well have seen you and be trying to make up his mind which side you're on. If you go without seeing him as likely as not he'll think we're all in the plot. He already thinks Carole is and he's a bit suspicious of Sydney. And Henry locked up in the pool-house. Wouldn't take much to make him think we're all against him, I shouldn't be surprised ...' He saw Elaine coming through the sitting-room. There remained just one more thing to tidy up. Important, yet not to be given time for long-drawn-out deliberation.

'Oh, one thing more P.J.,' he said.

'What's that?'

'Carnival. Don't mention it.'

'Wouldn't have dreamed of mentioning it.'

'No. But ... it might have cropped up.'

'Sets him off on something?'

'Something like that ... Oh, darling, there you are ...'

He got no further. Jeffery-Smith took over: 'My dear Elaine, I'm so sorry about this dreadful business ...'

'Oh, you know.' Her voice was dry.

'Yes, Joseph's told me all about it. I'm so sorry, my dear. And all my fault. If only I hadn't wished the blighter on you ... Look what I'm going to do is this. I'm going to have to talk to them before I go because it's just possible they may have seen me coming and if they have and I don't see them Joe thinks they may think we're all involved in this ... this damn silly revolution.'

'Oh, very likely,' said Elaine.

'Oh, you think so too.'

'Maybe they won't at once ...' She was looking at Joseph. 'But they'll probably be convinced of it before too long.'

'Quite,' said Jeffery-Smith. 'So what I'll do is humour them ... and I do think, my dear, it would be a good thing if you do as well ...'

'You know, I find it very difficult, Sir Peter,' Elaine interrupted in a formal way, 'to go along with what I know is a lot of damn foolishness.'

'Yes, I realise that. But it's what happens in the end that counts.'

'How right you are,' said Joseph. 'So, my love ...'

'Go on,' said Elaine to the Administrator.

'Your promise first.'

'Very well,' said Elaine. 'But don't forget I didn't want to.'

'None of us want to behave like idiots.' He smiled. 'But I've been mixed up with Governments too long not to have learnt there are times when it's unavoidable.' He paused. 'Now I'm bringing Oswald back with me as early as I can and as soon as I get back to Dukestown, arranging a flight so that we can ship the blighter out tomorrow and let that lot have the problem ...'

'You don't think it would be simpler,' Elaine said ironically, 'to cable London a revolution's about to happen. Then they could send a gunboat for him!'

In all his years of knowing Elaine Mordecai, Jeffery-Smith had never been personally subjected to her devastating irony—he had seen others demolished (and, as they had usually deserved it, been inwardly delighted) but he had been spared. They had had an understanding. Often, at Government House dinners and the like, she had caught his eye and much had been exchanged between them without so much as a word spoken; occasionally, even, he had, under cover of a tablecloth, squeezed her hand when a glance might have been too obvious. Now (temporarily, he hoped) their rapport seemed to have been destroyed. He was a little sad, a little rueful—but he did not blame her. Really this was too much for any woman to have to bear.

'And collect me while they're at it,' he answered gloomily.

Elaine was at once vexed with herself. It was bad enough for poor P.J. to be manipulated by Joseph without her adding to his troubles.

'Oh, surely it's not as bad as that?' she said, intending to be soothing but unwittingly merely echoing Joseph's approach and setting Jeffery-Smith off again.

'Isn't it? What d'you think they're going to do'—he nodded his head as if Whitehall were merely across the terrace 'when they hear about all this!?' And he repeated his diagnosis, although in words less trenchant than those he had used to Joseph, ending with an irony almost a match for hers. 'Been better for me, Mrs Mordecai, if there *had* been a revolution!'

Joseph rose like the wise, experienced trout which has lived for many, many years master of a deep slow pool and is able to select unerringly from amongst the wide variety of things it observes dropping like thistledown upon the surface. He rose gently as does such a trout taking what is offered to him without so much as a swirl upon the water.

'You mean,' he suggested innocently, 'one of those small and harmless blow-ups where no one gets hurt and it all gets swept underneath the carpet.'

'Damn right!' Jeffery-Smith agreed, although in fact it hadn't been what he'd meant at all—but he was in that confused state of mind which leads people into agreeing to almost anything which brings them comfort.

'And you know,' said Joseph in the slightly nostalgic manner of one who sees an opportunity (one not of course ever to be taken up) slip by, 'if there had been, I believe he'd have been just the man to put it down. And she'd have helped him ... don't you agree, my love?'

Elaine nodded silently. What else was there for her to do?

'I wonder ...' said Jeffery-Smith rather cunningly. And then, when Elaine had obviously not cottoned on. 'Yes, I wonder?'

'What?' said Elaine.

'You know ...' It was as if he'd had many hours of reflection. Often in his long career, Sir Peter Jeffery-Smith had been called upon to deliver judgements on matters he privately considered quite asinine and he had long since learnt that the more apparently considered the delivery, the more likely were his conclusions to be accepted. He had, as is often the case with civil servants, now become enmeshed in the *method* of handling the problems to the extent that he was beginning to lose sight of the problem itself. 'You know ...' he repeated, 'I have the feeling that if we keep playing this damn nonsense down we may get away with it. Now look, Mordecai, this is what I suggest. Firstly we humour him—all of us. Keep our faces straight. Right?'

'Right,' said Joseph.

'Elaine?'

'Of course.' He did not miss the coolness.

'Secondly, we keep it up in front of that wife he has. Tip her the wink we understand.'

'How?' said Elaine.

'My dear,' said Joseph in a beautifully succinct and unfinished sentence rather lacking in grammar. 'If Sir Peter with all his experience as Administrator ...'

'Kind of you,' said Jeffery-Smith. 'Thirdly, I'll do what I can to persuade him to stay here and not come back with me. Once he gets loose in Dukestown ... my God!' He winced at the thought. But then he remembered he had other obligations. 'If you agree, of course,' he added to Elaine. 'You don't have to and I'm not going to try to persuade you. There is really no reason why ...'

'Go on,' said Elaine in a level voice.

'Thank you ma'am.' He bowed his head a trifle as if to royalty. 'I'll go along with any suggestions he has to make ...'

'Cable for a gunboat?'

'Sometimes'—for the first time for quite a little while he chuckled 'we get faults on the line. Very small island, St Barbara, and technicians can be hard to find.'

'The Nelson touch?'

'In other words, the Nelson touch. The thing to do is keep the poor chap happy until I can get Oswald here. But one thing you can do for me, if you will. Would you have a quiet word on the side with Mrs Masterman ... after I've gone. Assuming of course he doesn't insist on coming back with me ... If he does.' He shrugged. 'Well let's meet that when it happens, If you would do that, Elaine ... explain I'll be back later. And bringing a doctor with me.'

'Very well,' said Elaine. 'But she isn't going to like it.'

'That I realise. But it can't be helped. Dammit, we're doing all we can. And they weren't *invited*. I mean, I'm sorry for the woman ... must be a hell of a thing to have to put up with. And if it's happened before, maybe she can snap the blighter out of it. Maybe by the time old Oswald gets here ...'

'He'll have put it all down,' suggested Joseph.

'Single-handed,' chuckled Jeffery-Smith, falling for it hook, line and sinker.

'What a brilliant idea!' burst out Joseph with high eyebrows—while Elaine listened, mesmerised.

'Uhm?' said Jeffery-Smith.

'I said what a brilliant idea. Don't you think that's a brilliant idea of Sir Peter's, my love? ... I wonder if it would work. Of course we'd *have* to have Mrs Masterman's co-operation. But I'm sure we would. I mean she's been so loyal ... even over that business of the arms drop. I told Sir Peter about that, you know. And about poor Henry being locked up in the pool-house. And Carole in her bedroom. But'—he was speaking to Jeffery-Smith again—'as you suggested earlier ... one of those small and harmless blow-ups where everything gets swept under the carpet and no harm done ... Would you care to suggest it to her?'

'No,' said Jeffery-Smith hastily. 'I'm sure you'll do it so much better. After I've gone.'

'Well,' said Joseph, 'I wouldn't say that, you know. But I'm willing to try. Now,' he looked around him. 'Darling,' he said, with some slight irritation, 'where is that boy?!' And he called out loudly: 'Sydney!'

Sydney soon appeared.

'Sydney,' said Joseph, 'where *is* that sangaree?'

'Mistress told me not to bring it till you called, Sir.'

'Oh. Did she? Well bring it now. We're very hot.'

'Yes, Sir.'

The ploy had the effect intended. The door to the radio rooms opened. Sybil came out.

'Mr Mordecai,' she called, 'do you really think it wise ...' She broke off at the sight of Jeffery-Smith. 'Good heavens!' she said, advancing towards them, then stopping again, irresolute.

'Good morning, Mrs Masterman,' said Jeffery-Smith hastily crossing towards her, hoping against all hope to be able to have a few words with her alone.

But she pre-empted this in a tone which struck Jeffery-Smith as brilliantly contrived and confirmed all the loyalty of which Mordecai had spoken so highly.

'How on earth did you get here?' she demanded in a sort of stage shout whisper as if she feared (as she did) a possible revolutionary behind every bush.

'By boat,' said Jeffery-Smith, responding

well, speaking loudly enough for anyone else in the radio room to hear him while at the same time winking at her broadly.

'Why are you ...' began Sybil, about to object to being winked at, but getting no further partly because Masterman, hearing the voices, came out to join her, a coil of wire in one hand, a revolver in the other—but more because Jeffery-Smith, quite misunderstanding the motive for this objection, hastily yanked a handkerchief from somewhere and began to dab at his eye whilst apologising:

'I'm afraid ... something ... in my eye ...'

But Sybil had already moved on—or, rather, turned.

'He got here by boat,' she explained. 'I daresay ...' she turned back again '... the road was ...' She broke off, puzzled.

'Trees down everywhere,' put in Jeffery Smith, taking the easy way.

'Ah!' said Sybil—and not without satisfaction.

'You're damn lucky to get through, Sir Peter,' said Masterman. 'How the devil did you manage it?'

'Oh ...' He spoke vaguely. 'We slipped through the islands.'

'Wouldn't have done if we hadn't nabbed Cicurel. Mordecai's told you we've got him safely under lock and key?'

'Yes.' Jeffery-Smith still found it hard to believe. But not so hard to believe as he would have had Masterman been showing anxiety. His cheerful grin, the twinkle in his eye, his easy, even relaxed manner confirmed all that Mordecai had said. This was a man who, holding such preposterous beliefs, ought to have been anxious; instead he was as much at home as if dealing with revolutions was a perfectly normal part of the life of a British Chancellor of the Exchequer. How did you cope with such a man?

'He'd got himself a sort of watching post, you know,' Masterman was going on meanwhile. 'Mordecai's gazebo. I managed to catch him a real fourpenny one from behind with a sort of cudgel.' The grin became, infectious. 'I bet he's got a headache he won't be losing in a hurry.'

'Well done,' said Jeffery-Smith weakly He could think of nothing more intelligent to say. 'Well done, indeed,' he added for good measure. 'Er ...' he noted that Sybil Masterman was staring at him rather hard, clearly expecting some contribution. 'Mordecai tells me you've got him safely under lock and key. Er ... you don't think there's any risk of him ... er ... escaping?'

'The worse for him,' said Masterman

cheerfully. 'They'll only shoot him. They've already tried it.'

'We can't be sure of that, Ernest,' Sybil said. 'For all we know it was you they were aiming at.'

Masterman shook his head.

'Doesn't make sense. They outnumber us heaven knows how many times, they've given up trying to keep it secret ...'

'Oh?' said Jeffery-Smith blankly.

'You mean you haven't seen any of them yet? No, that figures ... so far as they know it's only us who have an inkling of what's afoot, trees blocking roads can be accidents ...'

'You've *seen* some?'

'My wife, actually.'

'Thirty or forty,' said Sybil, exaggerating a little. 'All with rifles. And the police mingling with them.'

'Good God!' said Jeffery-Smith, conveying shock with little difficulty.

'You were lucky to get through ...' Masterman broke off; Sydney was emerging with an immense jug of sangaree choked with ice.

'You were saying?' Jeffery-Smith prompted.

Masterman briefly shook his head. Thoughtfully he watched Sydney putting the jug down on a convenient table and setting out glasses round it. No scene could possibly have been more peaceful. The full heat of midday had settled on Spoon Point. The coconut palms hung limp, their fronds barely rustling, the trumpet trees being without motion were all but invisible against the background of mangoes themselves etched out by the redness of the stalks of infant fruit in huge abundance and the ground between them and the terrace was shimmering. The sea showed its midday quiet, so calm that the movement of waves upon its surface was no more than the beating of a pulse beneath its skin and the necklets of surf around the islets were slim. In a cloudless sky a score of vultures circled lazily, borne by upcurrents, now and then dipping a wing to adjust their paths. It was blazing hot and brilliant bright—it was appropriate that a servant should be putting out glasses for cool drinks for five well-dressed men and women on a splendid terrace; only the young were missing, gay and laughing, to smash the surface of the swimming-pool, to add their own especial gaiety to the kind of scene which fills the pages of the glossy travel brochures.

'What's ... what's, er, in it, d'you know?' Masterman enquired.

'Eh?' said Jeffery-Smith.

'Sangria. Thought it was a Spanish thing.'

'Oh, yes ... yes, I believe that's where it did come from. Originally.' He sounded nervous.

Masterman was a little disappointed with him, Joseph delighted.

'That's a different thing, sangria,' Joseph said. 'This is sangaree. Made from madeira, water, spices and all sorts of aromatic herbs.' He gazed benignly at the jug in front of him, delicious-looking, with thin curls of lime floating on its surface. 'Very old St Barbara drink, you know. Takes half an hour to make and only Sydney knows how to put it together properly.'

Ah, well, thought Elaine, he's got that alibi in for Sydney—wondered how he would. She was almost beyond caring. It was a mad, mad world.

'I really do not think ...' Sybil began to protest ... But Masterman stopped her.

'I can't wait to taste it, Sydney,' he said easily. 'I'm sure I'm going to enjoy it very much.'

'Feel so, Sir,' said Sydney with a blaze of white square teeth.

Masterman took Sybil gently by the elbow and propelled her a trifle towards a chair, then took one himself. Sydney was busy pouring. Joseph lit a cigar. Elaine examined her nails, briefly. Jeffery-Smith felt in limbo. In the silence Gertrude could be clearly heard:

302

'... seein' as how the boy who fetches the beef from Port Lucea is busy, when you go to fetch the mail tomorrow, Hazel ...'

It was absurd to think of revolutions on St Barbara.

'How is it in Dukestown?' Masterman asked when Sydney had withdrawn.

'In Dukestown? Oh, quiet. Very quiet.' And hastily: 'I'm glad to say.'

'No sign of people gathering, showing excitement ... that sort of thing?'

Jeffery-Smith thought of Carnival, remembered not to mention it, but used it:

'Well it certainly is ... I don't know quite how to put it ... There's an atmosphere.'

'One moment,' Masterman turned casually to Joseph. 'You know,' he said. 'I think it would be a wise precaution if you had Sydney as it were keep guard on the pool-house door where we can watch him. Just in case.'

'But my dear fellow ...'

Masterman dealt smoothly with this outburst of righteous indignation.

'I quite realise,' he said, 'that it must be very difficult for you to doubt the loyalty of a servant who's been with you as long as Sydney has and your faith in him's probably quite justified. But there's no sense in being careless. And no sense in having anyone pass on the fact that Sir

303

Peter's here if we haven't got to.'

'Oh, very well, very well!' said Joseph huffing and puffing to his feet, his mouth drawn up in annoyance so as to cause a deep downward curve to appear in the fleshiness of his chin, his brows forming a veritable roof above his eyes.

'And while you're about it,' went on Masterman cheerfully, 'I think it'd be a good idea for you to make sure those two ladies you employ don't leave the premises.'

Joseph shrugged massive and eloquent shoulders but went off to carry out his instructions while Sybil began to make suggestions.

'Ernest,' she said. 'Don't you think it would be wiser if we went inside?' She cast a doubtful look at the distant bush.

He shook his head.

'I very much doubt if they'll be messing about in that lot any more. Where's the point? And if they are they'll have seen Sir Peter coming, so the best thing's to look casual. Frankly,' he was speaking to Jeffery-Smith, 'I'm not all that worried we're at immediate risk. If you'll excuse the expression, Mrs Mordecai, and I'm sure you will'—the smile was irresistible—'I imagine they're rushing around like a lot of blue-arsed flies ...'

'Ernest ...'

'Like a lot of blue-arsed flies' (What a pity, thought Jeffery-Smith—such a splendid fellow otherwise) 'wondering what they're supposed to do.'

'Well,' said Sybil crossly, 'you might easily have been killed.'

'Not a bit of it. If that shot was meant for anyone it was obviously Cicurel. Most likely it was just to scare the daylights out of us and give the blighter a chance to get away.'

'So how do you read it?' Jeffery-Smith enquired, amazing himself, as Elaine had done, by the lulling effect on common sense all this talk, all this quiet practical talk, of revolution was having on him.

'Well, of course, we don't know, do we? You say there's an atmosphere in Dukestown. But nothing overt is happening presumably?'

'Oh no, nothing. Nothing.'

'And yet, *you* know.' Masterman's eyes narrowed a little, yet without losing the glint which gave the man so much of his charm.

'Oh, yes ... er ...' He saw Joseph and Sydney emerging from the house farther along by the swimming-pool. Almost as though the sight of the shimmering water gave him final encouragement, St Barbara's Administrator took the plunge. 'We have our sources, you know.'

'Then I'm surprised ...' began Sybil with some heat—only to have Masterman quickly cool it.

'Sir Peter had his instructions, Sybil,' he pointed out. 'We were here for a rest. And ...' He turned back to Jeffery-Smith. 'And you didn't imagine it was imminent—as most probably it wasn't ... I wonder ...' He leaned back, idly sipping the sangaree he was finding refreshing and delightful. 'Do you think it's connected with this Christiana business? I think it has to be, don't you? Too much of a coincidence otherwise. No, you were asking me ... My own feeling is that this bunch on Spoon Point are here as much as anything to guard the arms supply. It's obviously been their dropping-point ... Mordecai told you about the drop we had last night?'

'Yes.' Jeffery-Smith cast a covert glance at Sybil as he listened to Masterman going on. Mordecai was damn right, he thought, the woman's marvellous. Not a blink.

'Pretty smartly done, you know. Not all that easy dropping stuff as close as they managed it, not on a moonless night. Of course it being a peninsula helps. Probably one of the very reasons they chose the place.'

Joseph came back, heavily, to rejoin them.

'I've told him to stay where we can

watch him,' he said trifle sulkily. 'He's not very pleased about it.'

'Well it won't be for long.' Masterman was back to talking to Jeffery-Smith. 'Good of you to come over ...'

'Well, I tried to contact you by radio ...'

'Sabotaged.'

'Yes, I imagined that it might be.' Jeffery-Smith was even beginning to enjoy his role. Once you got into the swing of it, it really was quite fun. He took a mental breath. 'Chancellor,' he said, 'if you want to, and of course you might think it wiser, you could come back with me ... you and Mrs Masterman, I mean ... and I suppose Mr and Mrs Mordecai, although ... well it's not a very big boat and if you think there's no immediate danger ... Well what I mean is that it probably doesn't arouse suspicion, an Administrator having a bit of a trip on an old friend's fishing cruiser ...'

'Dressed as you are?'

'Oh.' Jeffery-Smith had overlooked this point.

'No,' said Masterman, taking charge. 'Either they know you're here or they don't. Quite likely they don't. What they're looking out for is no one leaving Spoon Point, not someone landing on it. All the emphasis will be on the gateway side.

They know we haven't got a boat of our own and no means of getting a message out ... incidentally, Mordecai, did you mention Cicurel's boat pulling out?' Joseph shook his head. 'During the night,' Masterman explained. 'I heard it go. Took everything with it, every last hand-grenade or whatever it is they've got. I suppose Cicurel got someone else to drive the thing. Thought it more important to be here. Actually I wondered if it was pulled in out of sight to let him come ashore ... but you'd have seen it.'

In fact, Jeffery-Smith had seen it. Port Lucea was hardly a marina. He was glad it was an assumption not a question he had to deal with. He stayed silent.

'Anyway ... we oughtn't to be too long ... if they know you're here we shall find out soon enough when you leave.'

'Oh, you aren't going to come back with me?'

'No.'

'Nor the ladies?'

Masterman shook his head.

'No. That would be forcing things. As I've said, I think there's not too much risk as things are. They don't know how much we know, only that we've nabbed Cicurel and, for the moment at least, they're quite likely leaderless. Waiting for instructions and that takes time. There's a pretty good chance they don't know you're here and, if you don't hang around too long, not a bad chance you'll get away unnoticed. But if we set off in a gaggle ... well apart from being more conspicuous it really might force their hand. The best thing's for Mordecai to stroll down with you and at the distance there's a good chance if they do see you, they'll think you're me. In fact ...' He put down his glass emptied. 'Delicious.'

'Would you like some more?' asked Joseph.

'Well yes, I would.'

'Darling, I wonder ...'

'Only too glad,' Elaine said drily, 'to have something to do.'

'I take it,' said Sybil, seizing her opportunity, 'you are finally convinced, Mrs Mordecai, that my husband isn't talking out of the back of his head?'

'I never thought that,' responded Elaine coldly. 'Only that he'd been misled.'

'But you don't think that now?'

'How could I possibly against such weight of opinion.'

'Thank you,' said Sybil, with the most irritating complacency.

'Finished?' enquired Masterman pleasantly. 'Good. Now, Sir Peter. My wife and I have been spending the last hour or two, and it makes your fingers sore,

I can tell you, winding miles of wire to get a message out. But now that you're here ... How long should it take you to get back to Dukestown?'

'A little over an hour.'

'Is that all?'

'The road's clear the other side of Port Lucea ... or at least it was,' said Jeffery-Smith, repairing a tear in his performance.

'I'll give you an hour. By then the radio should be functioning and you can call me. If I don't hear from you, I'll do what I can to get a message out myself. When you get into Dukestown, I want you to call the P.M.'

'Call the P.M.' Jeffery-Smith tried to keep the dullness from his tone.

'And advise on the situation. You must make your own judgement as to how grave it is. Frankly, I doubt if it's very much to bother with. A frigate off Dukestown if there's one handy ought to do it. Lot of people think that'd've been enough to stop the Falkland's business in its tracks. The important thing is speed. Nip it in the bud and it'll get in the press as little more than a rumour.' He was on his feet.

Jeffery-Smith rose, putting his shoulders back.

'And what will you be doing meanwhile, Chancellor?' he asked in as grave a tone as he could manage.

'Oh come on now, Sir Peter, cheer up,' said Masterman. 'We aren't going to be massacred, you know. What am I going to do? ... I'm going to have a little chat with friend Cicurel—and find out exactly what this is all about. Unless you know?'

Jeffery-Smith shook his head.

'I've simply no idea. But then, I never really understood what Grenada and Anguilla were all about, either.' But a thought occurred to him. 'This ... er ... Cicurel. If he ... well I don't know, denies there's a ... a revolution ... or says if there is he doesn't know what it's all about. Or he's nothing to do with it. Or something. You won't ... er ... I mean ...'

'Torture him?' Masterman was chuckling. 'Hardly. But ... have you ever knelt on a piece of bamboo?'

'Knelt on a piece of bamboo? Good God, no! Why on earth should I?'

'No reason. But would you call that torture?'

'Well, no. Of course not.'

'Say no more,' said Masterman. 'Say no more, Sir Peter.'

He watched them go, Joseph and Sir Peter Jeffery-Smith, along the path between the hibiscus hedges towards the cliff. He had a revolver half-hidden by his side but little worry he would have to use it.

While he was watching, Elaine asked quietly.

'That business about bamboo?'

He turned his head to smile at her wickedly.

'A Japanese trick,' he told her. 'You kneel on it. It's surprising how little you enjoy it. Not something I'd recommend you'd try.' He chuckled. 'There's plenty of bamboo on Spoon Point, isn't there?'

'Incredible,' said Jeffery-Smith.

'Isn't it,' said Joseph. 'Very worrying.'

'Such a decent fellow. Be the end of his career, of course, when this comes out.'

'What a tragedy.'

'Won't do mine much good either.'

'Didn't you think *she* was marvellous?'

'Amazing. You know, though, what was the most amazing thing of all?'

'What's that, P.J?'

'I half found myself believing in his bloody revolution.'

'One does. One does.'

'You found the same?'

'Yes, man. I found the same. It all goes to show ... the power of suggestion.'

'But to take it to that extent ... imagine being shot at, seeing arms dropping from the skies ...' He remembered something else. 'You'll apologise to Carole for me, won't you? And Cicurel. Damn decent of

312

him to put up with it. Damn decent of both of them.'

They had reached the edge of the cliff. Now the fishing cruiser could be seen, moored to a stone arm which ran quite a little way out to sea, then turned to form a tiny dock. The light off the water was searing to the eyeballs but here it was cooler, under the shade of manchioneels. The path ran down, twisting, towards the jetty—a rough sort of path with occasional irregular steps, cut through the rocks. Crotons and spiky plants, succulents, anthuriums and so on, wild and planted, grew in abundance. Through this growth the sea, closer in, could be seen in patches, turquoise over sand, brown over weed, many-coloured over coral, inviting, exquisitely beautiful. The air was humid, heavy, smelling of earth and beach.

'Don't bother to come down, Joseph,' said Jeffery-Smith.

'If you don't mind.'

'I should be back around five ... with any luck.' He half laughed. 'Assuming, of course, I'm not torpedoed on the way to Port Lucea. Oh, by the way, I noticed your boat in.'

'Yes. It's being re-varnished.'

'You didn't try telling him ...' a nod towards the house.

'My dear fellow,' Joseph said.

Jeffery-Smith gazed at him for a moment or two in silence. St Barbara without Joseph Mordecai was unimaginable.

'Tell you what,' he said.

'What?'

'You manage to get him sane again before I let old Oswald loose on him and I'll make sure you get that K.B.E.' And he chuckled. 'Even if I have .to give you mine.'

Joseph watched him go, carefully, yet surely down the steps. Dignified, assured, well-groomed, immensely likeable and nobody's fool—Sir Peter Jeffery-Smith, Her Majesty's representative on St Barbara. He watched him all the way, seeing him in and out of the trees, and then in to the clear, harsh sunlight on the jetty. Watched him go aboard, nimbly for his age; saw him chat to Willie Matthews, waited for Willie's wave and then returned it. And he still stood there, panama-hatted, massive, rather hot. He heard the engine start, throaty, gurgling, watched the ropes being neatly stowed while the small boat pulled away carving a line of pure white in the blue. Then it was turning, threading its way towards the passage between the many islets, its antennae rocking, magnifying the small swell. Then it was lost between the

314

overlapping spiders of coconut palms on a small island and Joseph turned away, to walk back to the house—to play his part in the final act of this small comedy.

ELEVEN

The pool-house had been designed for the sole purpose of housing the water supply, the filtration plant and the equipment which controlled the temperature of the swimming-pool and it had not occurred to its designer to make allowance for storing revolutionaries. In consequence, apart from being in, as it were, the vertical as compared with the horizontal, Henry was possessed very much with a sense of *déjà-vu*. He was also very hot and the continual clicking on and off of the machinery (whose sole purpose after all was to keep at perfection a large quantity of cool fresh water only feet away from him) was particularly irritating. In fine, Henry Irwin Cicurel was not in the best of moods and only too ready to do battle with anyone he could lay his hands on.

Yet even, so, he was haunted by the delicious memory of Carole's long, firm yet yielding body pressed hard against his own, of mobile lips which (surely this had not been self-delusion) had been more expressive than the mere circumstance of persuading Masterman at a distance required. There had been a last pressure of a hand, that queer, mysterious yet somehow encouraging final smile. Her back had been towards the bush; Masterman could never have seen that smile. There had to be a reason for it. In just such manner as all young lovers through countless ages have read in the tiniest compliment, in the fluttering of an eyelid, in the brush of soft fingers on their cheek, messages of hope, so Henry was sustained through his hour of trial and, to some degree at least, his anger muted.

He was very much aware that, so far, his had been a negative role. He had been given his instructions and he had carried them out faithfully and, he told himself, pretty damn efficiently. After all they had wanted a desperate-looking revolutionary locked up in the pool-house and (and he passed a hand across his scrubby face, and felt the stinging of his scratches, the itching of his lumps and the aching of muscles, head and sinews) by any reasonable standard he'd provided that. But you didn't win babes like Carole just doing what you were told ... (he wouldn't normally have regarded Carole as a 'babe', that wasn't Henry's kind of language, but somehow it seemed appropriate thinking for a guy bruised by a revolver muzzle and put on ice) ... no, you didn't win them that way. You had to be *positive*. But how the hell could you be positive when what you were supposed to be part of did not exist? When everything was going on around you but no one briefed you on what was happening? When your eyes felt as if someone had run red-hot pokers through them? When your head was buzzing with the clicking and the grinding of a damn machine? When your body was as wet with sweat from scalp to burning feet as a pair of bathing-trunks hung on a line to drip?

Any time now that sonofabitch with the crooked smile and that 'don't think you can bug me' manner (Henry was still thinking Tom Wolfe style) was going to let him out and grill him. Well it was one thing being grilled about things you knew about and had to pretend you didn't but quite another about things that didn't exist and you had to pretend did. He could (or so he assumed) endure the death of a thousand cuts if necessary to acquit himself well in Carole's eyes, but how did you impress when no one told you what was expected of you?

Asking a great deal of himself, Henry attempted to rationalize the situation in a cool, calm and collected manner. His instructions had been succinct; he was to 'leave it to Daddy' and 'not do anything that might wreck it all.' He had in his pocket a piece of paper which the British Chancellor of the Exchequer, the guy with the crooked smile, who'd obviously been railroaded into believing all this garbage, was to find and who, when he found it, would believe that some other guy named (and would you believe it but it was true!) ... named *Rochambeau* was masterminding the revolution and had issued instructions to all the various units to rendezvous with other units at various places, prior to marching on Dukestown. His own unit was the Ninth Battalion which, presumably, as he was a colonel, he was leading. Carole, meanwhile, was known by Masterman to be in the plot but he believed he'd persuaded her that he thought he'd persuaded her that he believed it was no more than some small gang doing a little bit of illicit arms horse-trading. Was that right? It sounded complicated. He ran through it again. Yes, it was right. It didn't sound right, but it was, Carole was locked up in her bedroom (although Masterman knew she'd got out of it to tip him off) and therefore she was supposed to think Masterman didn't know she knew he'd slugged the guy she was crazy about. (Crazy about! I should be so lucky!) But he had been tipped off. About what? About the fact that Masterman had blown their cover. Okay. Suppose he was Masterman, what would he want to find out from someone he'd caught who was sufficiently high up to be receiving battle instructions? Well what would he? Who was Rochambeau?—he'd think that was a code name sure as Frank Sinatra's trees had little apples in the summertime! What was it all about? Who was going to run St Barbara if they pulled it off?

Well the answers were simple. There were just four of them involved, or five if you threw in Mrs Mordecai—or put it back to four if you let Sydney out because he thought it was some sort of game. Arms? No arms. Masterman had 'em all. Rochambeau? He almost laughed in the hot, clammy darkness of his cell. Rochambeau! He could answer that. He'd be supposed to answer that. The principle was you told no lies. That after it was over you could come out with your perfectly logical and accurate explanation if you had to. Rochambeau was The Mighty King! He'd tell him. See what he made of it. He'd probably think that Rochambeau was a second Ugandan Idi and he a second Major Bob!

The notion appealed to him enormously, so much so that he dwelt on it and forgot about thinking up answers to other questions. Major Bob—Colonel Henry! If the Ninth Battalion could co-opt him without as much as a by your leave, they could take the consequences. They were all colonels, weren't they, successful revolutionaries? Grivas, Nasser, Gaddafi. Started off as military henchmen and then took over. Why shouldn't he do the same? If that didn't impress Carole, nothing would. The imagery was delightful. He saw himself taking the parade with Carole at his side. It was all very clear and certain. It just showed how simple things suddenly became when you controlled yourself to look at situations in a cool, calm, collected manner. He became impatient. It was time they got down to business. Time the cards were laid down on the table.

What the hell was all this waiting?

He started to hammer with both fists on the door. He could see it was the door because of the bright edge where it didn't close accurately on the frame. He hammered and hammered and at the same time shouted.

This had a result. It brought Henry who, through a night of little sleep, a clout on the back of his head, considerable stress and the soporific effect of being locked up for an hour in a stiflingly hot and practically airless pool-house, had become mentally irrational, partially back to reality. But the daydream which briefly had taken charge of his consciousness left a lasting influence. He had been treated like a pawn—as no more than a piece which could be sacrificed for positional advantage! For the best part of twenty-four hours he had slogged it out and to what purpose? That at the end of it he was to 'leave it all to Daddy!' He was 'not to do anything that might wreck it all.' And if he complied, what would be the result? That Carole, and with justification, would regard him as being what he had been—a pawn! Not a shining knight, the one piece on the board of St Barbara who could clear all obstacles, who could not be hemmed in by interfering other pieces as even a king and queen could be. Not that. But a pawn! A poor, miserable, crawling, subservient and obedient pawn!

To hell with that!

And he banged his fists harder than ever against the pool-house door and shouted all the louder.

And Masterman unlocked the padlock and let him out.

The light was dazzling, painful.

Ernest Masterman was aware what it was like to be dragged out from a cramped and unlit cell (the Japanese had called it a *cheesai uchi*—in other words 'a little house') into the blazing sunshine. The eyes hurt as if acid had been thrown in them, the mind reeled from the impossibility of immediate adjustment. One felt desperately alone.

His sympathy was entirely with Henry Cicurel, to whom he felt no antagonism whatsoever.

But he had always played his games to win and when you played a game, so long as you stuck roughly to the rules, a little gamesmanship didn't come amiss. While the goalkeeper was reeling from the ball bouncing off his forehead into play, you slammed it in the net; while the tennis player was struggling to recover his footwork after that net cord, you smashed it to the corner.

'Ever knelt on a bit of bamboo?' he said.

'What?' said Henry.

'Not something I'd recommend. Worse than having your nails pulled out. Get along.'

And he shoved the hard circle of a revolver into Henry's back to encourage him to make his way along the terrace.

From a little distance, Elaine was watching. It really was, she thought, remarkable. And she was not meaning that it was remarkable that the British Chancellor of the Exchequer should be herding along her terrace at gunpoint an unshaven, dirty and absurdly attired business associate of Joseph's, but that she should be able to regard such proceedings with equanimity—it was amazing how capable the human mind was of adjusting to the most bizarre circumstances. Amazing too how detached one could be. How odd, she thought, this man who really does believe, and why should he not believe, that he has captured a dangerous criminal, is a man whose normal utterances cause the British Press to scrap one set of headlines for another and the British television to clear all channels to let him have his say; and how ironical that it should be Henry—poor, kind, uncomplicated, hardworking and earnest Henry—who should be cast in the role of Judy to his Punch. Why did he ever knock on Joseph's door? Why didn't I tell him to turn round and head straight back to the peace and sanity of old New York?!

As to what the end would be ...

She turned to Joseph, who had only moments before returned from seeing off St Barbara's Administrator and was watching the approach of Masterman and Henry with masked satisfaction.

'We shall,' she told him quite serenely, 'all end up in prison.' And not without a little malice: 'You certainly will.'

'Not at all.' Only the voice was urbane. Joseph was remembering that he at least had been convinced as to the validity of

Masterman's analysis and had drawn his eyebrows close together and given himself a stern, censorious expression. 'For me to go to prison the British Government would have to admit its second senior Minister had been hoodwinked into requesting the Queen's representative of one of its last remaining Colonies to indent for a gunboat or a force of paratroopers to invade a small, unimportant and perfectly peaceful island. It would be in the political wilderness for years. My love, I shall not go to prison. I should be far more likely to go to the House of Lords ... And what have you got to say for yourself, you rascal?!' This last was, of course, addressed to Henry, now thrust before them.

'Please, Mordecai. I think it would be better if you let me handle this.'

'Well naturally I don't want to interfere, Chancellor, but this was a man I trusted. A man I gave business to ... Oh, very well.'

And Joseph bowed out.

'Mrs Mordecai, would you be kind enough to bring your daughter down?' Masterman said politely.

Elaine favoured him with a look, then, without speaking, went off to carry out his instruction.

Sybil, meanwhile, hearing this conversation came out of the radio room into which she had gone to resume her winding.

Masterman refrained from sending her back; with the advent of Jeffery-Smith, getting the transmitter functioning was of rather lessened importance and he saw a degree of mileage in this.

'You may as well stay while we deal with this fellow, Sybil,' he suggested, waving the gun towards a chair.

'But what about the transmitter?'

Masterman replied obliquely.

'You may as well know,' he informed Henry, still busy trying to blink away the sunlight, 'That we've got a message out. Sir Peter Jeffery-Smith ... You know who I'm talking about?' Henry nodded. 'He managed to get through to us. By boat. He's on his way back to let the Government know what is happening. By this time tomorrow there'll be enough troops on St Barbara to deal with any of this silly nonsense you and your lot are tying to put together. Sit down.' Again he gestured with his gun. Willingly enough, Henry sat. 'It's rather hard luck,' Masterman went on, 'that the property which is normally deserted on your dropping nights ...'

Henry interrupted: 'Who the hell are you, anyway?'

'You know perfectly well who I am.'

'You're Mickey Mouse.'

'Ernest ...'

'Please, Sybil. You know perfectly well

who I am,' Masterman repeated in a relaxed sort of way. 'Mr Mordecai's daughter would have told you when she went to the gazebo.'

'Oh,' said Henry. He said this to give himself a little time. It was a very complicated business working out what he was supposed to know and what he was supposed not to know. Almost as difficult as knowing what to say and what not to say. Mister Mordecai wasn't giving him any guidance, just looking at him as if he was something just crawled out from underneath a stone. Besides, the discovery that Jeffery-Smith believed in the revolution too and had gone back to report it to the British Government had set him back. He was still determined—but more confused than ever. And this thing was dangerously close to getting out of hand!

'As I was saying,' Masterman resumed meanwhile, 'it was hard luck my wife and I happened to be diverted here because of the Christiana business. The two are connected, aren't they?'

'Go to hell!' responded Henry, this seeming both harmless and appropriate.

'You know,' said Masterman easily. 'You really are being rather stupid. St Barbara's a very tiny island and there just isn't any way of keeping anything from us in the end. There isn't going to be a revolution.

Whatever you had in mind isn't going to happen. And it'll be better for you in the long run if you decide to be helpful rather than obstructive. And' (just then Elaine, followed by a sullen-looking Carole still in mauve cords and short-sleeved lilac sweat shirt, came out on to the terrace) 'if you won't think of yourself ...'

He got no further. Throwing herself with huge enthusiasm into her part, Carole shouted: 'Cy!' and racing across the terrace flung herself at Henry so swiftly and unexpectedly that even Masterman was taken unawares.

Sybil rose to her feet, Elaine looked up to heaven, Joseph frowned.

'Stop that!' called Masterman, stretching out a hand to grasp Carole's shoulder.

She turned. As with any girl whose advances have been rejected out of hand, contriving a look of hatred wasn't too difficult.

'You pig!' she spat at him. 'You bloody English pig!' And she was consoling Henry. 'Oh, darling, darling! What have they done to you?'

'Mordecai,' Sybil was screeching. 'Can't you control your daughter?!'

'Carole, really ...' said Joseph rather helplessly.

Elaine merely shook her head. No one was watching her.

Henry, meanwhile, was enormously encouraged. The sweet closeness of Carole's body, the smell of her hair, the touch of her lips, were balm to his soul and gave strength to his resolve.

'Leave this to me,' he said. And gently, he put her from him.

'Okay,' he said to Masterman. 'Let's talk.'

'My dear fellow ...' Joseph, somewhat alarmed, began.

'Henry,' said Carole.

'Okay. Okay. I said it was okay.' Inspiration had come to Henry Cicurel.

Reluctantly Carole drew back; Joseph stared—fiercely trying to combine warning with apparent censure.

Henry stood, facing Masterman, who gently reminded him of the gun.

'It's okay,' said Henry. 'Take the weight off your wrist.' He stood, stuffed his hands into his pockets and adopted a swaggering air.

'Nothing you can pin on me,' he said. 'Revolution? Don't know what you're talking about. You should take more water with it, Mister. Never heard such eyewash. Revolution on St Barbara ...'

'Oh, for God's sake,' interrupted Masterman, becoming irritated. 'You strut about in uniform. You carry a gun. You help collect a crate of arms dropped by parachute. You run your boat out of its hiding-place ...'

'Any law saying I shouldn't?'

'Where is it?'

'Mind your own bloody business. This ...' he pulled at his uniform. 'It's a new fashion I'm starting. That ...' he pointed to the gun. 'I gotta licence. Crate of arms? You must be dreaming ...'

Carole was impressed. Henry was undoubtedly making progress. Timing is as important in affairs of the heart as it is in other fields. And when a girl, normally self-confident, has been shaken out of her usual calm, she turns instinctively to one of her own generation who is exhibiting assurance and decision. There were, she was forced to admit to herself, qualities in Henry Cicurel she had obviously overlooked. Joseph, too, was reassured, if in a different manner. The boy, he told himself, was doing splendidly. The effect on Sybil, however, was to require her to essay a contribution.

'Ernest,' she said. 'Don't you think we ought to search him?'

It had occurred to Henry quite some time before that the best revolutionaries when captured ate their battle orders; but he had worked out a solution—double bluff. 'I ate it, lady, don't you know,' he said. 'All twelve pages.' And quickly, as it were passing on to the next thing, to Masterman: 'This revolution of yours, what's it all about?'

Henry had been clever. Masterman was taken in.

'Turn out your pockets,' he said. And, as Henry drew back a trifle, jabbed him. 'Do as I say!'

'Oh, for Pete's sake ...' Henry began— but the bang of a bullet fired, of a glass shattering to pieces, silenced him. And brought a gasp from Joseph.

Masterman lowered the gun.

'One can manage without toes,' he observed. 'But it's much more difficult to get about, you know.'

A change came over Henry.

'Okay, okay! You win!' And he undid his tunic pocket, took out The Mighty King's instruction and flipped it to the floor.

Masterman picked it up, watching him carefully all the time. He read it. The glint in his eyes became a little brighter.

'Where's Bathsheba Halt?' he enquired of Joseph.

'Bathsheba Halt? It's a railway station. But ...'

'Railway station! On St Barbara?'

'Banana line. You know, taking bananas ...'

'Into Dukestown?'

'To the outskirts. They get loaded on to

lorries ... But my dear fellow ... What does that say?'

'Read it yourself.'

Joseph took the paper and read its contents in feigned astonishment. He wasn't necessarily to have heard of the Ninth Battalion, the Solitaires, the Highland Warriors or of Rochambeau. Carnival bands didn't publicize their names; and businessmen didn't have to rub shoulders with calypso singers.

'Good God!' he was able to gasp. 'How remarkable!' He then took his calculated risk. 'But the twenty-third,' he said, 'that's ...'

'Next week,' interrupted Masterman. (Had Joseph finished, which of course he never would have, he would have gone on to say: 'the first day of Carnival') 'We seem, Mr Cicurel, properly to have thrown a spanner in the works by dropping in on Spoon Point, don't we?'

'If you think what's fixed for ...' Henry fizzled out.

'But even you do,' Masterman said. 'Let's stop playing, shall we? The party's over. There isn't going to be a revolution. It just isn't possible to reorganise something fixed for a week ahead at five minutes' notice. By tomorrow morning at the latest it'll all be cold potatoes. So I'll go back to what I said before—if you won't think of

333

yourself you might at least think of her.'
He nodded to the decorative Carole, who
had decided that staring disconsolately at
the terrace floor was the safest thing to
do. 'So far as I'm concerned, if you're
prepared to be helpful she was merely
under the impression you were smuggling
arms. I never even saw her at the gazebo.'
His attitude towards Carole was not at
all as hers was to him. He would always
remember with nostalgia her standing half
naked, offering herself—he would, he knew,
for the rest of his life be torn between
relief at having shown common sense and
regret at not accepting what would never
be offered to him again.

'At the gazebo?' Joseph, meantime,
interjected, thorough to the last. 'When?
When was this?'

'About an hour and a half ago. Just
after she came back from showing me
your cave.'

'But she was locked in her room ...' He
showed indignation. 'Carole! Your mother
told you ... Did you disobey her?'

'You wouldn't understand ...'

'You mean ...'

'Daddy ... don't you see? I love him.'

'That's all very well ...' Joseph broke
off and pulling out his handkerchief
began to mop his brow. 'What an
extraordinary business this is,' he said. He

stopped mopping and looked with alarm at Masterman. 'My dear fellow ... I'm sure ... so far as Carole was concerned ... well how was she to know? ... I, mean, Henry ... Cicurel ... well, we've done business together. He's stayed here with us. Met my daughter ...' He rounded on Henry. 'How dare you? You know what you are? You're a cad, man! A cad!'

'Stow it!' said Henry.

It was all Carole could do not to laugh. She contrived a stifled sob instead.

'Well?' said Masterman.

But Joseph was not yet done.

'You said you didn't see her at the gazebo. That was what you said.'

'If Cicurel is prepared to be helpful, I didn't see her at the gazebo.'

'Well that's very decent of you ... but ... Henry! ... I've only shown you kindness. Tried to help you. Offered you my hospitality. And my daughter is apparently in love with you ... I can't imagine why ... but ... Man! Can't you see? The time has come to tell Masterman ... I'm very sorry, Sir ... to tell the Chancellor everything he needs to know to bring this dreadful business to an end.' The message was clear as crystal.

Henry shrugged. 'Okay, Okay. I know when I'm licked.' And, adopting, a careless attitude, he turned to Masterman. 'Shoot,' he said. Then gilded the lily. 'Cigarette first.'

Masterman threw a packet at him, pre-empting Carole.

'Light.'

Matches followed.

Henry lit his cigarette and slung both packet and matches back, one following the other, with a definite air. Masterman caught both neatly.

'Ready?' he said. Henry nodded. 'Two questions. Who? And why?'

'Who what?' said Henry, enjoying it. 'I'm not with you.'

'He means,' said Joseph helpfully. 'Who signed that piece of paper?'

'Can't he read?'

'Rochambeau?' queried Masterman.

'The Mighty King.'

'Oh, my God,' said Masterman.

'Well what about the other, then?' said Joseph hurriedly. 'Why should a bloody revolution break out on St Barbara?'

'A revolution has not broken out on St Barbara,' Masterman reminded him. 'And even if it had, it would not necessarily have been bloody. But why, Cicurel?'

Henry shrugged, drew on his cigarette, held it away from him high in the air, insolently.

'Guess any place that gets cold-shoul-dered the way this one has been compared with other islands in the Caribbean ...' he pronounced it in the American manner 'be entitled to blow its top.'

'What are you talking about?' demanded Masterman—and Joseph knew it was all over bar the shouting. Really Henry had done very well. What a splendid son-in-law he was going to make.

'You want to know?' Henry was in full flood. 'I'll tell you. Think I came here to go about like this?' He pulled at his torn and stained tunic.

'I certainly can't see why you should.'

'I came here,' said Henry, 'to make some dough. Straightforward, on the level, business. Got contracts all lined up to sell things like bras and bicycles guys like Mordecai could make because labour's cheap on St Barbara because there's not enough work going round. I could have sold those bras and bicycles. And a lotta other things. Given work to all those men and women you see lying around sleeping under trees because that's all they've got to do. That's what I could have done. But did I? Did I hell! Every time I got a contract lined up ready for signing on the dotted line, along comes some other island like maybe Trinidad, or Jamaica, or Barbados, that's had a hand-out from your lot, or from Uncle Sam, and pulls the skids from under me.'

'Is what he's saying true?' enquired Masterman of Joseph.

'Well, yes,' Joseph agreed reluctantly. 'They do get subsidies to build their factories. But that isn't any reason for starting a revolution! I never heard of such a thing. How ...'

'It's all right,' said Masterman. And to Cicurel: 'Go on.'

Henry shrugged.

'That's it. You can write the rest yourself.'

Masterman nodded. 'Yes. I think I could.' Deliberately he put down the revolver and, crossing the terrace, stared for a few moments at the brilliant sea, thinking. Then he came slowly back.

'This ... this Mighty King?' he said.

'What about him?'

'He's organising all these ... these various groups who're due to march on Dukestown a week today?'

'Right.'

'Mostly people without work to do?'

'Right.'

'And of course there'll be a pay-off for you.'

'Ever heard of Major Bob?'

'I wouldn't,' suggested Masterman drily, 'have thought wanting to follow in his footsteps the best of all ambitions. But, yes, I get the point. Call a spade a

338

spade, Cicurel, you're in this for the money, aren't you? The money and the power.'

'Aren't we all? Aren't you?'

This brought an angry outburst from the predictable Sybil, who, with the grimmest of determination, had been keeping silent.

'How dare you? How *dare* you? My husband is a politician, not a revolutionary!'

Henry flicked his burning stub nonchalantly in the air. 'There's a difference?' he enquired.

'Ernest ...'

'All right, Sybil.' He chuckled. 'He's got quite a point.' He looked down at Henry, who had sat down again and stuck his legs out in the best self-satisfied manner.

'Suppose,' he suggested, 'you were able to achieve your ends by more peaceful means ...'

'You are not,' interrupted Joseph indignantly, 'suggesting we make accommodation with this rascal!'

Seeing all this, unbelievably, yet inevitably, heading towards the exact end planned by Joseph, Elaine decided she might as well lend a hand.

'As Mrs Masterman says, Joe,' she pointed out, 'her husband is a politician.'

'But this man,' protested Joseph, 'is

ambitious. The cost of finding accommodation could run into millions!'

'And of not doing so,' said Masterman, 'perhaps be incalculable.'

'But surely a matter of principle ...'

This was altogether too much for Sybil. 'You dare to talk of principle! To my husband!'

'Don't forget,' said Elaine to Joseph, 'he is an Englishman.'

Masterman shot a sudden, searching glance at her and Elaine knew she had gone just that little bit too far.

'You were the one person, weren't you, Mrs Mordecai,' he said, 'who never believed in this revolution. But you believe in it now, don't you?'

Elaine knew without the least doubt that she had all but queered Joseph's pitch. That the whole question of success or failure hung on her reply. Small, neat and very personable, she held Masterman's eyes unwaveringly:

'I will only repeat to you,' she answered, 'what I have already said. Who am I to stand out against the opinion of so many people with vastly more experience than my own?'

There was a moment's silence. Then, smiling, Masterman responded: 'You know, Mordecai, your wife ought to have been in politics. And, who knows, maybe she will

340

be yet.' And he turned back to deal with Henry.

'This ... Mighty King. You obviously have influence with him.' Henry held up two crossed fingers. 'And you have admitted you are in it for the money. So ... if there was another way which might avoid trouble all round, shall we say ...'

'Making me an offer?' Henry dared.

Joseph thought this was going a little bit too far.

'Oh, nothing so sordid as that,' he intervened hastily. 'What the Chancellor is saying ... or at least what I think the Chancellor is saying ... is that if there were a more peaceful way for you to achieve your aims ... and the St Barbara people too, of course ...that is what you were saying, Chancellor? I did get it right?'

'The words out of my very mouth, Mr Mordecai. Tell me ... if other islands get grants-in-aid and undercut you, why didn't you apply?'

'Oh but we did,' said Joseph. 'Four times. Mind you that was when your opposition party were in ... And ... well, frankly, Nethersole's not the most tactful of men.'

'And how much money are we talking about?'

'Well,' said Joseph, 'I wouldn't know

341

of course but ...' hopefully 'three million pounds?'

'Is that all?' said Masterman blandly.

'Perhaps five would be safer, Joseph,' said Elaine.

'How about settling for four?'

Joseph did not reply.

'Do you think, Cicurel,' Masterman said, 'that if the British Government were to issue a grant-in-aid of four million ... no, why be mean? ... of five million pounds to St Barbara, you would be able to exert sufficient influence to, shall we say, ensure there was no revolution?'

'Well, man,' Henry said, stretching his legs if possible even further out and regarding his toe-caps with interest. 'That depends.'

'On what?'

'Two things. How we goin' to know the British Government's going to come across ...'

'You may take it that if I leave St Barbara promising St Barbara a grant-in-aid, it will get that grant-in-aid. The second point?'

'How're we gonna know it won't all melt away?'

'I don't follow you.'

'I think he means,' said Joseph helpfully, 'that one has so often heard of money vanishing in administration costs, getting into the wrong hands ... you know, that sort of thing.'

'You've never heard of Captain Morgan?'

'That dreadful pirate?'

'They settled his hash,' said Masterman cheerfully, 'by making him Governor of Jamaica.'

'You're not suggesting ...'

'The British,' said Masterman, 'have their own peculiar way of dealing with revolutionaries ... or would-be revolutionaries. They put them in control. And you know, Mordecai, it works. Gandhi. Kenyatta. Need I go on?' Joseph shook his head encouragingly. 'Usually,' Masterman continued, 'they have to go to prison first—but in this case there just doesn't seem the time for that. Cicurel, you mustn't misunderstand me, this is in no way a bribe. But *prima facie* there does seem to be a case made out for the issuing of a five-million-pounds grant-in-aid to St Barbara and, as Mr Mordecai points out, I should have to be sure before recommending it that it did arrive intact at where it was intended. So a necessary pre-condition would have to be that you would sign a contract to administer the fund with, I think, Mr Mordecai, as a respected St Barbaran national, assisting you. Do you agree?'

'Do I get a salary for my trouble?' said

Henry outrageously.

'Of course.' There was not even a pause. 'The British Government is never mean with the taxpayers' money.'

'But, Ernest ...' Sybil's feeble protest petered out at a brief shake of her husband's head.

'Well?'

'It's a deal,' said Henry.

Sybil tried again: 'Ernest, you don't think ...'

'You're quite right, Sybil,' Masterman interrupted. 'We must get through to Dukestown right away. If, while I'm drawing up this agreement with Mr Cicurel, you wouldn't mind finishing off winding that transformer?' And he looked at her very directly. Sybil shrugged and went into the house.

'Perhaps,' Masterman went on to Henry, 'it would be as well if we went inside to draw up some sort of temporary document. Incidentally, Cicurel, how do you spell your name. Is it C.Y.C ...'

He got no further; Joseph could not resist it.

'C.I.C.U.R.E.L.,' he said. 'The 'i' as in 'Prime' and not in 'Minister'.'

Masterman laughed aloud, his attractive laugh which came from deep inside his chest. Carole was able to laugh as well. It was all Henry now.

344

'Daddy,' she said, 'wouldn't it be a good idea if someone ran the Chancellor into Dukestown?'

'But,' objected Joseph, 'the cars won't start. And all those revolutionaries.'

'To say nothing,' put in Elaine, 'of all those fallen trees.'

'Oh, I daresay,' said Carole, 'something could be arranged. And if it was Henry who drove Mr and Mrs Masterman in and I came too ...'

'Well,' said Joseph thoughtfully, 'if that were possible it would certainly be a good thing. I mean ...' addressing Masterman '... you might pre-empt Sir Peter getting his message out—bearing in mind how unreliable everything is these days ... But I'm forgetting. You came here for a few days' rest after your dreadful experiences in Santiago and here we are after less than twenty-four hours ...'

'Trying to get rid of us?' The smile belied the words. 'My dear Mr Mordecai, change is often far better than a rest and staying with you, and your charming family, has certainly been a change. I haven't felt so well or rested for years. It's time we left ... before we outstay our welcome.'

'But Government House ...'

'We shall manage. Oh, by the way, Jeffery-Smith mentioned something about

345

your being in the honours list for public services to the people of St Barbara. His recommendation shall have my support. After all, quite apart from providing us with splendid hospitality, and entertainment, under the most difficult of circumstances, you, and your wife,' he smiled at Elaine, 'and your daughter'—again he smiled, but wryly now—'have enabled me to do something very few men have ever had the chance to do—to put down a revolution as if it never was.' He paused, just long enough, and then said briskly: 'Come on, Cicurel, let's go inside and knock something out, shall we?'

Joseph said to Carole: 'You know where we keep the Havanas?'

'Yes, Daddy.'

'A box, I think. And the Courvoisier Napoleon?'

'Yes.'

'A crate.'

'They were all taken out of the crates, weren't they?'

'I imagine,' said Joseph chuckling, 'Sydney will find an old one somewhere.'

'He knows,' said Elaine, when they were alone.

'Yes, my love, he knows. You pulled out a card and the house came tumbling down before his eyes. And in the process you got us an extra two million pounds which is not too bad for just one remark.'

'I might have ruined it.'

Joseph shook his head. 'If you work it out, either way he had to pay up and smile.'

'She doesn't know?'

'No.'

'And he'll never tell her.'

'No.'

'Because she'd never really understand. And yet they've been married for more than thirty years.'

'I thought Henry did rather well, didn't you?'

'Poor Henry.' But she said it without over-sympathising; after all, it wasn't only Joseph who had pulled off something which twenty-four hours before would have seemed impossible.

'I still find it difficult to believe,' she said.

'My love, it was never in doubt from the moment he heard that aeroplane.'

'No,' admitted Elaine. 'I suppose it wasn't. But I still find it difficult to believe.'

'In politics things are often difficult to believe,' said Joseph. 'For example did you never hear of the War of Jenkins' Ear?'

'Jenkins' Ear?'

'Yes. The poor fellow had it cut off round the corner from here. He managed to get hold of it again somehow and he carried it round with him in a leather purse and persuaded George the First to take a look at it ...'

'You're not serious, man!'

'My love, I am absolutely serious. To continue—the ear was examined some years later by a committee of the British House of Commons ...'

'Some years later?'

'Some years later. And they decided the best thing was to go to war with Spain about it. This in due course developed into the War of Austrian Succession ... You didn't know about Jenkins' Ear?' Elaine shook her head. 'But you believe me now?'

'I suppose so.'

'Tell me, my love,' said Joseph. 'Which is the more difficult to believe? The Revolution on St Barbara? Or the War of Jenkins' Ear?'

'That,' said Elaine, 'is a good question. A very good question, Joe.'

She looked ahead of her, beyond the neat Bahama grass partly shaded by creaking palms, to the brilliant blue and turquoise sea and its scatter of islands. She noticed the surf ringing each of them was more distinct than it had been before, that a breeze had sprung up cooling the day. The Trade Wind, she thought, the Spanish Main. Why not? Perhaps it was just here that poor Mr Jenkins had lost his ear. It was certainly possible. And she wondered what use Joseph Mordecai would have made of that if once he'd got it in his clutches.

The publishers hope that this book has given you enjoyable reading. Large Print Books are especially designed to be as easy to see and hold as possible. If you wish a complete list of our books, please ask at your local library or write directly to Dales Large Print Books, Long Preston, North Yorkshire, BD23 4ND, England.

This Large Print Book for the Partially sighted, who cannot read normal print, is published under the auspices of

THE ULVERSCROFT FOUNDATION